ECLIPSE

Recent Titles by Hilary Norman

The Sam Becket Mysteries

MIND GAMES
LAST RUN *
SHIMMER *
CAGED *
HELL *
ECLIPSE *

BLIND FEAR
CHATEAU ELLA
COMPULSION
DEADLY GAMES
FASCINATION
GUILT
IN LOVE AND FRIENDSHIP
LAURA
NO ESCAPE
THE PACT
RALPH'S CHILDREN *
SHATTERED STARS
SPELLBOUND
SUSANNA
TOO CLOSE
TWISTED MINDS

IF I SHOULD DIE (written as Alexandra Henry)

* *available from Severn House*

ECLIPSE

Hilary Norman

This first world edition published 2012
in Great Britain and 2013 in the USA by
SEVERN HOUSE PUBLISHERS LTD of
Salatin House, 19 Cedar Road, Sutton, Surrey, SM2 5DA.
Trade paperback edition first published
in Great Britain and the USA 2013 by
SEVERN HOUSE PUBLISHERS LTD

British Library Cataloguing in Publication Data

Norman, Hilary.
Eclipse.
1. Becket, Sam (Fictitious character)–Fiction.
2. Police–Florida–Miami–Fiction. 3. Serial murder
investigation–Florida–Miami–Fiction. 4. Suspense
fiction.
I. Title
823.9'2-dc23

ISBN-13: 978-0-7278-8224-0 (cased)
ISBN-13: 978-1-84751-457-8 (trade paper)

All Severn House titles are printed on acid-free paper.

Severn House Publishers support The Forest Stewardship Council [FSC],
the leading international forest certification organisation. All our titles that
are printed on Greenpeace-approved FSC-certified paper carry the FSC logo.

Typeset by Palimpsest Book Production Ltd.,
Falkirk, Stirlingshire, Scotland.
Printed and bound in Great Britain by
MPG Books Ltd., Bodmin, Cornwall.

For Gabriella
My beautiful little great-niece.
It will be many years before you're allowed
to read it – but this is for you.

ACKNOWLEDGEMENTS

My thanks to the following (in alphabetical order):

Howard Barmad; Diane Beate Hellmann; Daniela Jarzynka; Jeremy Joseph, MD, FRCS, FRC.Ophth.; Special Agent Paul Marcus and Julie Marcus (*still* putting up with me, and I can never thank you enough) and Scott Marcus, too; Annina Meyerhans; Wolfgang Neuhaus; James Nightingale; Katharina Peters; Sara Porter; Sebastian Ritscher; Helen Rose (who can answer *almost* any question); as always, gratitude to Dr Jonathan Tarlow; and special thanks to Euan Thorneycroft.

Finally, and most especially, to Jonathan.

The room was filled with dead things.

Some sham – things that had never been alive. Toys which might, perhaps, *almost* have lived in their owners' imaginations.

Some all too real.

A ginger cat in a coffin.

More than one tiny coffin in the room.

A white rat, too, nailed to a cork board.

Numerous butterflies.

And more.

There was an old beige teddy bear, lying on its back in a small crib.

A soft dog, part still fluffy, part threadbare, paws matted, testimony to small-child love, sucked on.

The toy dog had been laid out in the crib, front paws crossed on its chest.

Almost like a human corpse.

A doll lay nearby – a pretty blonde thing, carried back to Florida once upon a time all the way from FAO Schwartz in New York City by a doting dad and given to a daughter long since grown, with no time left for toys.

The doll was on her back too.

Her lower half covered with a tiny sheet. Her arms raised, twisted around in their sockets. Her hands covering her eyes, making it impossible to see if they were open or closed.

The eyes of every dead thing in the room were covered.

Some with hands or paws – in the coffin, the ginger cat's front limbs had been stretched, like the doll's arms, so that they, too, shielded its eyes.

The cat's paws were encased in white mittens.

The eye coverings were diverse. Everything from Band-Aids to miniature sleep masks to soft gauze and bandages.

Even the eyes of the butterflies were concealed.

In life, these were large and spherical, made up of thousands of hexagonally-shaped sensors, each directed at different angles, enabling the insects to see multidirectionally, albeit imperfectly.

The butterflies in this room no longer saw anything at all.

Their eyes blind now and invisible beneath tiny coverlets of white lace, like minuscule doilies at a child's tea party.

Unseen and unseeing.

There were photographs, too, on the walls.

Subject matter the same.

Dead creatures, terminated toys.

No eyes visible.

There was life, however, in the room.

A person, at work.

Stooped over a table, engrossed in a task.

Hard to see what the task was.

If you could have come close enough to peer over their shoulder, you would have seen.

Something horrible.

The stuff of nightmares.

The kind of thing it would be hard to forget.

The kind of thing to make you need to close your eyes.

And keep them closed.

May 8

On Sunday evening, Detective Sam Becket and Special Agent Joseph Duval were at Houston's in North Miami Beach, having dinner.

A first for them. The Miami Beach Police Department detective from the Violent Crimes Unit socializing with the man from the Florida Department of Law Enforcement – and not just a couple of beers in a bar after work. But Joe Duval had formerly been a Violent Crimes police detective in Chicago, and since he'd relocated to Florida the men had cooperated on a couple of major cases; Duval – fifty-something, sharp-nosed, sharp-jawed and slim – was an instinctive investigator and happy family man and, bottom line, he and Sam got along.

So when Duval had called a week ago and mentioned that his wife and son were going to be busy Sunday evening, Sam had suggested dinner, because Grace, his wife, would be out of town, and in her absence her sister, Claudia, would be staying at their house, helping to take care of Joshua, their three-year-old.

In fact, Sam had seen Grace off at Miami International just hours ago, and she would, within the hour, be boarding her flight to Zurich, Switzerland.

So tonight he was dining out, and tomorrow evening he'd be rehearsing Act Three of the South Beach Opera's production of *Carmen*.

Long time since Sam had sung with S-BOP, his old amateur company.

Almost like being single again.

Just the thought of that made him shudder.

It was seven p.m., and hectic. No such thing as a quiet table at Houston's, but on the other hand, in all the hubbub there was no big risk of neighbors listening in. Not that they had official work to discuss.

Except Sam could not help being interested in and disturbed by Duval's current big case. Another sicko loose in Florida, and just about *everyone* knew something about it. At least, as much as the investigators working the cases were letting the media know.

It was often the way in bad serial killings that the crimes themselves, or their perpetrators, collected unofficial names. This one had started in Orlando, where the first victim had been found, and it had stuck fast.

'Black Hole' was the individual they were hunting.

Ugly name, and so far, off the record.

Three victims. The first in Orlando back in January, the second in Jupiter, Palm Beach County, almost a month later; the most recent in early March over in Naples, Collier County.

Everyone hoping, but not really believing, that it would be the last.

Details had been entered into ViCAP, the FBI's Violent Criminal Apprehension Program. Matching fingerprints found at two of the scenes had thrown up no corresponding prints in the IAFIS – the Integrated Automated Fingerprint Identification System. Restricted details were on the FBI's Most Wanted website, and Joe Duval had entered the picture after the second murder.

No case yet in Miami-Dade County, and everyone in the MBPD wanted it to stay that way, and Sam Becket, for one, had heard more than enough about these killings to hope and pray that if Black Hole was coming this way, he might just bypass the Beach.

'No fresh links?' Sam asked Duval now, quietly.

'Nothing,' Duval said.

No more than Sam already knew. All three victims had been female and Caucasian, and the only other established common ground between them had been the manner of their deaths. The youngest twenty-two, the oldest forty-nine. One blonde, two brunettes. One married, one divorced, the youngest woman single. Two of them mothers. One not working out of choice; one in real estate; the last victim, Lindy Braun, owning and running her own bar.

'And not so much as a sniff of a lead,' the FDLE man went on.

Which was when his Hickory Burger and Sam's ribs arrived, and after that their conversation rolled around family, the Heat and the Hurricanes, then to the fact that Duval, who'd been living close to MROC – Miami Regional Operations Center – in Doral, was hoping to move house, and they'd been looking around Pembroke Pines, had liked what they'd seen.

'Grace and I were considering a move a while back,' Sam said, 'but I think we're kind of glad we stayed put.'

'Our son's a little tentative about relocating,' Duval said.

'It can be tough on teens,' Sam said.

Duval's cell phone rang.

Sam picked up another rib, and knew, from the expression in the other man's intent gray eyes, that their dinner was at an end.

'Fort Lauderdale,' Duval said grimly, his call over. 'Another one.'

Not Sam's jurisdiction, but Duval had told him he should come along.

It wasn't an invitation to be relished, nor was it one he could refuse. Not just because it would be impolite, but because he was a homicide detective, and a part of that man wanted to see this.

Fort Lauderdale Police Department's homicide unit were already all over the scene. A nice little single family house, a corner unit in the quiet, tree-lined Shady Banks neighborhood.

A pleasant place to live.

Standing in the victim's bedroom, Sam Becket – the part who was just a man, rather than a cop – wished to hell that he'd passed on Duval's invitation.

Some sights a human being ought to avoid if possible.

'Oh, man,' he said softly, seeing her, his mind recoiling along with his stomach.

He looked away – because he could, because this was not his case, so he could afford the luxury of averting his eyes from the horrors that had been visited on this poor woman.

Amelia Newton, age thirty-three. Living alone in her two bed, one bath, nicely-appointed, tidily-maintained, one-story house. No signs of a break-in or of a struggle anyplace, not even in the room where she lay.

Two photographs on her dressing table attested to the fact that she had been attractive. A slim, smiling woman with short blonde hair and blue eyes.

Sam looked over at Duval, knew he was doing what they all had to at such times. Shutting down their human side. Starting the process of doing the only thing they could for the victim: getting her justice.

He forced himself to look back at Amelia Newton.

The crime perpetrated on her was – even by the standards of an experienced homicide detective – bizarre and appalling.

She lay in the center of her double bed, tidily positioned. Her body, from the shoulders down, lay on a patchwork-style quilt covering the bed. She appeared fully clothed in turquoise cotton slacks and white T-shirt.

Her clothes and the quilt were blood-splattered.

Beneath her neck and head, someone had spread a sheet of latex, covering, but not really protecting, the pillows propping her up.

Three pillows, Sam counted, and a lot of blood.

A rectangle of foam lay on the floor to the left of the bed. It looked like the foam insert of a cushion, and it was scarred, burned-looking, had probably been used as a silencer.

If the killer had been true to form, toxicology would eventually show that Ms Newton had been sedated not long before death with a large dose of Diazepam. Almost tasteless, easy to mix with food or drink.

Duval came over, holding a Polaroid shot.

'This was how she was found,' he said. 'By her sister, who was coming for dinner. She had her own key. She'd brought wine, says they were going to order takeout and watch a movie.'

In the Polaroid, Amelia Newton was wearing a pair of oversized, very dark sunglasses.

'Her sister says she's sure the glasses weren't Amelia's.'

'Were the other victims wearing sunglasses?' Sam asked.

Duval shook his head. 'In Orlando, it was a sleep mask. The victim's husband said he thought his wife had kept it from an overnight airline flight. In Jupiter, it was gauze covered by Band-Aids. In Naples, the victim's white-gloved hands were covering the wounds.'

Sam made himself look back at Amelia Newton again.

At her face.

Her eyes.

Or rather, the hideous, dark cavities where her eyes had been.

Two deep, round wounds.

Black holes, probably created – like the first three – by .380 ACP cartridges.

Not big slugs, but enough to do the job.

Sam suddenly wished he hadn't finished his ribs. He took a breath, became aware of the mix of odors in the room, tried separating them – blood and death, the lingering smell of burned foam, and something else . . . And then he reminded himself that he was not the investigator here, and quit trying so hard.

'Some night off, huh?' Duval said quietly.

'Yeah,' Sam said. 'Thanks for sharing.'

Grace Lucca Becket sat in her airline seat, sipping a martini, contemplating the days ahead and admitting to herself that as much as she would rather have been making this trip with Sam, it was kind of fun sitting up here with her drink ahead of dinner and, she hoped, a reasonable night's rest.

A pleasant kind of limbo.

'And don't go spoiling it with guilt,' Claudia had told her yesterday.

'As if,' Grace had answered wryly.

All her family knew her talent for that most pointless of emotions. Though having committed herself to this trip, Grace's intention was to make the most of it. A good hotel outside Zurich, and the conference itself, with the stimulus of fellow professionals all with the same fundamental interest at heart.

Helping troubled kids.

Which was, of course, what she tried to do at home in her role as a child and adolescent psychologist. No need, therefore, for trips to Switzerland or any other place.

This was Magda's doing. Dr Magda Shrike, fellow psychologist, long-time mentor and valued friend, with whom Grace had been sharing work space for about a year.

The theme of the International Conference on Child Developmental Psychology to be held in Zurich, Switzerland, from May 10–12, was to be 'Emotional education: drawing together the best to help give troubled young people the best'.

The speakers had been booked long ago, but illness had created an opening in the teenage psychology group, and an acquaintance of Magda's had asked her to suggest someone who could step up.

'There must be any number of more suitable people,' Grace had said.

'No one more suitable that I can think of,' her friend had told her.

'That's very flattering, but I'm not sure it's true.'

'From my perspective, it is.'

'And is this the next stage, perhaps, of your therapy plan for me?'

Because Magda Shrike, as her own psychologist, had been helping Grace to continue her recovery from a series of traumatic events and, most notably, her all-consuming guilt over what had happened last May.

When Grace had killed a man.

It was extraordinary, she often thought, the horrors that people did manage to get past, if not over. Sufficiently, at least, to continue their lives; to go on, in her case, being a wife and mother, sister, daughter-in-law, aunt, and psychologist.

She had argued against accepting, but with Sam and Claudia both backing Magda, Grace had capitulated. So here she was tonight, wishing she had a satellite phone to use for a goodnight call to Sam, even if it would be disproportionately expensive.

But worth every cent.

May 9

At night, he read ceaselessly, driven by insomnia and his never-sated hunger for learning.

He had studied for so long, filling his brain with knowledge, had a passionate love for his chosen profession, yet that never stopped him exploring other fields. The mind, after all, being an infinite repository, requiring constant exercise and restocking, at work even when the body slept.

Excess sleep was the greatest waste known to man.

His walls were covered with diplomas and certificates attesting to his achievements and qualifications, and his shelves were filled with books. He had the facility to speed-read, but preferred to take his time.

Words and images reaching his brain courtesy of rods and cones in the outermost layer of neurons in his retinas, sending their signals to the middle layer of bipolar neurons, relaying their signals in turn to the optic nerve fibers in the third layer – and this was what he was reading about right now, the myriad miracles of vision.

Eyes, presently his area of fascination.

He was a proud man. No strutting peacock, but proud of what he had achieved. Of what he could do for others. Prouder of two letters after his name than of anything else.

MD.

He was a medical man.

A doctor.

That sang in his brain.

The most important thing a person could aspire to being.

A *doctor.*

'Someone leaked Black Hole.'

Alejandro Martinez, Sam's partner and close friend of many years, a stocky, middle-aged Cuban-American with dark, sharp, expressive eyes, was already at his desk when Sam arrived in the Violent Crimes office.

They'd spoken last night, Sam bringing Martinez up to speed on his evening. Now Martinez held up the *Herald* for Sam to see.

'Black Hole Killer Strikes in Fort Lauderdale
Florida Victim # 4!'

Sam took the newspaper, scanned the piece and shook his head.

'Getting too close, man,' Martinez said.

'Tell me about it,' Sam said.

'Grace arrive safe?'

Sam smiled. 'Sure did. She called soon as they landed. Sounded a little tired, but fine.'

'She has the day to rest, right?'

'And take a look around.'

'Meantime, we're due at the range,' Martinez said.

Sam grimaced, always a little antsy about the yearly State Qual.

Shooting not his favorite pastime.

Especially when the targets were human.

At the seven-bay range on the fifth floor of the Miami Beach Police Department headquarters building, waiting with Detectives Mary Cutter and Joe Sheldon for the range master to give his first order, Sam's mind returned to the odor he'd smelled in the victim's bedroom last evening.

'I still can't nail it, and it's bugging me.'

'The FLPD and Duval got noses too,' Martinez said. 'Don't worry about it.'

'You're right,' Sam said. 'Not our problem.'

'Let's hope it stays that way.'

'You'd better believe it,' Sam said, putting on his headset.

'Make your weapons ready, and holster.' The range master's voice came through loud and clear.

Sam, Martinez and the other detectives loaded up their magazines, moved to their respective bays, made ready and holstered their firearms. Unloaded again, reloaded, holstered.

Sam was tense now, his mind clear, knowing the routine – holster, fire, holster; good with his weapon, fast and effective, but never complacent.

'When the target turns, you have two seconds to draw and fire two rounds from the hip position, cover your target, then holster,' the range master instructed them. 'Ready on the line. *Gun.*'

The target turned.

Sam fired.

'I think you might need glasses,' David Becket told his wife, Mildred, as they sat in their backyard on yet another gorgeous morning, reading and drinking coffee.

Both in their mid-sixties, they had only married a year before. A second marriage for David, Sam's adoptive father and a retired pediatrician; a first for Mildred, whose life up until a couple of years ago had been far from easy.

They were very happy together.

'I do not need glasses, old man,' she said. 'I can read as well as I ever could, maybe even better.'

'Uh-huh,' David said.

'What does that mean?' Mildred set her book on her lap.

'Just that you've been peering at things lately. And frowning too.' He paused. 'Look down there.'

'What am I looking at?'

'That bird to the right of the pond.'

'What about it?'

'Describe it to me.'

Mildred's mouth tightened. 'I'm not a child.'

'You can't see it, can you?'

'Of course I can see it,' she said. 'It's a bird. It has wings. Now lay off.'

'It's a white-winged parakeet,' David said.

'Whoop de doo,' she said.

'You've never been nearsighted before,' he said.

'I can see the damned bird,' Mildred said.

David looked at her sideways. 'Mildred, are you having problems with your eyes?'

She sighed. 'You want me to have an eye test.'

'I don't think it would hurt,' he said. 'I'll come with you.'

'I may possibly need glasses' – Mildred was scathing – 'but I am far from helpless.'

'I'm glad to hear it, but I'd still like to come.'

'You didn't come with me the last time.'

'You said you preferred to be independent, as I recall.'

'As I still do,' Mildred said.

'Who was it you went to?'

'I don't recall offhand.'

David smiled. 'That's OK. We can go to my optometrist.'

'I'd prefer to go to my own,' Mildred said.

'What's going on, Mildred?'

'Nothing is going on, except that you're starting to get me mad.'

'Why?' he persisted. 'I've expressed the mildest concern that you might not be seeing as well as you used to.'

'You're bullying me,' she said.

'Nonsense,' David said.

The parakeet flew away.

'The bird left,' Mildred said.

'You had to screw up your eyes to see that,' David said gently.

She sighed. 'I guess I did.'

'And is the glare bothering you?' He smiled. 'I only ask because you've been wearing sunglasses more than you used to.'

She didn't answer.

'Mildred, why are you reacting this way?' he persevered.

She took another moment. 'Because I'm scared.'

'Of what?' David was surprised and concerned.

'If you really insist on knowing,' she said stiffly, 'I'm squeamish about my eyes. I'm afraid of going to the eye doctor.'

'But you've been before.'

'No, I haven't,' Mildred said quietly. 'I just told you that I went.'

'You said your vision was perfect.' Now he was astonished.

'I don't believe I used that word.'

'You led me to believe it.'

Mildred's cheeks were warm. 'I'm not proud of this.'

'So when did you last have an eye test?'

'When I was a teenager. In New York City.' She paused. 'I hated it so much that I ran out and vomited.'

'How horrible for you,' he said. 'Do you know what upset you so much?'

'The whole thing.' Mildred had grown pale. 'The doctor sat very close, and . . .' She shook her head. 'I don't even like talking about it. I know it's idiotic, but I can't help it.'

'It's not idiotic,' he said.

'Yes, it is,' she said. 'It's foolish and irrational and cowardly.'

'You're no coward,' David said. 'You're a remarkable, brave woman with a tiny weakness, which we can deal with together.'

'I can deal with it,' Mildred said, 'by staying away from eye doctors.'

'No,' David said. 'That has to stop.'

She leaned back in her chair, and then, after a few moments, sighed.

'So what do you think is wrong with my eyes, Doctor?'

'I think it's possible that you might have the start of cataracts.'

'Will I go blind?' she asked bluntly.

'Only if you ignore them for long enough.' He paused. 'Will you let me help you with this?'

'I don't want to go blind,' she said.

'Is that a yes?' David asked.

'I guess it is,' Mildred said.

In the room of dead things, the one who made them, who took them, living or inanimate, and turned them into little corpses, was working again.

Another doll, this one wearing turquoise cotton slacks and a white T-shirt.

The T-shirt was stained with dark red splatters.

Like blood.

The doll had short blonde hair.

And one blue eye.

The other eye having already been removed.

Cut out, neatly and precisely, to leave a small black hole.

The work was exacting, the air in the room hot and fetid, and the doll maker, the *corpse* maker, was perspiring as the short, sharp blade of the tiny scalpel blade began its next circular incision; the blade attached to a pencil grip handle, worked with the tips of the thumb, index and middle fingers, the handle resting between the index finger and thumb.

Over to one side, waiting on another table until the work was complete lay a pair of doll-sized sunglasses and a roll of gauze.

The corpse maker found this part of the job the most fulfilling.

It felt like an ending, almost like closure.

But it never was.

Grace's hotel, the Dolder Waldhaus, stood on a hill high above Zurich, surrounded by forest and prime real estate, most of it old and solid. Her room had a balcony with a fine overview of the city, its lake and the Alps way over on the horizon.

On arrival, she'd showered, eaten a light, excellent lunch and dozed off in an armchair. Waking upset with herself for having wasted time, she'd revived downstairs with a delicious cup of coffee and a swift but glorious walk in the forest just across the street, before catching a little red cogwheel train down to Römerhof, then a tram to the town center – and now, finally, she was in the heart of Zurich.

For a city renowned for banks, it was astonishingly pretty. A large Swiss national flag presided over a big bustling square where a host of tramlines intersected. Smooth modern cobbles underfoot, linden trees lining the street, attractive, expensive-looking stores and boutiques, people everywhere, hurrying or strolling, a church bell tolling someplace nearby – and Grace was debating whether she should begin with the lake or the Bahnhofstrasse when she saw, over to her left, one of the places she remembered Magda telling her about.

'If you have no time for anything else,' she had said, 'go to Sprüngli, sit upstairs, drink coffee, eat cake and watch people.'

A priority then, clearly.

The *confiserie* downstairs smelled like heaven, and Grace made a mental note to go home laden with foodie gifts. But for now, she climbed the staircase to a spacious old-fashioned restaurant where well-heeled locals and tourists waited for tables, and spied, by luck, a small, free window spot.

She ordered, then relaxed back in her seat to await her chocolate ice cream – which came in a misted silver flute with whipped cream, and was extraordinarily fine.

If she lived in Zurich, Grace reflected, she would grow fat.

She pictured her family sitting here, several tables pushed together. Cathy, their adopted daughter, studying at Johnson & Wales University's College of Culinary Arts, would relish choosing from the delectable-looking goodies behind the counter where customers were patiently queuing . . .

'Are you OK?'

It took a moment for Grace to realize that the man at the next table was speaking to her.

'I'm sorry?' she said.

'You're from the States, right?' he asked.

He was no more than thirty, with wavy brown hair and blue eyes behind fashionable rimless glasses. His smile was friendly and natural, his accent French.

'I am,' Grace answered him.

'You were looking very pensive,' he said. 'I wanted to make sure you were all right. I didn't mean to intrude.'

She smiled. 'I'm fine, thank you.' She looked at the remains of her ice cream. 'The food here seems as good as I was told.'

'Swiss food is excellent, and Zurich is filled with fine restaurants.'

Their waitress brought him a small glass of white wine.

'Are you here with your husband?' the young man asked.

Grace hesitated only briefly.

There was something in his eyes, she thought, something possibly flirtatious.

'I'm here to attend a conference.' She felt unsure why she'd told him that, why she hadn't simply lied, said that yes, her husband was with her.

The check was on her table. She picked it up, looked around.

'You pay over at the desk,' the young man told her.

'Thank you.' Grace stood up. 'It was kind of you to be concerned.'

'It was not so much concern,' he said.

He stood up too, and momentarily she thought he might want to leave with her, that she might have to be less pleasant. But instead, he extended his right hand, and she gave him her own, found his grip cool, firm.

'I wish you a good stay in Zurich,' he said.

And sat down again.

Probably waiting for his girlfriend, Grace thought, standing in a short line at the cash desk. Not remotely interested in a woman at least a decade older – absurd of her even to think that.

She paid, walked back down to the first floor and bought herself some dark chocolate truffles.

Perfect to nibble on later, while she rehearsed her conference speech.

Gorgeous sounds.

Filling his ears, his head, his mind and soul.

My, but it felt good to be back.

Sam Becket doing one of the things he loved best.

Way, *way* down his list of loves, of course.

Grace and Joshua still tied at Number One.

It had, of course, been Gracie who'd steered him gently back to S-BOP. Amateur operatics, for sure, but *hot* amateur, and a great bunch of people, some of whom he'd known for years, some new and none the worse for that.

'It's exactly what you need,' she'd begun telling him soon after New Year's, after their prolonged period of high stress, and she was right, he had needed something more, something therapeutic.

Singing again, releasing his deep voice, working at it, doing his vocal exercises, learning the libretto, listening to the others. Some of them way superior to him, some not as good, but all of them sharing that *shine* that got right inside them, that soaring sensation; and sharing the down moments, too, when they screwed up, forgot the words, hit the wrong notes, ruined the timing.

Letting down the geniuses who'd given them their music.

Georges Bizet in this instance, and Sam had been cast as Escamillo, the matador – a ton of swagger *and* the Toreador song *and* his very own fight sequence – what more could an amateur baritone homicide cop wish for?

'How's the diet going?' Toni Petit was S-BOP's long-time, dedicated and tireless costumier and dresser; a diminutive woman in her thirties with short dark hair and black cherry eyes, now regarding Sam critically, as the rest of the company assembled in the backyard of Tyler Allen's house on Lime Court in Coconut Grove.

Tyler Allen, a forty-something choreographer. His yard and good-sized converted garage their rehearsal venue till they could get into their theater. A great spot for rehearsing, if the neighbors didn't object.

They were grouped on benches around Tyler's long trellis table, set with large pitchers of water and paper cups – regular tea, coffee, cola and alcohol banned for the rehearsal's duration – the fragrance of night sage growing in the flower beds powerful, almost intoxicating.

It was Linda Morrison, directing *Carmen* (known as 'La Morrison' by the company), who'd first suggested to Sam, right after she'd cast him, that he might want to drop a few pounds.

Linda was the proprietor of a clothing store near Lincoln Avenue, an old pal, a cast member from way back: statuesque, red-haired and a talented mezzo-soprano.

'Grace's cooking.' Sam had taken no offence at Linda's remark about his weight. 'What can I tell you?'

'Bullfighters don't have paunches,' Toni pointed out this evening.

'Now I'm a little hurt,' he said.

'Don't be,' she told him. 'Just remember you're a big guy who's going to cut a dash with your dagger.' She smiled. 'So to speak.'

An interesting and eclectic cast had been assembled. Billie

Smith – the daughter, Sam had learned, of an old school pal, aged twenty-three and gorgeous, with a mezzo-soprano from heaven – singing the lead. Gossip had it that she'd been asked to leave UM's School of Music – reason unknown – but was now taking classes at the Lincoln Park Music School near the New World Center.

Jack Holden, tenor, a handsome, fair-haired, blue-eyed Scottish-born lawyer, singing Don José. Carla Gonzales as Micaëla, the village maiden – the role a little tame for the ambitious, thirty-two-year-old Cuban-American – and if her vocal range had been just a little lower down the scale, Sam thought there might have been a real battle for Carmen.

Tyler Allen, a specialist in stage combat, had relocated from upstate New York four years ago, out of work for some time due to sickness, but now raring to go. Whippet-thin with fearsome energy levels and, according to Linda, not always the kindest of men, Sam felt sure that Tyler was the one most likely to challenge the hell out of him.

Too many years of sitting, in the car, at his desk and in interview rooms, and though the occasional pursuit got the detectives up and running, and Sam had thrown a few punches over the years, a prolonged stage fight while *singing* . . .

Oh, man.

The rehearsal over, Sam felt tired, but content. His voice had held up quite well, and the choreographer had been less harsh with him than some of the others. Allen had openly humiliated Carla by referring to her 'big backside', had said Jack Holden was graceless, had referred to Toni Petit as 'the little seamstress', twice snapping his fingers to get her attention, rewarded both times with a chilly stare. Petit could clearly handle him, and Holden's ego was in need of a little downsizing, but Carla Gonzales was not, Sam felt, nearly as confident as she liked to make out. Linda had said that Tyler Allen could be unkind, but there was, Sam decided, something of the bully about him.

Not a trait Sam Becket could tolerate for long.

'Everything OK?' La Morrison asked him as they were packing up.

'Except for my lousy dancing,' Sam said.

'Seems to me you move pretty well,' Billie said.

Tyler Allen made a small, derisive sound, and Sam understood why, because it had seemed to him that Billie was actually looking him up and down. Which had discomfited him, considering she was an old friend's daughter.

Imagination, he told himself. Maybe even wishful thinking from a forty-four-year-old with a *paunch*, according to Toni Petit.

Though Allen had noticed it too, and hey, what the hell.

A compliment from a lovely young woman could only be good for a middle-aged guy's self-esteem.

May 10

The conference facility was less than fifteen minutes walk from Grace's hotel; sleek, modern, and beautifully appointed. The welcome breakfast at eight-thirty was delicious, and her name tag identifying her as 'Dr Grace Lucca' was boldly colored in a prize-winning design by the children of a primary school in the alpine canton of Graubünden.

'We're so happy that you could step in,' Dr Elspeth Mettler, one of the organizers, elegantly suited, wearing Chanel spectacles and sensible shoes, told Grace. 'And I'm personally very grateful to Doctor Shrike for her recommendation.'

'I'm honored to be here,' Grace assured her. 'Though to be frank, it's been a long time since I've spoken anywhere, let alone in such illustrious company. I hope I won't disappoint.'

'I'm sure you won't,' Dr Mettler told her. 'And yours, I understand, is to be an interactive event.'

'That's my hope,' Grace said.

She looked the part, at least, in a new linen dress bought with Sam's encouragement two weeks ago, but though she wasn't scheduled to speak till tomorrow, she felt suddenly intensely nervous.

Abruptly, she realized why.

It had been a long while since she'd stood on a podium.

The closest to it last year, in court.

In the past, she'd felt reasonably equal to this kind of gathering, but so much had been ripped from her during that terrible time, and though she accepted that she was slowly getting back on track, there was still a long path to travel.

In the old days, Grace Lucca Becket had believed she knew who she was.

A contented, grateful woman, at ease with herself.

Not quite back there yet.

Mildred was finally at the optometrist's.

David had made the appointment with Ralph Sutter, a man he had known for about a decade, a good optometrist with his own practice on NE 29th Place, an experienced and kindly doctor.

Mildred seldom took pills, had a repugnance for illegal drugs which had spilled over into wariness of prescription medication. But despite her best efforts to disguise her fears, after a virtually sleepless night, David had seen that she was pale, tremulous and agitated.

'I'd like you to take a very mild tranquilizer,' he'd said, expecting her to refuse. 'It won't give you any loss of control, but it will help take the edge off your anxiety.'

'How about two?' Mildred had said.

'That won't be necessary.' David had smiled.

'I wasn't joking,' she had said.

She already knew, from television programs, how much these places had changed since her last visit to an eye doctor's office.

That had been in her first 'respectable' life as Mildred Bleeker. Long before she had met Donny, her first love, had given up everything to become his fiancé, and had then lost him and, with him, her very identity, becoming a homeless person, sleeping on a bench down in South Beach. Which was where she had found a whole new Mildred Bleeker, a woman with the kind of perspective on life that only a person living on the edge of society could achieve.

Where she had first met Sam Becket, the tall, broad-shouldered African-American detective who had become her friend.

Where she had come close to losing her life – after which she'd met Dr David Becket and the rest of his family.

Her family now.

The tranquilizer was keeping her in Dr Sutter's office, but neither the doctor nor David were in any doubts as to her high level of anxiety.

'I don't know if it helps,' Dr Sutter had told her, 'but I can assure you that you're by no means alone. I've encountered many nervous patients in my time.'

Mildred had thanked him, and the doctor had suggested they keep questions for later, and get the exam over and done with first, and she knew it ought all to have been easy as pie, but she had hated every second of it, though she'd just about managed until it came to the slit-lamp examination.

Dr Sutter asked her to rest her chin and forehead on a support, and Mildred had already done that several times, but perhaps the tension was cumulative, because suddenly she didn't know how much more she could take.

He inserted dilating drops, which stung a little.

'A small waiting period now,' Ralph Sutter told her. 'The drops can take fifteen minutes or a little longer to work.'

'I don't know,' Mildred said.

'It's necessary,' David said, 'so that Ralph can see the back of your eye.'

'It may be *necessary*, but it doesn't mean I can tolerate any more.'

'If you can't, Mrs Becket, that's OK,' the doctor said. 'Though now the drops are in, it would be a shame to miss the opportunity to complete the exam.'

'I can taste them,' Mildred complained. 'How come I can taste them?'

'They drain down from your tear ducts,' David told her.

'I wasn't asking you,' she said.

She knew she was behaving badly, but she couldn't seem to help it, and the truth was that her vision had been growing foggier for a while now, and if it hadn't been for the fact that she could still read, she might have feared she was going blind.

She'd dealt with it in a manner she'd grown expert at during her years as a homeless person. Some things you dealt with head-on, even if they were tough. Sometimes, though, there were things you just could not face, and if you thought you could get away with it, you simply buried your head in the sand.

Which did not, of course, make you wise.

But she had married a wise and sensible man.

So here she was.

Didn't mean she had to like it.

Paperwork Tuesday for Sam and Martinez.

The last two weeks had been quiet for Violent Crimes. One armed robbery with a firearm – suspect placed under arrest within hours. One sexual battery – suspect arrested at the scene. One felony battery, also with a result.

Good jobs.

Detectives Cutter and Sheldon were seeking an armed carjacker. On the streets and in a couple of nightclubs, people had been getting in fights – the usual – but if anyone had pulled or used a knife or a gun lately, it had not been reported to MBPD.

Maybe not love in the air, but peace of a kind.

And a lot of paperwork to complete.

The usual.

Grace called from Zurich at five after one.

'I'm about to have an early dinner with a few of the delegates,' she told Sam. 'I don't know where we're going, but they seem a nice bunch.'

She was hungry for details about Joshua, wanted to check on the rest of the family, to know how Sam's rehearsal had gone.

'Your day first,' he said.

'It's been good – interesting session on parenting, tougher afternoon dealing with serious depression in adolescents.'

'Certainly your territory,' Sam said.

'I did contribute,' Grace told him.

'How did that feel?'

'Good,' she said. 'Stimulating, I guess.'

'I'm feeling a little sore,' he told her. 'All we really did last night was block the moves for the fight, and even that felt like a damned workout. Jack Holden might weigh less than me, but he's no lightweight, I can tell you.'

'Tell him I said to be gentle with you,' Grace told him.

And then they both said how much they missed each other.

Both knowing it was true.

Both liking that.

'Cataracts,' David told her, 'are nothing in the scheme of things.'

'Except they make you go blind,' Mildred said.

'If left untreated, yes, they do.'

She had been very quiet on the short drive home, had let David take her arm getting in and out of the car because her eyes were still blurry, had then sat thinking dark thoughts about how much worse things might become if she did not start doing as she was told.

Mildred had never appreciated being *told.*

David had waited till they were safely back home in the comfortable old living room that had been little altered since his late wife Judy's days. Not that David hadn't encouraged Mildred to make changes if she wanted to, but though she had bought some cushions and had expressed a great liking for a painting of South Beach – which David had promptly gone out to buy for her – the room was still much as it had been.

'I'm not minimizing anything,' he said now. 'But I can't help feeling relieved.'

'You thought it might be worse.' She was assailed by guilt. 'You've been afraid for me. I'm so sorry. I've been selfish.'

'You've been scared,' David said. 'It's allowed. And I know you're still scared because of what comes next, but it's going to be fine. In fact, once it's done, it'll be better than fine.'

'I know that's true, and I know I'm generally regarded as having good common sense. But now I have to go see an ophthalmic surgeon, and you'll have to give me two tranquilizers that day' – her voice shook a little – 'and then there'll be the surgery . . .'

'Which you will know nothing about,' David said gently.

'But Doctor Sutter said that most people have cataracts removed under local anesthesia.'

'He also said that plenty of other people opt for sedation or general anesthesia. And in your case, I can't think of a single reason why you should have to put yourself through any ordeal that isn't absolutely necessary.'

Mildred looked at him through the lingering blur of the drops. 'I'm still a first-class coward,' she said.

'No one's perfect,' David said. 'Not even me.'

The waiting room was almost full.

No more than usual in a busy, multiphysician Miami Beach practice. Patients with sore throats or asthma or gynecological problems or sunburn or any number of ailments or issues, waiting for their respective doctors to summon them.

Several women flicked through old copies of *Elle*, *Good Housekeeping* and *Reader's Digest*. A skinny man of about thirty, dressed in black, appeared immersed in *GQ*. A visually-impaired woman with dark glasses, a cane propped beside her, popped a green Tic Tac into her mouth. A woman beside her listened to music through tiny headphones, her eyes closed. A man with badly-dyed blond hair read something on his iPad. A woman with retro Rita Hayworth-style red hair stared into space. A couple in their twenties, in T-shirts and shorts, texted endlessly on their BlackBerrys, and once, briefly, the man laid a hand on the young woman's knee, and she smiled at him.

When the door opened and two newcomers walked in, Rita Hayworth, the man in black and the iPad guy glanced up briefly, then lost interest.

Just a mother and daughter, at least twenty years apart, yet lookalikes, dark-haired with tawny lights, expensively dressed, both slim, both wearing large, dark Tiffany sunglasses which neither removed.

The mom checked them in with the receptionist as the teenage daughter chose a seat, picked up an old copy of *Cosmo*, opened it, then closed it again and dumped it back on the table.

She waited until her mother sat down beside her.

'I'm not going in,' she said quietly.

'Sure you are.' The mother's accent was lightly Hispanic.

'I'm not.'

'You promised you'd let the doctor look at you.'

The tension in the mother's tone carried, made several people glance up.

'I've changed my mind. I can't bear it.'

'You're being foolish.'

'And who taught me that, Mama?'

Hysteria bubbled under the teenager's tone, and her mother tried to take her hand, but the daughter snatched it away.

'I understand, baby, if anyone does, but they're so sore.'

'You're such a hypocrite. You can't even say the *word*.'

'Stop it, Felicia,' the mother said.

'Eyes,' the girl said, and shuddered. '*Eyes*,' she repeated. 'You made me a freak, and you're cruel to make me come here.'

Everyone was listening now, most trying not to stare openly.

'This is hard for me too,' the mother whispered. 'You know that.'

'So I'll make it easier for you,' the teenager said.

And stood up.

'What are you doing?' the mother said.

'Leaving,' the daughter said.

And went out the door.

The mother took a distraught breath, then stood up, looked helplessly toward the receptionist. 'I'm very sorry,' she said.

'Mrs Delgado,' the receptionist began.

But she had already gone.

The young couple grinned at each other; the blind woman's lips compressed a little; the skinny man raised his eyebrows; Rita shook her red head.

The receptionist sighed softly, picked up a pencil and crossed through something in one of her appointment books.

A little after four, Billie Smith called Sam, surprising him.

'I'm having a bit of a crisis of confidence,' she told him.

'I can't imagine why,' he said, 'but how can I help?'

'You could help me a lot,' she said, 'by agreeing to a couple of extra rehearsals of our scenes. Especially our duet.'

'Small beer for you, surely, compared with the rest.'

'To be truthful,' Billie said, 'what I'm really hoping is that you might help me work through my Act Four stuff with Don José.'

'Then surely it's Jack you should be asking.'

'He's not as approachable as you are, Sam.'

That surprised him.

'Have you talked to Linda about it?'

'No *way*,' Billie said.

She sounded horrified, like a teen scared of exposing weakness to a tutor, reminding Sam again of how young she was.

'I'm sure Linda would gladly organize some extra rehearsals,' he said. 'Though it's Mondays and Thursdays from next week, so that should help.'

'I'd rather it was just the two of us, just this one time.' Billie stuck to her guns. 'So I could really feel I was getting somewhere before next week.' She paused. 'I'll understand if you say you don't want to, only please don't.'

It was exactly like talking to a kid.

Sam sighed. 'You'd have to come to my house. We could work in the lanai.'

And Claudia would be around.

Grace's sister, who'd been horrifically widowed last year, had moved to Sunny Isles Beach a few months back, close to where Saul – Sam's adoptive, much younger brother – and Cathy shared an apartment. And with his dad and Mildred just up in Golden Beach, all of them in easy reach of the Bay Harbor Islands, where Sam and Grace lived, they were spoilt for choice when it came to babysitting.

And in this case, chaperoning.

Better safe.

'That would be just great,' Billie said. 'Tomorrow?'

'I'll have to run it by my sister-in-law,' Sam said. 'She's staying with us while my wife's away.'

'Taking care of your little boy?' Billie said. 'Joshua?'

'That's right.'

'Seven o'clock, if it's OK with her?'

'Sure,' Sam said.

May 11

Grace's address – titled 'Irrational fears and phobias in the young teen' – began at nine a.m. on the penultimate morning of the conference.

She was buzzing with tension, her pulse racing, but she took a calming breath, conjured up a favorite image of Sam and Joshua playing, and took in her audience.

Those whose faces she could see looked expectant, interested.

Having no viable alternative, she began. 'The title of my talk this morning is misleading. One of Merriam-Webster's definitions of the word "irrational" is "not based on reason".'

She paused, plucked a single face out of the front row.

Female, fortyish, anonymous.

She talked to her.

'It seems to me,' she went on, 'that any young person has an incalculable number of reasons to experience fear of some sort. Being a still-growing, developing, unfolding human is both fascinating and terrifying. And even those children and young teens most capable of superficial toughness – the ones who appear to skate through – are often deep-down scared.

'I know I was,' she said. 'Weren't you?'

In the long, narrow foyer just outside the conference room, a young man watched and listened through the slightly open glass doors.

And smiled.

He had wavy brown hair and rimless glasses, and he was dressed in a well-cut gray suit, blue silk tie and perfectly polished shoes.

A middle-aged woman in a navy-and-white-spotted dress came out of the room, moving carefully, quietly, so as not to disturb the speaker or her audience. The young man held the door open for her, and she nodded her thanks.

He stepped inside the room, took out his phone.

Went on listening and watching.

And, every now and then, discreetly, took photographs.

Sam called Grace before he took his shower.

Five a.m. in Miami. Eleven in Zurich.

Her printed schedule stated that the talk after her own was set to begin soon, which meant that Grace's phone was probably switched off.

She picked up instantly, which told him she'd been hoping he'd call.

Which he loved.

Something to be said about separation, perhaps – so long as it was brief.

'It's early,' she said. 'You should be asleep.'

'I should be speaking to my wife,' Sam said. 'How'd it go?'

'Quite well, I think,' she said.

'Good questions?'

'Better than that,' she said. 'A real back-and-forth debate.'

'Better than "quite well" then,' Sam said. 'Congratulations, Gracie.'

'How's our son?'

'Still sleeping, angelic till he wakes. How was dinner with those nice people?'

'Good fish restaurant,' she told him. 'And they are nice. I miss you.'

'Me too, sweetheart. Roll on Friday.'

'Is Claudia OK?'

'She was last night,' Sam said. 'I've had to ask her to chaperone me this evening.'

'How come?'

'Billie Smith wants to run through some scenes before the next rehearsal.'

'Billie Smith as in young and gorgeous?' Grace said.

'Billie Smith as in the kid of my old school pal,' Sam said. 'But yes, definitely as in young and gorgeous.'

'I'm glad Claudia's chaperoning.'

'You are kidding, I hope,' Sam said. 'Old enough to be her father, remember?'

'Still pretty handsome for an old guy,' Grace said. 'And your eyes still work.'

Sam heard a hum of approaching voices over the phone.

'I have to go,' Grace said.

'I love you,' Sam told her.

But she had already gone.

Eight a.m., and Mildred and David were seated in another waiting room.

She'd requested a first appointment, figuring that at least she'd be done with it early, and she'd considered turning down David's tranquilizer, then caved in.

Dr Ethan Adams, according to her husband and Ralph Sutter, was a distinguished, well-respected ophthalmic surgeon with his own clinic, though this morning they were seeing him in an office he occupied twice weekly at Miami General Hospital.

Right now, waiting, Mildred felt far worse than she had yesterday.

No real possibility of escaping, because the diagnosis had already been made, so now it was just a question of precisely how this new doctor – this *surgeon* – decided to deal with it.

'OK?' David asked her.

'Wonderful,' she said.

She felt nauseous, cold.

David took her left hand, but she pulled it away, laid it in her lap.

'Sorry,' she said.

'It's fine,' he said. 'It will be fine.'

'I just want it to be over,' Mildred said.

Ethan Adams was around fifty, she surmised, with beautiful silver hair, silver-rimmed spectacles to match, immaculate skin and well-kept, elegant hands. He looked like the kind of super-rich man with staff at home to help him with personal care and dressing – and of course, that was nonsense, she was being judgmental and unfair, but the fact was, Mildred did not care for him.

There was something about Dr Ethan Adams that disturbed her. She did not feel that he was a *nice* man.

Which probably did not matter nearly as much as his talent for operating on cataracts. Yet for someone as scared as she was, it seemed to matter a good deal.

She told herself it was just imagination, fear taking over.

'Shall we make a start?' Ethan Adams asked her.

No.

Mildred stood up.

'Of course,' she said.

Grace, two of her fellow delegates and Elspeth Mettler had come to a restaurant two streets down the hill from the conference center, a small, pleasant place with embroidered white tablecloths and gleaming cutlery. The menu was small but with enough variety for most tastes, and the aromas emerging from the kitchen were mouth-watering.

'I was expecting a sandwich,' Grace said.

'Don't worry,' Dr Mettler told her. 'The portions here are quite small.'

'Certainly by American standards,' said Natalie Gérard, a slim, suntanned teacher from Provence.

'Doctor Lucca hardly looks like a huge eater.' Dr Stefan Mainz, a children's advocate from Frankfurt, smiled warmly at Grace.

'Maybe not huge,' she said. 'But I do enjoy fine food.'

'Marvelous food in Tuscany,' Dr Mainz said. 'Or is your surname a red herring, Doctor?'

'Not red or any other color herring,' she said. 'But please call me Grace.'

'Perhaps we should order,' Ms Gérard urged. 'We don't have long.'

A small bowl of fragrant fish broth, an excellent mushroom risotto and a glass of Valais white wine later, Grace felt more like snoozing than returning to the conference, but she hoped the uphill walk back would revive her.

'I need to pick up something from the pharmacy over the road,' Dr Mettler said. 'I'll see you all back there.'

She hurried across the street and into the *Apotheke*, just as a young man emerged from the shop, paused to slip a small paper bag into the pocket of his leather jacket, and took out his cell phone.

For a moment, Grace, still standing outside the restaurant, was unsure.

His glasses were dark today, and though he appeared to be glancing in her direction, he showed no sign of recognition.

Yet she was almost sure that it was the man who'd spoken to her on her first afternoon in Zurich.

Suddenly, belatedly, he raised his left hand absently in a kind of salute.

'Coming?' Dr Mainz prompted her.

Grace returned the wave, and quickly turned back to her colleagues. 'Yes, of course. I'm sorry.'

'A friend?' Natalie Gérard was curious.

'Just someone I encountered the other day,' Grace said. 'A coincidence.'

'Ah,' Stefan Mainz said. 'But do we believe in those?'

'My husband doesn't, on the whole,' Grace answered as they walked up the hill. 'But I think I do, for the most part.'

'Your husband's a detective, I heard,' Ms Gérard said.

'A police detective, yes,' Grace said.

'Some parallels in his work and yours, don't you think, Doctor Lucca?' the advocate said. 'Detection and deduction.'

Grace smiled. 'Sometimes.'

A scrap of recall came to her abruptly from that first afternoon. The young man in Sprüngli had asked her, at the outset, if she was OK, but then, when she'd got up to leave, after she'd thanked him for his concern, he had said: 'It was not so much concern.'

Which she hadn't really understood, but which had probably meant nothing whatsoever, like her mistaken impression that he'd been flirting with her.

And she supposed that Zurich was a small enough city for coincidences.

Slow, slow morning at the office.

Sam could not remember the last time his desk had been this clean.

Martinez's looked about the same, except he was relaxed about it, whereas Sam felt restless and bored.

It was hard to know what to feel at times like these, since none of them wished for brutality anyplace, let alone in their jurisdiction, and the other detectives in Violent Crimes sure as *hell* did not want to see first-hand the handiwork of a monster like Black Hole . . .

A vacation might be nice, Sam pondered. Maybe he'd ask Claudia if she'd mind caring for Joshua on her own for a few days, and he could fly to Zurich, meet Gracie . . .

Except Grace was not on vacation, and she was flying back Friday and the fare was not flexible, and he had this damned rehearsal with Billie Smith tonight, and the next official S-BOP rehearsal in a few days.

And anyway, this restlessness was mostly on account of Grace not being home, so, Lord willing, only another two days to go.

Dr Magda Shrike was about to see a new patient.

Actually, the patient's mother had phoned to make an appointment with Grace and, in her absence, had agreed that her daughter should see Magda.

Felicia Delgado, age fourteen.

Her mother, Beatriz Delgado, had said that she just couldn't cope anymore, and she knew she ought to have sought help long ago, but she'd been too afraid, because this was, of course, 'all her fault'.

They'd arrived together, two brunettes, both wearing ultra-large and impenetrably dark designer sunglasses.

Beatriz Delgado had requested a few minutes with Magda before her daughter's appointment. Magda had asked the teenager if that was OK with her, and Felicia had shrugged and sat down to wait.

In Magda's office, the reason for the dark glasses was swiftly revealed.

'My daughter has a phobia,' Mrs Delgado said. 'And the reason I say I'm to blame for her problems is because I have the same thing, so I've passed it on to her.' Her clasped hands were white-knuckled. 'It's called ommatophobia. A fear of eyes.'

'Do you know the origin of your problem, Mrs Delgado?' Magda asked.

The other woman shook her head. 'I don't think I can remember a time when I was normal.'

'It's not uncommon,' Magda said, 'for sufferers of phobias to have no conscious understanding of what might have sparked their fear or aversion, though in some cases they've buried the source deep because of its painfulness.'

The need for this consultation, Mrs Delgado explained, had been triggered by an eye infection that Felicia had developed some days ago. Yesterday, after her daughter had refused to keep an appointment with a doctor, her mother had bought antibiotic eye drops and attempted to administer them – which had been hard for her, Beatriz said, had made her feel sick to her stomach – but her daughter had become completely hysterical.

Magda waited.

'My husband – a decent man – left me when Felicia was seven, because he couldn't bear to go on living with a crazy person. I have no other family, I don't talk to our neighbors, and over time I've pushed away all my friends.' Her voice was choked. 'I'm only telling you these things, Doctor Shrike, because of how badly they've affected Felicia, and I've already caused her so much damage.'

'You've brought her here now,' Magda said.

'But what if I'm too late?' Beatriz Delgado said.

It was a long, long day for Mildred. Dr Ethan Adams nothing if not thorough.

Questions came first for him.

'Couldn't we please get the exam out of the way first?' Mildred asked.

'I'm afraid not,' he said.

Dr Sutter had asked her similar questions about her vision and general health, but this man was not prepared to take her word as gospel. Her assurance that she did not have either diabetes or high blood pressure made little impression on him. He took her blood pressure and pronounced it a little high, which surprised neither Mildred nor David in the circumstances, and ordered basic blood tests – which Mildred supposed she didn't mind, having no fear of needles.

Eyes, so far as she knew, were her only real Achilles' heel.

Dr Adams explained about the different types of cataracts and their causes, and Mildred tried to tune out, nodding occasionally and trying to visualize happy situations. But then Adams began describing the various methods that might be used to treat and remove each kind of cataract, and Mildred could bear no more and cut him short, feeling angry with him because he had been made aware of her anxieties.

'I'm afraid I'm much too nervous to listen to that right now,' she said.

Dr Adams smiled, but Mildred saw that he was unimpressed. Which was just too bad, so far as she was concerned, and she was perspiring now – she seldom perspired – and her heart was beating too fast, and he hadn't even *begun* his examination.

'Maybe later,' she said, 'after you've discovered which type of cataract I have, you can tell me what you're going to do.'

His smile did not reach his eyes. 'I'm pretty sure already what we're going to find,' he said.

'Good for you,' Mildred said.

She could feel David's eyes on her, ignored him.

Barely hanging on as it was.

He repeated every test that Dr Sutter had done, and by the time they reached the eye drop stage, she disliked him even more intensely, though she knew she was being irrational, because patently these tests were vital, and for Pete's sake, her *eyesight* was the prize at the end of all this.

So she gritted her teeth and went on, through extra exams and tests to rule out far more serious problems like macular degeneration, and nothing bad befell Mildred. Except for blurry vision, plain old-fashioned fear, and a growing revulsion at having Ethan Adams sitting so *close* to her.

Over soon, she kept telling herself.

Which, of course, it finally was.

Except that she knew that it was only the beginning.

Magda seldom expected much from a first encounter with a troubled teen. In this case, little more than gauging how resistant Felicia Delgado was to talking to her or any psychologist, though conversely – less probably – she might discover a young person craving professional help.

Felicia came to the point fast.

'Don't ask me to take off my glasses, because I won't.'

'All right,' Magda said.

'I'm sure my mother told you that already.'

The big sunglasses covered the teenager's oval face from her eyebrows down to her cheeks and horizontally to her ears. Her hair, long, shiny and brown with reddish lights, was cut with long bangs. She took care with her general appearance and her exposed skin was clear, but her fingernails were chewed, her sitting position slightly hunched.

'She told me that you have a problem regarding your eyes,' Magda said.

Felicia shifted in her chair.

'What color are they?' Magda asked.

'Brown,' Felicia said. 'I don't want to talk about them.'

'Is there anything you would like to talk about?'

'I'm only here to get my mother off my back.'

'Your mother wants to help you, Felicia,' Magda said.

'She says she does.'

'Don't you feel that's true?'

'She feels guilty,' Felicia said.

'Why do you think that?'

'I don't just think it, I know it.'

'OK,' Magda said. 'Why should your mother feel guilty?'

'Because she knows she's the reason I'm like this.'

'Like what?'

'Like mother, like daughter.'

'How exactly?' Magda asked.

'Both crazy,' Felicia said.

Grace had been to the cinema.

She'd had no appetite at the end of the working day, and she'd noticed that *The King's Speech*, the big British Oscar-winner, was playing at a cinema in town – subtitled, not dubbed, and the hotel receptionist had advised her that Kino Corso on Theaterstrasse was a large, clean cinema in a busy part of town, close to cafés, restaurants and bars, with good tram connections.

It felt strange sitting in a cinema alone, but the movie was every bit as fine as she'd heard, good enough for her to see it again with Sam, if he liked. But for now, she was finally hungry, wondering whether she should find someplace down here to eat, or go straight back to the hotel to eat in the bar . . .

She spotted him about five seconds before it happened.

The young man *again*, crossing the street about twenty yards away, wearing jeans and the same leather jacket he'd worn earlier, carrying shopping bags. And as Grace wondered about the odds of this second coincidence, he dropped one of his bags, bent to pick it up – then stumbled and fell on the tramline.

A tram was speeding towards him.

'Hey!' Grace shouted, halfway across the street, realizing that something was wrong, because he looked dazed, was not moving. 'Tram coming!'

He tried rising, gave a startled yelp of pain, his right leg folding under him.

'Let me help.' Grace reached him, bent, pulled at his left arm. 'Come *on*.'

She heard the tram's bell, heard its brakes screech, saw its lights looming, and the young man was up now, but trying to retrieve his bags.

'Just *leave* them!' She dragged at his arm again, and this time he came with her, clearing the line, leaning on her as the tram halted, just feet away.

She looked back at the bags, realizing suddenly how close they'd come.

Joshua and Sam flew into her mind, and maybe she should have been more careful, though she knew she'd had no choice.

'*Ist alles in Ordnung?*' a woman shouted.

Grace looked up, saw people staring, heard another louder voice, realized that the tram driver was shouting at them in Swiss-German, incomprehensible to her, though it was clear that the poor man had been frightened into anger.

'I'm very sorry,' she called to him.

'*Sind Sie verletzt?*' another woman called.

'She's asking if you're injured,' the young man translated.

She turned to the woman, shook her head, managed a smile, turned back to him. 'What happened to you?'

'I don't know. My leg just gave way.' He looked shaken. 'You could have been killed.'

'No,' Grace said. 'The driver stopped in time.'

'But he might not have.'

'How's the leg now?'

He tried a step. 'It feels OK, but back there . . .' He smiled at her. 'You were incredible. So fast.'

Last year flashed into her mind, as it often did.

Taking a life.

Perhaps the reason she'd felt she had no choice just now.

The young man had gone to speak to the driver. Their audience was melting away, and now both men were coming back to her.

'This gentleman needs to make sure we're not injured. For his report.'

Grace smiled at the driver, showed him that her arms and legs were in good order, thanked him, and looked back at the young man, who was gathering up his bags. 'You seem fine now.'

'My dignity aside,' he said.

The driver, restored to calm, bade them farewell and returned to his tram and waiting passengers.

'I don't know about you,' the young man said, 'but I could use a drink.'

'Good idea,' Grace said.

'Will you join me? There's a good restaurant close by, but I'm sure we could just have a drink.'

Grace thought about calling Sam. 'I really should get back.'

'I wouldn't keep you long.' the young man said.

He looked quite pale, she thought, perhaps still shocked.

'Why not?' she said.

David and Mildred had left Miami General a while ago, traffic slow.

Mildred sat silently, the blur in her eyes worse than last time, making her feel a little nauseous.

'I wish you'd say something,' David said.

Mildred took a breath. 'Remind me, please, why you took me to that man?'

'I gather you didn't like him.'

'Please,' she said, 'just tell me.'

'Because he's one of the very best,' David said. 'Because his clinic has a fine reputation with a virtually zero rating on infection issues.' He glanced at her. 'And because he's happy to perform the procedure under general anesthesia and to keep you in overnight – which I like the sound of, because it'll put you under less pressure.'

'I know I'm very lucky that it's only cataracts.' Mildred paused, remembering something the doctor had said about the value of good diet and lifestyle. 'Do you think that my old life might have caused this?'

Her years on the streets suddenly taking on a new perspective.

'I'd doubt it,' David said. 'Cataracts are very common.'

'I know. Doctor Adams said so.'

'How much do you dislike him?'

'I wasn't keen,' she said.

'Then we'll find someone else,' David said.

'And go through all that again?' Mildred shook her head. 'Not for anything.'

'You wouldn't have to go through it all,' David said. 'I'd see to that.'

'No,' Mildred said. 'I'm just being foolish again. I'm sure Doctor Adams is terrific, because otherwise you wouldn't have recommended him.'

'I wouldn't,' David agreed. 'But it's your call.'

They were both silent for a few moments.

'I'm so sorry you're having to go through this,' he said.

'But it's nothing,' she said. 'Compared to real sickness, nothing at all.'

'It's not nothing,' David said, 'to you.'

'It'll pass,' Mildred said.

Finally the young man had a name.

Thomas Chauvin.

From Strasbourg, France. The official seat of the European Parliament, located close to the German border.

They'd only reached introductory details after they'd been seated in *Sterne Foifi* for a few minutes, each quickly downing a small whisky, and then the delicious smells had become too much for Grace, and Thomas had recommended and ordered the *Geschnetzeltes Kalbfleisch* with *Rösti* potatoes for two, and a carafe of Swiss white wine.

Grace took out her phone and checked for messages.

'Someone you need to call, Mrs Becket?' Thomas Chauvin asked.

'My husband,' Grace said. 'In Florida.'

He glanced at his watch. 'Six hours earlier?'

She nodded. 'He's still at work.'

'May I ask what he does?'

'Sam's a police detective,' Grace said.

'Sounds exciting,' Thomas Chauvin said.

Grace saw the flicker of intense interest in his eyes.

'Sometimes too much so,' she said.

'And you? You told me you're here for a conference.'

'I'm a psychologist,' Grace said.

'An impressive couple,' he said. 'I'm a photographer.'

'What kind of photographer?'

'All kinds. I take photos for recreation and for a living. My aim is to be a photojournalist.'

'Interesting work,' Grace said.

'I'd like to take a photo now,' he said. 'Of you.'

She smiled. 'I don't think so.' She looked around. The place was full, the clientele of all ages, the noise level moderately high.

'So,' Thomas Chauvin said. 'Small world, as they say.'

'Amazingly so, in this case,' Grace said.

'I'm no gambler or mathematician, so I couldn't begin to guess the odds of three chance encounters in less than as many days.' He paused. 'Lucky ones for me, especially the last.'

She skated over that, remarked instead on his fluent English, and he told her that his grandmother had been raised in London, and that he'd made a point of studying English intensively, since it was still the dominant language in the world he wanted to inhabit.

'And I spend too much time watching American and British movies.' He grinned.

'So what brings you to Zurich?'

'Just vacation,' he said. 'A few days to look around, get some ideas, watch people.' He smiled. 'Meet them, sometimes.'

She wondered, very briefly, if there was any possibility that he might have engineered that incident outside the cinema, then realized it would have been almost impossible to get the timing right – and in any case, it was a preposterous thought. Yet still, she was starting to wish that she had stuck to one swift drink, since now she had no choice but to wait for dinner with this stranger, their only common ground those few moments of shock on the street.

It was a relief when the food arrived.

'You like it?' he asked after her first mouthful.

'It's delicious.' She wished he would stop watching her so intently.

'I'm sorry for staring. But I never had anyone save my life before.'

'I didn't exactly run into a burning building,' Grace said.

'You shouldn't make light of it,' he said. 'It was very brave.'

'It was nothing. I didn't even stop to think.'

'That's what heroic people always say.'

'Oh, please.' She regretted her irritation, but his exaggeration rubbed like sandpaper on last year's wounds.

'I'm sorry,' Chauvin said. 'I didn't mean to upset you.'

'You didn't,' she said. 'But I can assure you that I'm no heroine.'

'May I at least say you were foolhardy?'

Grace smiled. 'I guess you can say that.'

'I never had such a thing happen before,' he said. 'I heard of a terrible freak accident involving an old lady and a tram a year or two ago, but for a young man to be so clumsy and stupid . . .'

'Accidents can happen to anyone.' Grace looked at her wine glass, decided against another sip.

'Foolhardy and brave,' Chauvin said.

She looked around. 'I wonder if they would call a taxi for me.'

'I've made you angry,' he said.

'Not at all,' Grace said. 'But I do want to get back.'

'To speak to your husband.'

'Yes,' she said.

She almost mentioned Joshua, then stopped. Past experiences, she guessed. Trusting strangers with personal information and coming to regret it. Especially a would-be photojournalist.

Chauvin requested a cab for her and asked for the check, and Grace took out her Amex card.

'No.' Thomas Chauvin's face was set firm. 'I promise this is the last time I will mention it. But whether or not that tram would have stopped in time, you did try to save the life of a perfect stranger, and I'd say that's more than worth the price of one small dinner.'

She found it hard to argue with that, and within minutes her cab was outside, and Chauvin wanted to see her into the taxi, and Grace knew it would be churlish to refuse.

'Thank you for dinner,' she said.

'Thank you for saving me, Grace.' Thomas Chauvin opened the taxi door for her. 'That name is, coincidentally, very special to me.'

She had neither time nor inclination to ask why.

He closed the door, and the taxi departed.

Thomas Chauvin watched for another moment as the car pulled away, and then he took out his iPhone, tapped into his photos and looked at the screen.

At one of the shots of Grace he'd taken earlier that day, as she and her colleagues had left their restaurant.

In the photograph, she was looking right at him.

God, she was beautiful.

Chauvin smiled, put the phone safely into his pocket.

Patted it.

'How's she doing?' Sam asked his father.

He hated the thought of Mildred being afraid, their relationship going back to her bag lady days when she'd shared occasional snippets of street information with him.

Tiny in stature, but brave, no cowardice in her.

'She's mad at herself,' David said. 'And she's doing her best to appear calm, but she's dreading the surgery.'

'Do you have a date yet?'

'Not yet,' David said. 'The doctor plans to do the eyes one at a time, and he wanted to discuss methods with Mildred, but she wasn't ready, so we have to go back again, which is a pity.'

'This Adams is a top man, obviously,' Sam said.

'He has a great reputation, though Mildred didn't care for him.'

'Shooting the messenger?' Sam asked. 'Or something more?'

He'd always had a healthy respect for Mildred's instincts.

'His empathy skills could use some work,' David said. 'But my contacts assure me he's damned good, and this is small fry for him.'

'What about going to someone else?' Sam asked.

'She says she wouldn't start over again even if the new doctor were Santa.'

When Grace called, Sam gave her family news and then they moved on to her day.

'As a matter of fact,' she said, 'I had quite an evening. Went to the movies, stopped a man from being hit by a tram and ended up having supper with him.'

'Really?'

She heard the startled note in Sam's voice.

'Young enough to be my son,' she reassured him, even if it was not strictly true. 'He'd had a shock, needed a drink. I needed food. He's a photographer, keen to be a photojournalist, and he was very interested in your occupation. I told him nothing, obviously, except that I wanted to get back to my hotel to talk to you.'

'OK, I'm convinced,' Sam said. 'Though he must have thought his birthday had come early, having his life saved by a sexy blonde.'

'I told you, he's young.'

'Young men have eyes too.'

'So they do,' she agreed, and tried not to think about poor Mildred.

'As a matter of fact, you'll recall that I have a young and rather beautiful woman coming to spend the evening with me,' Sam said, staying upbeat.

'So you do,' Grace said. 'Your gorgeous young diva.'

'To be honest,' Sam said, 'I could do without it.'

'It'll be fun,' Grace said. 'And good for the production.'

'I'll think of you,' he told her, 'asleep in your Swiss bed.'

'And I'll think of you,' she said, 'coaching Carmen.'

Magda had finished work for the evening when her appointments line rang.

She let it go to voicemail, screening.

It was Beatriz Delgado, calling to make another appointment for her daughter.

Magda picked up. 'Doctor Shrike here. How's Felicia doing?'

'Not so good,' Mrs Delgado said.

'Do you think our short session upset her?' Magda asked.

'Everything upsets her.'

'It's too soon even to say "early days", Mrs Delgado.' Magda walked into her office and opened her datebook. 'We haven't really begun.'

'Do you think you can help her, Doctor?'

'I'm certainly going to do my best,' Magda said.

'I have to go,' the other woman said suddenly.

'The appointment,' Magda said.

But Beatriz Delgado had already gone.

Billie Smith looked a treat, reminding Sam, a little, of a very young Halle Berry.

'This is so kind of you.' She stood on tiptoe to kiss his cheek, held out a bottle of red wine.

'Hey,' Sam said lightly. 'This is a rehearsal. No alcohol allowed, orders of La Morrison.'

'Who's not here,' Billie said, 'and I need to relax into the singing a little more, which is part of the point of tonight.'

'Extra practice is the point of tonight,' Sam said, like a schoolteacher.

Claudia came out of the kitchen into the hallway, the dogs behind her: Woody, the Becket's ageing mini dachshund-schnauzer cross, and her own three-legged spaniel, Ludo.

'Hi there,' she said warmly. 'I'm Claudia Brownley, Sam's sister-in-law.'

Billie shook her hand. 'Good to meet you. I'm Billie Smith.'

'Sam tells me your father's an old school friend of his.'

'Uh-huh,' Billie said.

'And you're playing Carmen,' Claudia said. 'I'm incredibly impressed.'

'I wish I was,' Billie said.

'You have a beautiful voice,' Sam told her. 'And nerves are just part of the whole process.'

'Do you suffer from stage fright?' Claudia asked her.

'God, yes,' Billie says. 'That's why I'm here, because Sam's so much kinder than our director, so I'm hoping he's going to give me a boost.'

Sam thought he almost saw his sister-in-law's brows rise.

'Well, let's hope,' Claudia said. 'It was good of you to bring wine, Billie, though I gather alcohol isn't good for the singing voice.' She took the bottle. 'A few sips will go nicely with our supper, though. I made a lasagna. I hope that's OK for you, Billie. I made it vegetarian, in case.'

'It sounds wonderful,' Billie said.

'You didn't need to do that,' Sam told Claudia. 'You're doing far too much for us already.'

'I'm enjoying it,' she said. 'You know that.'

The supper was delicious, if a little strained. Sam and Claudia asked Billie a few questions about her life, her job, her classes, about Larry and Jill, her parents; both trying to draw her out, relax her, but she seemed reluctant to give up much about herself, and Sam wondered if there were family issues.

Though it was later, while he and Billie were working through their Act Four scene – *'If you love me, Carmen'* – that the really awkward moment of the evening occurred.

Not a pass, exactly.

Just Billie brushing up against Sam.

In a way that felt more than merely accidental.

Enough to put him on alert.

Definitely not what he wanted.

'You guys want some coffee?'

Claudia again, right on cue, making Sam wonder if she'd been on patrol, and in other circumstances that might have been irritating, but right now it just felt welcome.

'I'll get it,' Sam told her. 'I want to look in on Joshua anyway.'

'Can I come?' Billie asked.

'He's been a little restless,' Claudia said. 'Better if it's just his dad.'

Before long they were back to rehearsing, and it was a real pleasure listening to Billie and good giving his own voice an extra airing. And a little later, Joshua came down and brought the dogs in with him, and Billie was sweet and natural with them all, so Sam let Joshua hang with them for about fifteen minutes until Claudia coerced him back upstairs with a promise of an extra story.

'You're a lucky man,' Billie told Sam.

'You don't have to tell me.'

'When's Grace due back?'

'Day after tomorrow,' Sam said.

For an instant, he thought he saw wistfulness in her eyes, and she'd spoken briefly about her parents' move up to Jacksonville a few years back, and he guessed she missed them. And for all Billie's natural beauty and talent and sweetness, Sam found himself feeling sorry for her.

You could never tell just by looking who were the lonely ones.

May 12

The call came in to Violent Crimes just after eleven on Thursday morning.

Bay Drive in North Beach.

Woman shot to death in the bedroom of a single-story house.

'Sounds like Black Hole finally hit the Beach,' Beth Riley, their sergeant, informed them, and appointed Sam lead investigator on the case.

Sam said little, Amelia Newton's deathbed still vivid in his mind.

'We got a name?' Martinez asked Riley.

'Beatriz Delgado,' she said.

Nice little house with a small, well-maintained driveway, pretty backyard, plenty of neat palms and flowers. Wood flooring inside, vaulted ceilings, marble in the bathrooms, granite and steel in the kitchen. Expensive.

No signs of struggle or forced entry.

Patrol officers put the detectives in the picture, fast and somber.

The man presently slumped on the couch in the living room, his face in his hands, had reported the crime. Carlos Delgado, the victim's ex-husband, whose cries when he'd found Mrs Delgado had been – according to a female neighbor – enough to ice her blood.

Even Dr Elliot Sanders, the Chief Medical Examiner, was grim-faced when he joined the party. 'I gather you saw Fort Lauderdale,' he said to Sam.

'Bad scene,' Sam said. 'Lot of similarities.'

As in that previous case, the victim was in the bedroom. The late Mrs Delgado looking even worse, or maybe just more bizarre, than Amelia Newton had.

No sunglasses this time.

A pair of small, old-fashioned white lace doilies covering her wounds.

Sanders took his first look beneath them.

'Gauze again, stuffed into the sockets under those things.'

'Holy Mother,' Martinez said quietly.

Sam stayed silent, pushing through these first tough moments so he could get straight to work.

The parallels with Fort Lauderdale were unmistakable. The victim tidily positioned on her own king-size bed. Fully clothed in an olive-colored linen dress, her underwear in place.

Same kind of latex sheeting over three stacked pillows.

'Why three pillows?' Martinez asked.

'Makes them easier targets, maybe?' Sam hazarded. 'But why bother with the rubber sheet if they're leaving it behind?'

'Maybe a thing about dirty laundry,' Martinez said. 'Not that it worked.'

'Seems almost theatrical,' Sam said.

Sanders went on working. 'I heard you're singing again.'

Sam didn't respond, knew no answer was expected, went on focusing hard.

The time frame here was obviously the biggest difference between this and the last scene, this crime perpetrated more recently, perhaps just an hour or two ago.

Not the only timing difference. The first three killings had been approximately a month apart, then nothing in April – now *two* in less than a week, and did that mean the killer was growing more frenzied (though there was nothing here, in this carefully set scene, to suggest frenzy) or making up for lost time? And if the hiatus had been in March, coinciding with spring break, they might have been considering a teacher or other school employee, but . . .

He quit trawling, and came back to what was in front of them.

Ballistics would probably confirm that the wounds had been created by the same weapon.

Just those weird little lacy coverlets seeming to make it a little worse.

And that *smell* again, Sam realized as it reached him through the rest. Past the smell of burned feathers from the pillow probably used as a silencer – feather pillow rather than foam this time, though more than likely that was simply because it had been available.

This time, though, he identified the other smell.

'Anyone else smell acetone?' he asked.

Elliot Sanders nodded toward the victim's feet, toenails polished bright pink.

'Recently applied?' Sam asked, trying to recall if Amelia Newton's toe or fingernails had been painted.

'Not this morning,' the ME answered.

'That smell always hangs about,' Martinez said. 'I've never liked it.'

'So no chance the killer applied that polish?' Sam asked the ME.

Sanders took another look at the victim's toes. 'Too hard to have been painted that recently. Unless the killer was here all night or longer.' He paused, added ironically: 'She certainly didn't die of inhalant abuse.'

'Drugged again?' Sam said.

'You'll find out when I do,' Sanders said. 'No sign of her being forced to swallow anything.'

Joe Duval, who'd arrived soon after the Miami Beach detectives, came into the room. Different kind of worry etched on his forehead.

'The daughter's missing,' he said.

Carlos Delgado had only just started making sense, was still a mess.

As anyone finding that scene, let alone his wife, would be.

Ex-wife.

Looking at him closely now, Sam had to ask himself how *much* of a mess. Anyone could yell loud enough for the neighbors to hear, work themselves up, bury their face in their hands.

This man was a whole lot calmer now than he had been.

No tears, no look of devastation.

Still, *ex*-wife, so who knew what had gone on?

Nothing so bad, so *terminal*, apparently, that he hadn't been able to come into her home and find her body.

Sam glanced at Martinez, knew they were browsing the same page.

They knew that everyone reacted differently to tragedy.

Certainly ex-husbands, especially after a lousy marriage.

Though it would have to have been a real bitch of a marriage for a guy not to be genuinely distraught on finding his ex, the mother of his child – presumably – so brutally and grotesquely slain.

Delgado's account was straightforward, so far as it went.

When his fourteen-year-old daughter, Felicia, had been a no-show at St Thomas Aquinas Middle School – less than two miles away – this morning, someone in the school office had called her home and, receiving no answer, had contacted her father at his office.

That part of the story had already been corroborated. Felicia had missed school time twice in the previous two days, taken by her mother to doctors' appointments, but Mrs Delgado was always correct, they said, about seeking permission or informing the school if Felicia was sick.

'You have a key to this house, sir?' Sam asked.

'I do,' Delgado said. 'It's my property, for one thing, but my wife likes – liked – me to keep a key.' The shake of his head was disbelieving. 'I tried calling Beatriz, and then I came to see what was up, and . . .' His mouth trembled. 'You know the rest.'

'And you have no idea where your daughter might be?' Sam asked.

'If I knew . . .' He shook his head again. 'I'm scared to death for her.'

The haunted look now in his dark eyes looked real enough to Sam, except that killers got *haunted* too, because of what they'd done.

Especially in crimes of passion.

And he felt that this man was holding back something.

It made no sense to figure him for Black Hole. Serial killers seldom spilt blood on their own doorstep, unless, of course, they were in a real tight corner.

If, say, their ex-wife had found out what they'd been doing.

Though after a thing like that, they were more likely to flee the scene or maybe commit suicide.

A killer calling in the crime and sticking around for questioning seemed more than improbable to Sam and Martinez.

The house was busy now, Crime Scene techs all over, Duval on the phone ensuring that teams in Orlando, Jupiter, Naples and Fort Lauderdale were being kept in the loop.

This case, though, belonged to Miami Beach.

Goddamned poison chalice.

Martinez was asking Delgado about his movements the previous evening and night, and early that morning.

'You have to be kidding me,' Delgado said, comprehending what he was being asked.

'It's routine, sir,' Sam assured him.

'I have no *alibi*,' Delgado said. 'If that's what you're asking.'

'It would help the investigation,' Martinez said, 'to know where you were, sir.'

'For elimination,' Sam said.

'I was alone,' he said. 'At home.'

'Which is where, sir?' Martinez asked, ready to note it down.

Home was a condo in Country Club Drive in Aventura, opposite the golf course. Carlos Delgado an affluent real estate broker.

'Last evening, I was watching the Heat beating the Boston Celtics, eating pizza. Later, I went to bed. This morning, I already told you about.'

Martinez asked if he'd had the pizza delivered.

Delgado shook his head. 'It was in my freezer.'

No way of confirming any of it.

They requested his cooperation with fingerprints and a DNA swab, assured him that these, too, were strictly for elimination purposes.

'We're guessing, since you have a key,' Sam said, 'you're a regular visitor.'

'Regular, no,' Delgado said. 'But sure, I'm here now and then, for Felicia.' He stood up. 'So who's looking for my daughter while we waste time here?'

'There are a lot of people working on this case, sir,' Sam told him.

'They'll find your daughter,' Martinez said.

Unless, of course, Delgado had done something to her.

Both detectives thinking the same ugly thought.

They went on with their questions.

The last day of the conference had ended at five.

It had, overall, been a good experience for Grace. She'd listened to fine speakers, had met caring people from many countries, enjoyed stimulating debates with more strangers than she had for many years. Her own expertise appeared to have stood up well, if Dr Mettler and Stefan Mainz's compliments were to be believed.

But she could not wait to go home.

She'd called Sam during recess, and he'd told her about his evening with Billie Smith, and she'd been glad when he'd mentioned that awkward moment, even if it was a reminder of what she already knew: that her husband was a handsome, compelling man, and that women of all ages noticed him. And when the woman concerned was young, beautiful and talented, it was probably wise not to be complacent.

Yet Sam had told her about it, and she trusted him, same way he'd trusted her when she'd mentioned her encounter with Thomas Chauvin.

All done now at the conference, but not quite over yet for her, because four colleagues were coming for dinner at her hotel; the same group she'd lunched with yesterday, plus an Italian child psychologist.

A pleasant way to end.

And then, a bouquet of large pink roses waiting for her at the hotel's reception desk as she and her guests arrived.

'How lovely,' Grace said.

Until she saw the message on the card: 'With my undying gratitude. Thomas Chauvin.'

'You have an admirer,' Natalie Gérard said.

Grace smiled and asked the receptionist to hold the bouquet for her.

'I'm guessing they're not from your husband,' the French teacher persisted.

'Why not?' Cecilia Storm, the Italian psychologist, asked.

'The evening before his wife's return?' Mlle Gérard said. 'Making her either waste the flowers or carry them with her luggage onto a crowded plane.'

'If I were fortunate enough to be married to Doctor Lucca' – Stefan Mainz was in gallant mood – 'I think I might send roses morning, noon and night.'

Grace laughed and thanked him.

'I don't know if we're even permitted to carry flowers onto planes these days,' Elspeth Mettler said. 'Regulations alter all the time.'

'Shall we have a drink first?' Grace changed the subject. 'Or go straight through to the restaurant?'

'I'm absolutely starving,' Cecilia Storm said.

'Dinner then,' Grace said.

Felicia Delgado had been found wandering on the beach near 80th Street shortly after two p.m.

Bloodstains on her school uniform.

Her clothes almost certainly fresh on that morning, placing her at home prior to and either during or after her mother's murder, and making it less likely that the killer – if a stranger – had been there overnight.

Sam and Martinez were still with her father in his ex-wife's living room when the news came in that she was safe.

'Thank God.' Delgado was up on his feet. 'Where is she now?'

'Apparently she's unhurt,' Sam told him, 'but she's distressed and confused, so she's been taken to Miami General as a precaution.'

Delgado seemed to hesitate, then sat down again.

Which threw Sam, since as a father he'd be through that door and on his way to the hospital, nothing short of restraints capable of stopping him.

'Do you know,' Delgado asked, 'if my daughter saw her mother after . . .?'

'We don't know that yet, sir,' Sam said.

'It's just . . .' Delgado stopped again.

'Just what, sir?' Martinez asked.

Delgado took a breath. 'You should probably know that my daughter being confused is sadly nothing new.' He paused. 'Much like her mother.'

Coming to it now, Sam realized. Whatever this man had been holding back.

'Go on, please,' he said.

Delgado shook his head. 'It seems wrong, speaking about my wife now.'

'It might help us find the person who did this to her,' Martinez said.

Delgado took another moment.

'The truth is, she was sick.' He paused again. 'In her mind.'

Sam waited, then asked: 'In what sense, sir?'

'In a sense that seems horrifically connected to . . .' Delgado stopped, covered his face with both hands, shuddered, then dropped his hands onto his knees. 'That thing – that nightmare – with her eyes.'

Sam and Martinez both waited.

'My wife had a phobia,' the other man said.

Black Hole's drug of choice clicked into Sam's mind.

Into his partner's too, he saw that in Martinez's sharp, dark eyes.

Diazepam.

Prescribed for all kinds of things from muscular pain to anxiety.

And sometimes, perhaps, for phobias.

'It has been such a great pleasure,' Stefan Mainz told Grace, kissing her hand. 'I look forward to the next time.'

The pleasure had been hers, Grace had assured him as they'd all taken their leave in the hotel driveway.

It was just after ten, and she felt a sense of relief. Dinner had been enjoyable, but during the evening her thoughts had veered to the possibility that Thomas Chauvin might show up in person, which would have been embarrassing. She'd thought, too, for a second time, about the faint chance that he might have set up that 'accident' on the tramline, and she knew it was absurd, but it had been odd that his leg had been fine just moments later. And it troubled her a little that she hadn't mentioned that suspicion to Sam, but she hadn't because it had patently been nonsense, and she might have worried him unnecessarily, and in any case, she would tell him about it and the flowers when she got home . . .

'Don't forget your bouquet,' Natalie had reminded her in reception.

Grace wondered now why she had not simply told her dinner companions about the encounters with Chauvin, which would have amused them all, perhaps set them hypothesizing.

A desire for privacy, she supposed.

In the event, he had not appeared, and she supposed that the flowers were a nice gesture of gratitude, that it was a shame, really, not to be able to thank him.

But tomorrow, thankfully, Grace was going home.

At five-thirty, at Miami General, Sam and Martinez were still waiting to talk to Felicia Delgado. Her doctor had confirmed that she was physically unharmed, but appeared to be in a state of deep shock.

Her father was at her bedside now, but the teenager had not spoken either to him or to anyone else.

Her condition added to the probability that she had found her mother's body.

Though until she spoke, there would be no way of knowing if she might not have seen something even more horrific.

Some*one*.

For all they knew, Felicia Delgado might be a witness.

The first known witness to Black Hole.

Joe Duval for the FDLE and the investigative teams from the other jurisdictions were all standing by.

'We need to take this gently,' Sam had said to Duval a while ago. 'Meantime, I'd like it if we could have someone watching her room.'

Duval had nodded. 'I'll get on that.'

* * *

'Weird thing,' Martinez had said quietly to Sam a while back.

Referring to Felicia Delgado's large, inky-dark sunglasses.

According to hospital personnel, she had become distressed and combative each time someone had tried to remove them.

Lending credibility to Carlos Delgado's description of his daughter's phobia, which he said she had shared with her late mother.

The sight of the glasses had really chilled Sam. Not because of what Felicia's father had told them, but because of the Polaroid shot that Joe Duval had shown him at the Fort Lauderdale scene.

Of Amelia Newton wearing those oversized dark glasses.

He remembered again the acetone smell.

Felicia Delgado's fingernails had no polish on them, but Sam asked one of the nurses if she'd noticed if the teenager had polished toenails.

'I didn't notice,' the nurse said, almost disapprovingly.

Sam asked her to take a look at her feet, told her it might be important.

Waiting, his thoughts slid back over the horrors of the day.

The doily coverlets over the victim's destroyed eye sockets. No more grotesque than the covers used in the other cases, except they seemed somehow *jokier* than the other items Black Hole had used.

And there was something else that was really getting to Sam.

It looked as if Felicia Delgado had washed blood off herself, though traces had remained beneath her fingernails and on her arms as well as her clothes.

Which had to make her a person of interest in the case.

Sam's best guess was that she had found her mother, had touched her, perhaps tried to hold her, and had then fled in a state of near catatonic shock.

But the way Felicia was now, hours later, just lying there in that hospital bed, reminded Sam too damned much of how Cathy had been when she'd been found following her own parents' murder.

Long time ago.

But some memories were never eradicated.

Like the day when he had been the one with no choice but to arrest her.

She had been fourteen, too, at the time. And totally innocent.

So many scars in Cathy's psyche.

And here was another fourteen-year-old in similarly terrifying circumstances.

They were going to have to interview this child as soon as she was fit, and they would, God help them, do their job.

But already Sam hated it.

The nurse was back.

'No polish,' she said.

Which meant nothing, since many nail polish removers contained acetone, yet with so little to go on at this early stage . . .

'Any chance it was removed here?' Sam asked.

The nurse shook her head. 'If she were undergoing anesthesia, some varnish might be removed from her fingernails,' she said, 'but not her toes.'

Sam thanked her, his mind flipping to the drug found in previous victims. They were a long way off toxicology confirmation that Beatriz Delgado had ingested a large dose of Diazepam prior to her death, but Sam had called his father a while ago to ask about the drug's role in the treatment of phobias, and David Becket had confirmed its use in some cases.

Though, in fact, Xanax and Prozac had both been found in Mrs Delgado's bathroom cabinet, but no Diazepam.

'You think they did blood tests on the kid here?' Martinez asked quietly.

Sam looked at him. 'No reason they'd be looking for that drug if they did.'

'I guess not,' Martinez said. 'But I'd sure like to know if she had any of that shit in her before she went walkabout on the beach.'

'And if she did?' Sam said.

'Would it confirm her as strictly victim?' Martinez shrugged. 'Since we have no cause to get her tested, we're not going to find out.'

Sam said nothing.

His thoughts slipped back again, to Cathy.

'Hey,' his partner said. 'Not the same.'

That was the way it went with them sometimes, almost reading each other's minds. Like a kind of marriage.

'I know it,' Sam said.

May 13

He was reading again, from a text entitled 'The Eyes Hold the Key'.

About forensic pathology and vitreous humor. The stuff that resisted putrefaction longer than other bodily fluids could manage.

'Where bacteria has begun to corrupt the blood alcohol level and render it inaccurate, the vitreous humor can still quite faithfully tell the ME what the blood alcohol level was shortly before death. Even after embalming, because embalming alcohol cannot enter the vitreous humor after death, a toxicologist is still able to test it for ethanol.'

He tossed that text aside, moved on.

To ancient Egypt. To one of his favorite myths about the battle between Horus, the god of the sky, and Seth, the god of chaos.

Though he was a man of science, chaos fascinated him in a manner that order never could.

According to the myth, Horus had fought Seth to avenge his father's death, in the course of which battle Horus's left eye had been damaged – part of a mythological explanation for the phases of the moon.

My, how he loved it all: knowledge, science, fiction, mythology, drinking in everything from classical Latin to the study of rainforests, to suicide methodology and even euthanasia – a subject which went against all his most deeply held beliefs.

His studies were eclectic, but his preference, always, remained science-based. Because he was a man of learning. A doctor.

First and last.

At one in the morning, Sam could not get off to sleep, and though he could have called Grace, who might already be breakfasting in Switzerland, she might *not* be awake yet and he was reluctant to disturb her.

Anyway, he didn't want to burden her with his present dark thoughts, at least not just before her long flight home.

His own evening had been pleasant. Martinez had come back to the island for dinner, and they'd dropped by Epicure on the way to pick up a bunch of Claudia's favorite foods. And Joshua had refused to go to sleep, had been allowed to stay up late, and they knew it was excitement because his mommy was coming home next day.

An excitement shared by his father.

The darkness was in him because of the case.

Mostly, though, because of Felicia Delgado. The sheer insanity of the fact that she might possibly be regarded as a suspect in her own mother's murder. Because she had psychiatric issues. And because she'd had her mom's blood on her – that now confirmed.

It made no sense, at least – small mercy – to consider her a suspect in the other Black Hole killings, and in this case, too, Felicia being a witness was a whole lot more probable.

But just thinking about the poor kid's state of mind stirred up another echo.

Grace had been the one, from the outset, who had steadfastly believed in Cathy's innocence.

Grace, who had become her psychologist.

That was the other thing burdening Sam tonight. He hated the idea of involving his wife in this new case, yet he couldn't help wondering if Grace might not be exactly the right person to try to penetrate Felicia Delgado's wounded shell when she was ready.

Sleep would not come any time soon this night.

At ten a.m. Zurich time, Grace was checking in at Kloten Airport.

Everything going smoothly, and she'd allowed extra time before her lunchtime flight to shop for gifts. Chocolates, of course, for everyone, from the terminal's branch of Sprüngli, but also a few small impulse gifts for the family.

And for Magda, and perhaps for Martinez too. And something extra special for Claudia, and she had no idea yet what to get Sam, though she was pretty sure there'd be no shortage of gifts for Joshua . . .

Eyes on her.

Watching from a distance as she walked – in her smooth, easy, graceful way, golden hair glinting beneath the lights – through to passport control and the departure area, finally vanishing from sight.

Thomas Chauvin sighed.

Took off his rimless glasses, wiped them with a small soft white cloth, put them back on.

Waited for another few moments, as if there were some chance that she might come back through, though he knew she would not, because people never did.

No return . . .

Gone.

He sighed again, and then he smiled, and turned, and began to stroll back toward the exit.

Humming as he strolled.

'*Je prends les poses de Grace Kelly . . .*'

The French version of the Mica song.

'I try to be like Grace Kelly . . .' The English version.

In his head now.

Not going away any time soon.

With Delgado still at his daughter's bedside, and with no justification for pulling him away for a full interview at this sensitive juncture, Sam and Martinez spent Friday morning running the usual checks, talking to neighbors in his condo, checking on the canvassing near the crime scene, then paying a visit to the head office of Delgado's real estate firm, CD Realty on Biscayne Boulevard.

The man had no criminal record, had weathered the downturn, his firm still successful, Delgado seeming on the level, with no known financial problems. His partner, Angelo Cortez, appeared fiercely supportive of him, told them that they could forget any possibility of his partner being involved in this terrible crime.

'No one's suggesting anything like that,' Sam told Cortez.

'These are just routine questions,' Martinez said.

'But everyone knows you always look at husbands first,' Cortez said, 'and I know that Carlos walked out on Beatriz, but only a saint could have put up with how she was, poor woman, God rest her soul.' He crossed himself. 'And Carlos always said he knew she couldn't help it, but it was obviously affecting the kid, and he just couldn't face dealing with two of them day after day.'

Delgado had always looked after them, Cortez said, financially and every other way. He paid all the bills, was always there when his wife needed him.

'He just couldn't live with them anymore,' Cortez said.

'Was there anyone else involved?' Martinez asked.

'Another woman, you mean?' Cortez shook his head. 'Not that I know about, and I would know, believe me. Carlos and I, we're good friends, not just business partners.'

'Good friends tell lies for each other,' Martinez said as they left the building.

'You're such a cynic,' Sam said.

'Who are you, Pollyanna?'

Sam grinned. 'No, but my wife's on her way home.'

Back at the station, an encrypted file from Duval awaited them, thoroughly detailing the previous Black Hole murders. Estimated dates and times included. Gruesome reading.

Arlene Silver, the first and oldest victim, in Fairview Shores, Orlando. Forty-nine, married, a housewife, her two kids grown, with their own homes, her husband at work when she'd died. Attractive brunette, a little overweight, a serial dieter according to her sister and friends.

Victim number two, Karen Weber, age twenty-two, blonde, single. Working in real estate in Jupiter, getting decent commissions, popular, renting her own apartment. Happy, healthy, everything to live for.

Lindy Braun, thirty-seven, divorcée with her own bar in Naples. A dark-haired, sparkling-eyed bundle of energy according to all who knew her.

Amelia Newton of Fort Lauderdale. Thirty-three, another blonde.

Making Beatriz Delgado the first Hispanic victim.

Sam and Martinez read every word, scrutinized each photo and sketch, searching for just a single detail from their own case that might highlight an area of common ground not previously spotted.

Nothing jumping out at them.

Except those women's deaths.

And, of course, eyes.

'Remember the "Moe Green Special"?' Martinez said.

'Hardly Mafia.' Sam shrugged. 'Could be revenge, though. The old biblical "eye for an eye" thing. Putting out eyes was a punishment.'

Martinez was already Googling. 'Happened to some guy called Zedekiah,' he said. 'Book of Jeremiah.'

'Happened to Samson, too,' Sam said.

Martinez was still browsing. 'Yeah,' he said. 'The Philistines did it to him.'

'Those guys didn't get sedated first,' Sam said. 'Makes Black Hole seem almost gentle.'

'A prince,' Martinez said.

'Could mean we're looking for a Bible fanatic,' Sam said. 'For now, though, we should check out Delgado's alibis for the other murders.'

Though Felicia remained the person they most needed to speak to.

Still silent.

At three, a multijurisdictional meeting was held in the squad room – ahead of the press conference arranged for Monday morning.

Lieutenant Michael Alvarez hosting for Miami Beach. Also present, Sam and Martinez, the detectives investigating for Orange County, Palm Beach, Collier County and Fort Lauderdale, with Joe Duval for the FDLE. On the table, Duval's own informal report which Alvarez had requested he read aloud.

'I'll tell you at the outset,' Duval said, 'that I doubt there's a single item here that every one of you has not thought through. You have the experience in your jurisdictions, you've seen the victims first-hand, conducted the interviews, had time to mull things over.'

'It never hurts to recap,' Alvarez said, 'as we've all had to do on every case that didn't jump up and solve itself.'

'This is more a summing up than a profile,' Duval went on. 'I'm not a psychologist, and though I once completed a criminal personality profiling program with the BSU, I am not a profiler by profession and my training is years out of date.'

'You helped catch the Inhuman Torch in Chicago,' Sam pointed out, for the rest. 'And Frederick Schwartz, the pacemaker killer.'

'We've all helped catch killers,' Duval said.

'Shall we get on?' Alvarez said.

Duval stood.

'As we know, we have ourselves an organized serial killer or killers, with a clear signature. Shooting out the victims' eyes could symbolize blinding as a punishment, but the character and lifestyles of the victims speak against that likelihood. That does not, however, rule out irrational "punishment"' – Duval made quotation marks with his index fingers – 'by an obsessive, probably paranoid individual, who might be targeting women because they're attractive, or because maybe they *looked* at the killer the wrong way, or maybe something about the victims' eyes upset him or her. None of the women had unusual visual issues, though the latest victim's phobia may have significance.'

He went on.

The killer had chosen a 'safe' time to strike, had found some way to be allowed into, perhaps invited into, the victims' homes.

Nothing suggested uncontrolled violence or sadism.

No indication of sexual assault or even interest.

No removal of clothing or undergarments.

Each victim had been drugged, then probably moved to their own bed, then shot through both eyes, resulting in immediate death or bleeding out.

'We don't know if the victims were drugged to stop them struggling or, just possibly, to minimize suffering. Certainly, any suggestion of mercy seems unlikely, yet the killer may feel *compelled* to carry out this specific end game, yet have no urge to inflict pain.'

Duval spoke about the weapon.

.380 Automatic Colt Pistol cartridges matched in lab tests to a Colt Mk 4 series 80, a self-loading, recoil operated, semiautomatic weapon produced from the mid-eighties to the late nineties.

'No way of knowing if this is a recently acquired gun or a collector's item or even an old family weapon.'

He went on to what he called the 'finishing touches' of each crime.

'The staging of these scenes has not appeared sexually motivated, and in only one case has the body been manipulated for effect; Lindy Braun's arms moved so that her gloved hands covered her eyes.'

The beds, themselves, had significance, Duval felt.

'Deathbed. Convenience. Comfort. Cleanliness.'

Three pillows – the number perhaps significant – piled up behind each victim's head, with a latex sheet separating the head from the top pillow. (The fourth pillow or cushion used as a silencer and, therefore, part of the MO, not the staging.)

The victim tidily positioned, clothing in place.

'Most meaningful of all, staging-wise, are the covers over the blasted eye sockets. Covering in itself comprehensible: the killer finding it tough, perhaps, to look at his or her handiwork. But the fact that the coverings have been the only notable variant at each scene suggests some different significance.'

The sleep mask.

The gauze, covered by Band-Aids.

The white-gloved hands.

The sunglasses.

The little doilies.

'Smacks of amusement,' Duval said. 'Game playing. Showing off. Having *fun* at this point. Yet still vicious and controlling. Quirky, but ultimately powerful.'

He returned to the probability that the victims had admitted the killer to their property. So, either an acquaintance or someone with an appointment, an arrangement, even an assignation – though no records in datebooks or on calendars or even Post-it notes had been found. So either these had been removed by the killer, or the victims had chosen not to make a note for some reason. Or perhaps the arrival of the killer had been unexpected.

'Detective Becket, noting a smell of acetone in the two crime scenes he visited, has provided a list of multiple products containing the substance. If this is a clue, even if only in two out of five cases, we could be looking for anyone from a house painter to a nail technician. Or it could be immaterial.'

Staging, as they all knew, was generally thought to be either a conscious effort to confuse and thwart investigators, or to further shock those who found the victim or whose job it was to investigate, or to give perverted pleasure to the murderer.

'So who are we looking for? Someone convincing enough to be allowed in and to give the women a drink containing Diazepam.' Duval paused. 'Mrs Delgado's tox results are not back yet, but we can include her for now.'

It was not known, he went on, if the victims had been very drowsy or asleep before being taken to their beds – the distinction crucial, since one individual, even a female, could assist a very sleepy woman from one room to another; whereas a virtually unconscious dead weight would require a strong male or two people.

'There was no evidence on the bodies, floors or rugs of the victims being dragged to their beds, and unless we're dealing with masochism, there's no way these women voluntarily lay down on those beds.'

Duval paused.

'A profiling expert might suggest gender, but I won't. Everything here could point to a single male or strong female – gay or straight – or even a team. Timing of no obvious help. The killings began in January, continued in February and March, then paused through April, and now we've had two in May.' He took a breath. 'I think this may be something that's been festering for years, and after it first blew its top with Arlene Silver, the killer felt better. Better enough to do it again and again and again.' Duval shook his head. 'More to come, unless we stop him. Or her.' Another pause. 'Or them.'

He sat down, tidied some papers, then stabbed at a pencil, which flipped off the table and landed on the floor.

'I wish I had more. As it is, it's just a consolidation of what you all already know.'

'You've concentrated our minds,' Alvarez told him.

'A refresher course on Black Hole.' Jerry O'Dea from Palm Beach was ironic.

'Guess the pressure's on you guys now,' Bobbi Gutierrez from FLPD said to Sam and Martinez.

The meeting continued a while longer, frustration building.

Sam remembered that just two days ago, he'd been bored.

'Be careful what you set your heart upon,' James Baldwin had once said.

Beth Riley came into the office at five.

'Something I think you should see, Sam.'

A copy of a piece of paper found in Beatriz Delgado's living room.

A note of an appointment on May 11.

'With Doctor Shrike,' Riley said. 'Isn't that Grace's colleague?' She handed it over.

Sam looked at the phone number written beneath the name.

Not Magda Shrike's number.

Grace's.

Grace's flight touched down at five-thirty p.m.

Sam had made it, was waiting with flowers.

He thought she looked a little weary, but more beautiful than ever.

He told her so, loving the feel and scent of her as she leant against him.

'I've never been happier to see anyone,' she said.

'There's a small boy waiting in a house on Bay Harbor Island who's going to make you even happier,' Sam said, picking up her bags.

'Does he know I'm coming?' Grace asked as they headed out through the throng of passengers and redcaps and drivers holding up name cards. 'Do you think he missed me? I know it's selfish, but I want him to have missed me a little.'

'We told him tomorrow,' Sam said. 'Just in case you were delayed. So you get to see his little face light up.'

A perfect homecoming.

Joshua wide awake, having wheedled the truth out of his aunt, rushing out whooping when his dad's car drew up, bombing his mom with questions about her airplane, squeezing the breath out of her with joyful hugs.

'I missed you so *much*, Mommy.'

'Not as much as I missed you,' Grace told him.

'How much?'

'All the way to Jupiter and back again.'

'Me too,' Sam said.

Claudia had prepared dinner, but was insistent on going home right away, adamant that they needed time alone and that she was ready for her own house.

'I think this may have been the best evening ever,' Grace said a few hours later, sitting in their den, Joshua finally asleep upstairs.

'Ever,' Sam agreed.

Except there was one thing he still had to talk to her about, much as he hated to.

No real choice.

'Al and I are meeting Magda tomorrow,' he said.

'How come?' she asked.

He filled her in, then, finally, asked:

'Any idea why Beatriz Delgado would have had your phone number?'

'I've never even heard her name before.' Grace shook her head. 'That poor, poor woman,' she said. 'And her daughter.'

In the room of dead things, another doll had been completed.

She had been, before her makeover, a 2006 Teresa doll, a Hispanic friend of Barbie's with a soft vinyl head.

All the easier to operate on.

Her original clothes had gone, and in their place she wore a 1965 Barbie olive-green dress.

Her pretty dark eyes gone now, too, the grotesque tiny sockets stuffed with red-stained gauze, and two dainty little white lace doilies covering them.

Black Hole's task fulfilled once more.

The miniature Beatriz Delgado already in her small white coffin.

May 14

Sam and Martinez met with Magda at nine-thirty on Saturday morning.

Beatriz Delgado had not been her patient, and was, in any case, deceased, so Magda was free to talk about her. Though she would not, she stated, disclose any information about the daughter, since as they well knew, Florida recognized psychotherapist-patient privilege, and since she had not even the smallest cause for concern that Felicia Delgado might present a danger to anyone.

She unbent just a little. 'I will tell you that, as it happens, I've only had the briefest of conversations with Felicia. On May the eleventh.'

The last day of Beatriz Delgado's life.

'So are you saying that even if you could talk about her, there'd be nothing worth telling us?' Martinez asked.

'I've said all I'm going to,' she said.

Sam showed her the phone number found in the Delgado house.

Magda nodded. 'Mrs Delgado initially called for an appointment with Grace. I told her that she was away, but that we have a mutual *locum tenens* arrangement. Mrs Delgado seemed anxious not to wait.'

'The poor kid's definitely in bad shape now,' Sam said. 'She hasn't spoken to anyone since she was found wandering on the beach.'

Magda shook her head, but said nothing.

'Can you comment on the mother-daughter relationship?' Martinez ventured. 'From the mom's point-of-view?'

Magda said that she could not.

Though she remembered very clearly the remark made by the fourteen-year-old, when she had seemed to align herself with her mother.

'Both crazy,' Felicia had said.

A disturbing statement from a young teenager, deeply troubled even before her mother had been murdered.

'Two things I think I can tell you,' she said. 'Mrs Delgado said that Felicia had refused to see a doctor the day before they came to me. She mentioned no name, but it would probably have been because of an eye infection.'

Sam noted that, thanked her.

'The second thing?' Martinez asked.

'Mrs Delgado phoned on the evening of the eleventh to make another appointment, but then, quite abruptly, she said she had to go, and hung up.'

'What time was that?' Martinez asked.

'Just after six-thirty.'

'Did you hear anything in the background at her end?' Sam asked.

'Nothing,' Magda said. 'My guess was that Felicia had come in.'

'You didn't try calling her back?' Martinez asked.

'It would have been inappropriate,' Magda said. 'With rare exceptions, we don't chase patients or their guardians. If they want to speak to us, they call back.'

Not this time.

In the corridor outside his daughter's hospital room, Carlos Delgado told Sam and Martinez that he knew nothing about any recent visits to a doctor by Beatriz or Felicia, though the report of his daughter's refusal did not surprise him.

'Another thing they shared,' Delgado said. 'Avoiding doctors. In fact, I'm surprised Beatriz managed to get her to the psychologist.'

'Your wife obviously wanted to help her very badly,' Sam said.

Delgado leaned heavily against the wall. 'Beatriz loved Felicia very much. I never doubted that.'

'One more thing,' Martinez said.

'Anything,' Delgado said.

'Do you know if your wife ever had beauty treatments at home?'

'Or maybe massage or physiotherapy,' Sam added.

'Not that I know of. But I wouldn't know, unless I paid for it.'

They asked him to check credit card and bank details with that in mind.

'It could be important,' Sam said.

'Is that what you think happened?' Delgado's forehead creased deeply. 'You think maybe someone like that came in and—'

'It's just one line of inquiry,' Sam said.

'But important,' Martinez emphasized. 'Even just so we can rule it out.'

'She used to go out to the hairdresser,' he said. 'I don't know where.'

'What about her nails?' Sam asked.

'I don't know anything like that.'

'One last thing,' Sam said. 'As the person who knows Felicia better than anyone, have you been able to get any sense as to whether this shutting down is from shock, or because she might possibly be too frightened to talk?'

'You mean if she saw the killer?' Delgado shook his head. 'I don't know what's going on inside my child's head right now, Detective. I'm not sure I've ever known. Shock, for sure, but I don't know what else. I wish to God I did.'

Delgado's alibi for the evening before the killing was holding up, so far as it went.

His neighbor had confirmed having heard his TV most of the evening of the eleventh, remembered because it had been a noisy sport event.

'Could have gone out and left the TV turned on,' Martinez had pointed out.

The surveillance cameras in the building's underground garage had recorded Delgado's BMW entering at five-ten p.m. on May 11, and not leaving until just after eight-forty next morning to go to his office, where the school had reached him an hour or so later.

'Could have gone out anytime before that without his car,' Martinez said, back in the office on Saturday afternoon.

'I know,' Sam said.

'But you're not getting a bad feeling about him,' Martinez said.

'I'm not.'

'Me neither.' Martinez paused. 'Which is more than I can say about the daughter. I hate to say it, but she creeps me out, lying there with those glasses.'

'She has a phobia.' Sam shook his head.

'I know it,' Martinez said. 'But still, if the mom were the only victim . . .'

May 15

On Sunday, the whole family were at Cathy and Saul's for brunch.

Rain forcing them to stay inside, a little cramped, but no one complaining.

Food in this apartment by Cathy or, sometimes, by Mel Ambonetti, Saul's girlfriend, an anthropology student. Furniture by Saul, who'd given up studying medicine some years back to learn woodcraft, and was now a modestly successful cabinet maker with a small workshop off North Bay Road.

Mildred was refusing to talk about her eyes, which left too much time for Grace to tell the family about her trip, and Cathy said she should do more lecturing, and Grace agreed that she wouldn't mind participating in the occasional future seminar.

'No more trips to Europe, though,' she said.

'Sam could go with you next time,' Saul said.

'I might cramp her style,' Sam said. 'Put off the gorgeous young men.'

Grace made a dismissive sound.

'What was his name again, Gracie?' Sam persisted, teasing.

'You mean there was a guy?' Cathy asked.

'No need to sound so surprised,' Mildred said.

'With a beautiful woman like Grace,' David said, 'it's almost inevitable.'

'Oh, stop,' Grace said.

'She's blushing,' Saul said.

'Tell us,' Mel said.

'There's nothing to tell,' Grace said. 'Sam's just teasing me.'

'His name was Thomas Chauvin,' Sam said. 'A Frenchman.' He grinned.

'Seems he and Gracie just kept bumping into each other everywhere they went in Zurich.'

'It's a small city,' Grace said.

'And then Gracie saved his life,' Sam said.

'That's just nonsense,' she said.

'Now even I need to know more,' Mildred said. 'And I'm nowhere near as nosy as the rest of this family.'

'It was nothing,' Grace said. 'He was crossing the street, took a tumble on a tramline and I went to help him.'

'She omits to mention there was a tram bearing down on them,' Sam said.

'Grace, that sounds dangerous,' David said.

'It wasn't,' she dismissed. 'The driver stopped in time.'

'But you didn't know he would,' Claudia said.

'It sounds very brave, Aunt Grace,' Robbie, Claudia's younger son, said.

'It sounds very *Grace*, period,' Mike, his older brother, said.

'It sounds stupid to me,' Cathy said.

Sam glanced at her, saw consternation in her eyes, their cornflower blue so uncannily similar to Grace's that strangers always assumed they were biological mother and daughter.

'Sweetheart, it really was no big deal,' Grace told her.

'After all we've been through,' Cathy said, 'I'd just think you'd know better.'

'I have to agree,' Claudia said.

'It's hard to leave another human being in trouble,' Mel said, 'if there's something you can do about it.'

'But what if the tram hadn't stopped?' Saul said.

'It did,' Grace said. 'Zurich is a very safe place.'

'Maybe we should change the subject?' David suggested.

'Can't I just mention the flowers?' Sam said.

'Oh, for heaven's sake,' Grace said.

At fifteen minutes after three, in North Miami Beach, a young woman, responding to a buzz that she had been anticipating, opened her front door and let two callers into her apartment.

'I'm not sure if I'm looking forward to this or not,' she said.

'A lot of clients get a little nervous,' one of the callers said, 'but there's really no need.'

They went into the living room to get organized.

'If you are a little tense,' the other visitor said, 'we have just the thing.'

All organic, apparently.

A kind of tea made from an herb that grew exclusively in Guatemala.

'We're not talking dope, are we?' the young woman checked.

'I'll show you the packet, if you like,' the first visitor said. 'Do you have any honey? It tastes great with honey.'

'I'm feeling really weird,' she said a little later.

'The tea does sometimes have a slightly stronger effect on sensitive people,' one of the visitors said. 'But you don't need to worry, it'll wear off soon.'

'Are you sure . . .?'

'Just relax and enjoy.'

The young woman's pretty blue eyes were closing.

She was already semiconscious when the two visitors assisted her into her bedroom.

Which had been made ready.

The last thing she was aware of was the comfort of her own bed.

The pillows beneath her head felt strange, but . . .

'It's time,' one of the visitors said.

'I don't want to,' the other one said. 'It doesn't feel right.'

'It's exactly right,' the other said. 'It's perfect. Do it now.'

The young woman on the bed, asleep now, gave a soft moan.

'*Do* it.'

The detectives had returned to the office for a one-on-one brainstorming session.

Felicia still hovering at the top of Martinez's agenda.

'So I know the chances of even a screwed up fourteen-year-old girl being Black Hole are zero. But what are the chances of Beatriz's killing being a copycat?'

Sam drummed his fingers on his desk. 'OK. So let's go over what's out there in the public domain. Dates of killings, victims' names and "Black Hole", which for now, at least, could easily refer to their all having been shot in the head.'

'And that the crimes were "gruesome" and "grisly",' Martinez added.

The families knew more, of course, had been asked not to speak about the condition of the bodies, but stuff like that still sometimes got out, because bereaved, shattered individuals often *had* to talk about what they had seen.

'So far as we know, no one's leaked *eyes* to date,' Sam said. 'So I don't see one single possibility that this vulnerable girl planned on killing her mom and making it look like the work of the latest Florida serial killer.'

'OK,' Martinez said.

'So are we done with this, finally? Felicia Delgado is ruled out as anything other than a witness?'

'Sure, though if we haven't totally ruled out Carlos yet . . .'

Sam saw where Martinez was going.

'You're thinking Felicia might have seen her father kill Beatriz,' he said.

'That's one possibility,' Martinez said. 'But suppose Carlos is Black Hole, and suppose Beatriz found out.' He paused. 'Though if mom and daughter had both found out, then the kid would be dead too.'

'Unless she ran,' Sam said.

'Dad's with her now practically twenty-four-seven,' Martinez said.

'Officer outside her door.' Sam paused. 'But Delgado could be talking quietly to Felicia, threatening her.'

'And we can't listen in,' Martinez said.

No probable cause, and they both knew it.

They went on playing with theories.

'Suppose Beatriz found out Delgado was a killer, and Felicia overheard and didn't believe mom, wanted to protect daddy?' Martinez said.

'That might play out if Beatriz had been stabbed or pushed down a staircase,' Sam said. 'Not the way it happened. No way.'

'Agreed,' Martinez said.

'So do you feel Felicia needs protection from her father?'

'Probably not.'

'Because I'm really starting to believe he cares.'

With nothing new to go on, they returned to the acetone smell.

Sam's researches had taught him all kinds of things – mostly of no use to them. That the compound occurred naturally in the human body, that acetone on the breath alerted doctors to serious diabetic situations; that it was used in a variety of cleaning products and in paints and varnishes, among other things.

It was sometimes used to cleanse skin prior to certain medical procedures, but to date, no common ailments or physical conditions had linked the victims. And it could also be used in beauty treatments as part of the 'defatting' process prior to chemical exfoliation.

No signs of chemical peels on any of the victims.

'Let's don't forget TATP,' Martinez said wryly.

Referring to triacetone triperoxide, aka acetone peroxide. A high explosive popular with terrorists.

Not looking for a bomb maker.

About the only good news they had.

'So what the fuck do we have?' Martinez said. 'For the investigation, never mind the press conference?'

'Not a whole goddamned lot,' Sam said.

Depressing as hell.

* * *

May 16

Monday morning brought more bad news.

An interview in the *Miami Star*.

Sandy Reiner talking in depth with Michele Newton, sister of Black Hole's Fort Lauderdale victim.

The young woman had seemed to understand the vital importance of keeping key details about Amelia's body out of the public domain. But at some low point, still stoked up with grief and rage, she had clearly changed her mind.

Sandy Reiner would have said that the public had a right to know, maybe even that her silent cooperation was only serving to ease pressure on the cops. Reiner was a slick writer, a master of persuasion, his scoops regularly lifting his paper's readership and picked up by TV news.

So before long, just about everyone in Miami was going to know about the full horrors of Black Hole's MO.

And Sam and Martinez knew, just by looking at the intent, hungry crowd gathered in the sunshine on Rocky Pomerantz Plaza for the press conference, that nothing Chief Hernandez or Captain Kennedy or Special Agent Joe Duval were telling them this morning would do anything to stem the flow.

They headed back inside when it was over, gloom pervading, certain that headlines by lunchtime would be set to terrify as many South Florida females as possible.

Intensifying the pressure on all concerned.

As was only right and proper.

Mildred having agreed to take the next step, she and David had returned to Miami General to see Dr Ethan Adams.

Almost resigned by now.

The doctor attempted again to discuss methods of cataract removal, but she asked him to stop. He said that he preferred his patients to understand what was going to happen to them, and she said that she appreciated that.

'And if we were talking about any other part of my body, I'd probably agree, but I've made my decision, so if it's all the same to you –'

'We'll skip right over it,' Adams said.

'Thank you,' Mildred said, grateful to him for the first time.

'There is a question you do need to answer,' he continued. 'And you may want time to consider it.' He paused. 'Within reason, you get to help choose the kind of intraocular lens we put in.'

David saw her pallor returning. 'This isn't about the procedure,' he said quickly. 'This is about choosing the best kind of vision to suit you.' He glanced at Adams. 'Forgive me, Doctor.'

'Go ahead,' Adams said easily.

David smiled his thanks.

'I believe it's possible these days,' he told Mildred, 'for a surgeon to restore your ability to see at all distances.'

'So to that end,' Adams said, 'it's helpful to know about your lifestyle and preferences. To know if you're a reader, if you swim or do embroidery.'

'I swim and read. I do not embroider, nor do I knit.' Mildred tried to smile.

'Fair enough,' Ethan Adams said.

'I think you have to do a little measuring, Doctor,' David said.

'I do,' Adams said. 'Though a few more tests and measurements will be done as close to the time of surgery as possible.' He smiled at Mildred. 'For pinpoint accuracy, you understand.'

'Of course I do. I know I'm a fool, but I do appreciate what you've been telling me.'

Not his fault, after all, that she had this problem.

'Do I have to stay at the clinic overnight?' she asked.

'In your case, I think it would be easier for you.'

'May I think about that?'

'Certainly,' Adams said. 'But though there's no need for particular haste, I do need to tell you that I'm going away in mid-June for two months.'

'Is there no one else who could do the procedure?' Mildred asked.

'Not in my clinic,' Dr Adams said.

'No pressure then,' Mildred said.

At noon, Sam had a call from Ida Lowenstein in the ME's office to say that presumptive toxicology tests – comparatively swift with their field narrowed to a search for a specific drug – had shown that

Beatriz Delgado had ingested a large dose of Diazepam some time before her death.

The drug's name one of the few details still not known to the public.

No big surprise for the police.

Black Hole for sure.

At six, Martinez picked up a message from Carlos Delgado informing them that Felicia had been moved to a private clinic in Aventura.

'He says she's still not fit for interview,' Martinez told Sam. 'But we're welcome to talk to the head honcho, Doctor Pérez. I'm checking out the place now.'

Sam called Joe Duval to appraise him, learned that Delgado had consulted with him on the subject of continuing security, since he wanted to arrange his own twenty-four-hour guard on Felicia's room.

'I was about to call you,' Duval said. 'It's hard to fault the guy, but it gets us no further with an interview.' He paused. 'Any chance this could be a smokescreen? Dad feeling he might have more control over her at this place?'

'We'll head over there soon as,' Sam said.

The Weston-Pérez Clinic on 190th Street gave a solid, comfortable appearance, and Dr Eduardo Pérez was affable and elegant, sporting a trim goatee and open-necked crisp white shirt. He expressed concern for his new patient, said that the clinic prided itself on its own state-of-the-art security, but that as a father himself, he understood why Delgado had chosen to make additional arrangements.

Delgado had only left his daughter for a couple of hours to go home to shower and change, the doctor told the detectives.

But at least he had left, Sam registered, was not standing guard twenty-four-seven.

They met with Delgado in a waiting room.

He looked exhausted, apologized for not yet finding time to look over payments made on Beatriz's behalf. Sam asked if he'd thought of anyone who might have had recent contact with her. Delgado pointed out again that they'd only communicated about Felicia, that Beatriz had no reason to keep him informed about her daily life.

Sam waited while Delgado took some Evian from a small

refrigerator. 'Did your wife suffer from her phobia when you first knew her?'

'Why do you ask?'

'No specific reason,' Sam said. 'When we have nothing clear-cut, we ask more questions, look for more tenuous links. Sometimes things that don't seem insignificant can be helpful.'

'Her problems weren't as extreme back then, but they did exist,' Delgado said. 'When we first met, she said she wore sunglasses because her eyes were sensitive to light. I found it quite attractive, even intriguing, back then.'

His sadness was almost palpable now.

Both detectives feeling it.

'Did she ever tell you the root cause of her phobia?' Sam asked.

'Never. She wouldn't talk about it.' Delgado drank some water, set the bottle on the table and stood up. 'Too late now.'

'Hopefully not for your daughter,' Sam said.

Delgado hesitated for a moment. 'Doctor Shrike said that Beatriz originally wanted Felicia to see your wife, Doctor Lucca, but she was overseas. Perhaps when she's ready, we could try again?'

'That's not something I can answer,' Sam told him. 'It would have to be between you and Doctor Lucca.'

And did that question about Grace take suspicion further off the man? Sam wondered. Or was that why Delgado had asked the question?

Cynicism, all the time, in this job.

Not one of Sam's favorite traits.

Impossible for a cop to avoid.

At rehearsal that evening, Billie Smith's singing was so fine that it drew a rare burst of applause from the company.

She came to find Sam during the break. 'That was down to you,' she said. 'You really helped me.'

'I didn't do anything,' he said. 'You're doing this all by yourself.'

'That is *so* not true.' Billie glanced around. 'Sam, could we talk?'

'Great job, Billie.' Linda Morrison came up behind them, checked her watch, clapped her hands. 'Three minutes, people. Billie, don't you even *breathe* too near Carla or Jack. They both swear they're coming down with the flu.'

It was late before they finished.

Sam saw Billie heading his way again, figured departure might be the wisest tactic, threw his libretto in his case, looked around for Linda.

'Gotta go,' he called to her.

'Rehearse, rehearse, rehearse, big guy,' she called back.

Sam blew her a kiss, gave Billie a friendly wave and headed out to his car.

He didn't look back until he was in his old Saab, motor started, and then he glanced in the rearview mirror and saw that she was halfway down the path, one hand raised, maybe calling to him.

He thought about his old friend, Larry, and felt a little guilty.

Hoped to hell that Billie wasn't in any kind of trouble.

Though the trouble he'd *thought* she might have been looking for the other night was the kind he was definitely not interested in.

And heck, Jacksonville wasn't that far away, and if Billie did have problems, maybe needed a parental figure, she surely only had to call them.

Less than a minute later, his iPhone rang.

Joe Duval calling.

'We got another one.'

Sam and Martinez arrived within minutes of each other.

Another young woman living alone, in North Miami Beach.

Found by her *mother*.

Unbearable scene, even worse than the others, because it had patently taken longer to find the body.

Victim's name Zoë Fox, age twenty-five. Photographs and horrified neighbors affirming that she had been pretty as a picture, fun-loving, adventure-seeking, sweet disposition, guys lining up.

Now all that horrifically destroyed.

Same as the others, right down to the one variable.

A Zorro mask covering the horrors this time, its eye slits filled in with black tape.

Impossible to guess how many retail or online outlets sold those masks, unless this one turned out to have some manufacturer's code or defining feature.

Neither Sam nor Martinez holding their breath on that.

No way of asking the mother yet if she knew if the mask had belonged to her daughter, because that poor woman had, for the time being, lost her mind.

'One thing,' Joe Duval said to the detectives. 'Maybe nothing at all, but the security pass in her purse says Miss Fox worked for Shade City in the Aventura Mall.' He paused. 'Selling sunglasses.'

Maybe something.

Zoë Fox had lived and died in the City of North Miami Beach.

Not their case.

Didn't make Sam or Martinez feel any better.

And by the time Sam got back in his car to drive home, he felt sick to his stomach and his heart.

And mad as hell.

Such a waste.

Such a sick, evil *waste*.

May 17

The doctor's reading tonight was, yet again, concerned with the eye. Specifically with the *macula lutea,* the small yellowish area of the retina near the optic disk that provided humans with central vision.

A tiny miracle, in its center a depression called the *fovea*, containing nerve cells known as cones, which were associated with color vision and perception of fine detail.

He had read this more times than he could count. About the wonder of perfect vision and about the disorders, accidents and degenerative conditions that could disrupt or destroy that perfection.

Some of them bringing darkness where there had been light.

Sometimes slowly, like an eclipse, sometimes terrifyingly swiftly.

And then, new miracles were needed.

Wonders of medicine.

Brought about by scientists and doctors.

Learned people.

The good and the great.

Like him.

He would always read, study, go on learning, no matter how complete his knowledge or finely honed his skills. He understood that there would always be room for improvement, and that was one of the things that would set him apart from the rest, raise him higher.

Make him the very best.

Grace had been waking earlier since her return, giving her and Sam a little welcome extra time together, while Joshua still slept and the demands of the day were not yet eating at either of them.

It had been late when he'd got home last night, his mind filled with poor Zoë Fox, but this Tuesday morning, Sam knew he should wait no longer to revisit the subject of Felicia Delgado.

'Her father intimated to me yesterday that when she's ready, he might like her to see you professionally, since it was you his wife had initially tried to approach.'

'How did that come up as a topic?' Grace was frowning.

'He found out you're my wife,' Sam said simply. 'I think he was just asking me to pass on the message.'

'Very inappropriately,' she said.

'As I told him. But if you and Magda were to feel you were the right therapist for Felicia . . .' He paused. 'You have very specific experience.'

The old package of dismay landed between them with an almost palpable thud, Cathy's horrific times returning again.

Not the same, but still . . .

'I just didn't want this to come out of left field,' he said. 'And though in some ways I'd rather it didn't come your way, I know there could be no one better qualified to help Felicia Delgado.'

'I'm not sure whether to thank you for that or not,' Grace said.

'Know just what you mean,' Sam said.

Duval called early from MROC to keep them in the loop.

Zoë Fox's work location had, as they'd thought, given them a glimmer of hope because of Aventura's sophisticated CCTV system.

If Black Hole had been a customer of Zoë's, or maybe stalking her, then he or she might appear somewhere on footage recorded in the days preceding her murder – or if they got real lucky, on the day itself. Even if the victims were not random, even if Zoë Fox had been preselected – or was on some kind of list – it did not preclude her being watched at work or approached under some pretext. So anyone recorded looking even remotely suspect would be tracked on their route through the mall into one of the parking lots. Maybe even to their car.

It would take time.

'I'd like to look at Shade City's records for our own investigation,' Sam said.

'Big sunglasses are being sold all over,' Duval said. 'Very fashionable, in case you hadn't noticed.'

'Hell of a long shot,' Martinez said.

'Anyone got any better ideas?' Sam asked.

May 18

Mid-morning Wednesday, Carlos Delgado called to say that Felicia had emerged from her semicatatonic state, had immediately become hysterical and was now under sedation.

City of North Miami Beach were studying CCTV footage at Aventura, but customer details from Shade City were going to have to be sought from their head office.

Nothing to stop Sam and Martinez getting straight over to the clinic, where Dr Pérez interrupted a meeting to confirm that his patient was still unfit for interview.

'Did she say anything before you sedated her?' Sam asked.

Pérez shook his head. 'She was incoherent.'

'Sometimes,' Martinez said, 'even in that state—'

'Miss Delgado said nothing.' The doctor cut him short.

'Just trying to do our jobs here, Doctor,' Martinez said.

'Trying to help Miss Delgado with what she's going to need most,' Sam said. 'For us to find who murdered her mother.'

'And scared her half to death,' Martinez added.

The doctor promised his full cooperation the moment Felicia was ready.

Neither Sam nor Martinez had reason to doubt his word.

From the clinic, they headed over to the Bay Drive crime scene to meet Duval for another scout around ahead of next day's second multijurisdictional meeting.

He was out on the sidewalk, blowing his nose.

'We got something new in Naples.'

Homicide number three. Lindy Braun, the bar owner.

'A neighbor's come forward – she's been in the UK for almost two months, didn't know about the killing, but claims she saw someone visiting that morning.' Duval sneezed. 'Sorry, guys. Damned head cold.'

'*Gesundheit*,' Sam said.

'The neighbor?' Martinez said.

'Says she saw a red-haired female – though she also says she wouldn't swear that she *was* female, because she was wearing a uniform with pants, and the hair was big and could have been a wig.' Duval blew his nose again. 'But she – or he – was wearing big dark glasses and got out of a black SUV with tinted windows, carrying two bags.'

'What kind of bags?' Sam asked. 'Purse or travel size?'

'Quite large and black, she *thinks*.'

'Was the redhead alone?' Sam asked.

'She only noticed her – or him.'

'No make or license plate for the SUV, I take it?' Martinez said.

'Why would she have looked?' Duval said.

'When she says this person was "visiting",' Sam said, 'did she see them go to Miss Braun's actual front door?'

'She did.' Duval's voice was husky with his cold. 'But she didn't see if they went inside.'

'So Lindy Braun might not even have come to the door,' Martinez said.

'Do we have an exact time?' Sam asked.

'Mid or late morning,' Duval said. 'I wouldn't depend on that.'

'Is she even sure about the date?' Martinez asked.

'She claims to be,' Duval said.

'Does she think she'd recognize the redhead again?' Sam asked.

'She says that if she saw the whole deal again – the vehicle, uniform, wig, sunglasses, carrying the bags – she might be able to tell by this person's walk.'

'Something special about that?' Martinez asked.

'Nothing noticeable like a limp,' Duval said. 'But the neighbor believes everyone has a unique way of walking, says she's made a study of it.'

'Fruitcake,' Martinez dismissed.

'Maybe not,' Sam said.

'I'm inclined to believe she saw a redhead in a uniform,' Duval said.

'Who might possibly be a scared witness,' Sam said. 'If she went inside.'

'Or Red could be Black Hole,' Martinez said.

'No similar sightings in Orlando or Jupiter?' Sam checked.

'Yeah, I just figured I'd leave that out,' Duval said, wry.

They went inside for another look at the crime scene.

Not a glimmer of new inspiration.

Nothing new here or anyplace else.

Just an unidentified redhead in Naples.

The doll maker was working on a sweet-faced *poupée*.

French in origin, taller than those that had come before.

Not as slender as Zoë Fox.

But with lovely, sky-blue eyes.

Their color not dissimilar to the late Ms Fox's contacts.

For just a moment, the hand gripping the scalpel clenched a little too hard.

Not good for control or accuracy.

Relax.

Breathe.

Better.

The work continued.

Sam and Martinez headed back to the station for the remainder of the day, Duval staying with them.

All trawling back again through each Black Hole case file.

Reading and cross-checking, duplicating the work of the other investigating offices, knowing that others were probably doing likewise, sifting for that one tiny clue that another jurisdiction had missed. Because cops were human and therefore fallible, and the victims deserved every ounce of resolve and indefatigability they could offer.

Nothing new.

They rechecked details of each woman's vision, found nothing significant. Arlene Silver had used glasses for reading and Lindy Braun had worn contacts for myopia. Amelia Newton had twenty-twenty vision, according to a recent eye test, the details found in a file at her home; Zoë Fox likewise, though she had sometimes worn striking blue contacts to enhance her paler blue eyes. Beatriz Delgado's eye problems of a different kind.

Three of the victims brown-eyed, two blue-eyed.

Eyes.

The three men strained, thought outside the box, went back over old ground, still finding nothing.

All the women reasonably affluent or doing OK.

Not one other single thing seeming to connect them.

They looked, increasingly, like random targets.

They discussed possible implications of the alleged sighting of the Naples redhead – detectives in North Miami Beach already busy canvassing Zoë Fox's neighbors again, Duval said, in hopes of a similar lead.

'So what might she or he have been carrying in those bags?' Sam wondered. 'Did the neighbor say they looked heavy?'

'Didn't say,' Duval said.

'Bibles.' Martinez returned to the archaic punishment theme. 'If they were heavy. Maybe selling them door to door.'

'Does anyone still do that?' Sam queried.

'Maybe Red was just a friend, stopping by,' Martinez said.

'Except a friend would have come forward,' Sam said.

'Could have been carrying samples,' Duval said. 'Wallpaper or color charts.' He made a note to see if anyone had heard Lindy Braun planning a makeover.

'Or any other kind of makeover?' Martinez said.

'Personal trainers carry equipment,' Duval said.

'So do beauticians,' Sam said. 'Manicurists.'

Acetone back on his mind.

'I think they call them nail technicians now.' Duval saw Martinez's face. 'Lot of women in my family.'

'So are we keeping this sighting quiet?' Sam asked.

Duval shook his head. 'Press release hitting the CCSO website as we speak. Public's help wanted for help in identifying an individual in order to eliminate them from our inquiries. The usual.'

'If Red's our perp,' Martinez said, 'the hair's a wig for sure.'

Sam turned to his PC, typed in 'mobile beauty therapists miami', then grinned wryly. 'Shoulda known better. Every "masseuse" in the county.'

'Might be exactly what the redhead was,' Duval said.

'That'll narrow it down,' Martinez said sourly.

Sam typed in 'home nail technicians miami', printed out the listings, did the same search for Naples and Fort Lauderdale, then scanned swiftly, cross-checking.

'I got an outfit coming up all over called "Gorgeous At Home",' he said. 'Might be worth following up.'

'Looking for Red, you mean?' Martinez was dubious.

They had no photo to ID, nothing more to go on than red hair, two bags and a black sport-utility vehicle, no make or tag.

'You have something better?' Sam said. 'Or do we just go on sitting here on our butts while Black Hole lines up another target?'

May 19

David had waited till late Wednesday evening before raising the subject again, and Mildred had requested one last night before reaching a decision.

On Thursday morning, when he woke, she was not in the house.

He found a note in the kitchen.

If we had a dog, I'd be walking it.
As we don't, I'm walking myself.
Don't worry, old man.

It was eleven before she returned.

'My God, woman, I've been climbing the walls,' David said.

'Didn't you see my note?'

She looked fresh-faced, vigorous, better than she had since this had begun.

'I did, but anything could have happened,' he said.

'I lived on the streets for years,' Mildred reminded him, sitting down on the ancient sofa in their living room. 'I may have become soft since we met, but I can still manage a stroll by myself.' She paused. 'What happens if something goes wrong with the surgery?'

'It won't.' David saw that wasn't good enough. 'In very rare cases, further treatment is needed, or a new lens has to be repositioned or replaced, but that is very unusual.'

'What if the first surgery goes well, but I can't face having the second?'

'Then I guess you'll have one excellent eye,' David said. 'But you'd almost certainly need glasses.'

'And in time I might lose the sight in the bad eye,' Mildred said.

'If you decided not to have it done,' David said. 'Does this mean you've made up your mind?'

'It doesn't seem to me that I really have much of a choice.'

'So you're going for it?'

'I am.' She paused. 'One request.'

'Anything,' he said.

'I'd like to have the rest of this week without doctors' appointments and without talking about it. I want to be normal.'

'You've got it.' David said. 'Whatever you want.'

'I don't want anything, that's the whole point. I just want us to be us.'

'I can't think of anything I'd like more,' David said.

At twenty past eleven, Billie Smith called Sam on his cell phone.

'Sam, I need to talk to you.'

'Bad time, Billie,' Sam said.

'No, I mean I need to see you.'

'We're seeing each other this evening,' he said.

'I want to tell you something before rehearsal,' she said.

Sam had already begun worrying about his right to a future in *Carmen* with the investigation making such lousy progress. This wasn't helping.

'Not possible,' he said. 'I'm sorry, Billie.'

'But I'm not sure it should wait.'

Irritation crept in now, made his voice a little harder.

'Like I said, Billie, I'm sorry, but it's going to have to.'

Felicia Delgado was still sedated.

Sam called David. His father always his number one medical adviser of choice, particularly when it came to youngsters.

'Aren't all these drugs potentially harmful?'

'Sure, if it goes on too long,' David said. 'Not to mention the poor child will have to start facing up to what's happened at some point. Is this her physician's inclination, do you know, or her father's influence?' He paused. 'Not that a good doctor would listen to him if it was against the best interests of his patient.'

'I haven't seen Doctor Pérez today,' Sam said, 'but a nurse told me that when Felicia woke this morning, she was so hysterical they thought she might harm herself, so it was a case of restraints or sedation.'

'That's rather different,' David said. 'No one likes to restrain a child.'

Sheldon and Cutter had already called at the Miami offices of Gorgeous At Home, and were not hopeful.

'The office manager was helpful,' Cutter said, back at the station. 'Showed us their Miami operatives' files and photos. One redhead, but she looked tiny, and her hair was cut shorter than Riley's.'

'Do the operatives work outside Miami-Dade?' Sam asked.

'Never, apparently,' Sheldon said. 'It's a territorial business.'

'One more thing,' Cutter said. 'Beatriz Delgado went to a hairdressing salon three days before her death.'

'Her regular stylist,' Sheldon said. 'She had her hair trimmed, and *then* she went right next door to the nail bar and had a manicure and pedicure.'

'Did they remember what color?' Sam asked.

Cutter nodded. 'They keep files for every client. Looked like the same bright pink as the day she died. And neither her hairdresser nor nail tech make home visits. Too busy at the salons, apparently.'

'Want us to run checks on them?' Sheldon asked.

Sam felt his acetone lead leaking away.

'I don't think so,' he said.

La Morrison was not pleased.

Billie Smith, her leading lady, was a no-show, with no explanation and no response from her phone.

Everyone else was at Tyler's tonight. Jack Holden was still complaining about his ailments. Toni Petit had come bearing homemade soup for his throat, and flowers from her backyard for their host, who had accepted them with reasonable grace. Carla Gonzales said she was in great shape, and the whole chorus was raring to go.

'I'll be damned if we waste the evening,' Linda said.

Which meant that Carla was going to have to sing Carmen as well as Micaëla, and here was the corny old stand-in cliché, because Sam could almost see her willing Billie to drop out altogether so she could talk Morrison into recasting her own role and allowing a soprano to take over the lead – not normally done, but not unheard of.

Sam was a little uneasy after Billie's call that morning.

'Anyone know where she works?' he asked during a break.

'I think she said she was waiting tables,' Carla said.

Sam knew that much. 'Any idea where?'

Carla shook her head.

Now he thought about it, that had been one of the things Billie hadn't volunteered in conversation that evening, or maybe he just hadn't been interested enough to press her.

No one here seemed overly concerned, other than for the production.

Which made Sam a little sad.

And a little guilty too.

He went into the house after his next scene, looking for the bathroom.

Clearly signposted, instructions within, like a scrupulously clean and remarkably well-decorated public john. Their host clearly fastidious and choosing to keep his property the way he liked it, and Sam couldn't blame him for that as he dried his hands on a small white towel from a generous stack, then placed it in the basket provided, lined with a plastic bag – hygiene high on Tyler Allen's priorities too.

Emerging from the washroom, he heard a sound.

The kind to stop a cop in his tracks.

Someone crying out. Male or female, hard to know.

Then a thump, like the sound of someone falling over.

Sam waited a moment, then moved down the dimly lit corridor that he assumed led to the main part of the house, and stopped at a closed door.

He heard another cry.

He looked back, saw no one, heard from outside the less jarring sounds of the *Carmen* chorus coming to a ramshackle halt, a couple of voices left stranded on high notes after the others had stopped.

Sam turned back to the door. 'Hello?' he called, not too loudly, not wanting to disturb the rehearsal.

Hearing nothing, he tried the handle.

The door was locked.

'OK, guys!' La Morrison was calling them to order.

Including him, if notes were to be given.

And this, whatever it had been, was none of his business.

He headed back outside to the yard, joined the rehearsal.

'. . . like strangled bagpipes,' Linda was castigating the chorus, a few of whom grinned, then got serious again. 'Nice of you to join us again,' she told Sam.

'Call of nature,' he said. 'Apologies.'

Tyler Allen appeared, coming from the side of the house, carrying two pitchers of fresh water. He set them on the table, then stopped to listen to notes.

He looked, Sam thought, flustered. 'Everything OK?' he asked him quietly.

'Why wouldn't it be?' Allen said.

'Only I was using the bathroom and thought I heard some kind of upset from someplace in the house.'

Allen's pale green eyes were cool. 'My cats. Two Siamese. They fight all the time, knock stuff over.'

'Why not let them out here?' Sam asked.

'They're indoor cats,' Allen said. 'And they don't care for singing or strangers.'

'Gentlemen!' La Morrison said loudly.

Sam held up both hands, palms to her, then zipped his mouth shut.

Siamese did have oddly pitched voices.

And if something else had been going on inside that house, it really was not his concern.

May 20

The sounds were still tweaking at his mind Friday morning, so first chance he had in the office, without knowing exactly why, he ran a check on Tyler Allen.

The guy had a record. Misdemeanors, mostly alcohol related. Accused of assault twice – once on a female, once on a young male – charges not brought. No good reason for Sam to nose any further.

Tyler Allen was a formerly successful choreographer – currently amateur, which had to be tough on him.

Live and let live.

He called Linda Morrison at her clothing store just after nine to see if she'd heard from Billie.

'Not a word,' Linda said. 'In fact, I'm a little concerned about her.'

'I have her cell phone number,' Sam said, 'but no address.'

Linda said she had it on file, would call him back.

He mentioned it to Grace when she called him mid-morning.

'If you're worried about Billie, go check on her,' she told him. 'Though I was calling to say I thought we might do a family Friday tonight.'

It was a tradition they'd been keeping to a little less often lately: the family dinner to celebrate the Jewish Sabbath that none of them had missed without good reason while Judy Becket had still been alive. Though Grace, despite her own Catholic-Protestant mixed upbringing, had taken to the custom with pleasure, relishing the Beckets' eclectic nature.

'Sounds good,' Sam said now. 'And even if I do drop by Billie's place, I should still be home in time for dinner, otherwise you start without me.'

'I just thought, with Mildred going into the clinic next Thursday . . .'

'Is that decided?' Sam was surprised.

'I only found out myself ten minutes ago because I called her to ask. She says she'll only come to dinner if we promise not to discuss her eyes. She's put a veto on the topic at home too.'

The day got away from him after that. Routine work, mostly, the dogged stuff that sometimes took the place of good luck in all kinds of investigations.

Nothing yet from the follow-ups on Gorgeous At Home.

Nothing useful from Aventura's CCTV.

Nor from Shade City.

Linda Morrison called at four with Billie's address, said her memory had been jogged by Toni Petit, who'd called to see if Linda had heard from her. Like the rest of the S-BOP company, Toni had never socialized with Billie, but she said she'd gotten the impression that Billie lived alone. Toni, raised in Louisiana, had also said that she couldn't imagine what was wrong with Florida men.

'Which I said was sexist,' Linda said, 'since living alone is probably Billie's choice.'

'Probably,' Sam said.

He detoured on the way home, traveling alone since this was not police-related, and Martinez was dining with a cousin in from New York.

Not work, yet Sam had an uneasy feeling about Billie. Not exactly one of the hunches he was prey to, but *something* nonetheless.

She rented a room in a small house on SW 29th Avenue near 13th Street in Little Havana, not far from Woodlawn Cemetery.

A small, unattractive house.

A plastic glued-on plaque beside the front door informed callers that the entrance for B. Smith was at the rear.

Sam took a moment, wondering if maybe calling on her uninvited might be a little *off*, if maybe he ought to have made contact with her parents first. But he was here now, and Billie would probably not have thanked him for calling Larry Smith about her, and why worry her parents if there was no need?

The path leading around to the back door was dusty, a few weeds to either side, but not overgrown.

Sam knocked, waited, stepped back.

No lights inside, no obvious signs of occupation.

He walked back around to the front door and knocked.

No answer here either, but he could hear a TV game show, so he persisted, finally rewarded by a slow tread moving toward the door.

'Who is it?' A woman, suspicious sounding.

'My name's Sam Becket. I'm a friend of Billie Smith's.'

'Can't you read?' She was irritated. 'Her entrance is out back.'

'I tried that, ma'am,' Sam said. 'She didn't answer.'

'Then I guess she's out.' Her voice was Southern, slow.

Being out of jurisdiction and here, in any case, on private business, Sam had no justification for using his police status, but there was no way this woman was going to let him in if he did not.

'Ma'am, I'm a detective with the police department. I need to ask you a few questions, so I'd be grateful if you'd open the door.'

She was silent for a moment.

'Do you have a badge?'

'Yes, ma'am.'

There was another pause while she slid a safety chain into place, and then the door opened a little way.

'Show me,' she said, hardly visible in the dim light beyond the door.

Sam held out his badge.

'Detective, huh?' she said.

'That's right, ma'am. From Miami Beach.' No point lying over this. 'And this is not official business, but Ms Smith is a colleague of mine, and I'm concerned about her.'

'She's a cop?' The woman sounded almost shocked.

'No, ma'am. All I need to know is when you last saw her.'

'I don't know,' she said. 'She has her own entrance, so she can come and go as she pleases.'

'Do you remember seeing her in the last few days?' he persevered.

'I don't think so.'

Sam gave her a moment. 'Ma'am, would you mind very much letting me take a quick look at her apartment? Just so I can see there's nothing wrong?'

'I don't know. It's her place. She pays the rent.'

'I'll take full responsibility,' Sam said. 'Goes without saying.'

'Let me see that badge again.'

'Of course.'

She took another look, sighed, then removed the chain, opened the door and let him in. 'I don't have the key to her front entrance, but there's a connecting door we can use.'

Billie's landlady wore a pale blue housecoat and slippers, and was younger than she'd sounded, no more than forty, Sam reckoned, with mousy hair and a small, pale, pudgy-cheeked face. She moved like a woman with little energy, and Sam thought she might be unwell.

She walked ahead through a small, barren hallway, took a key off a hook on the wall, moved on past her kitchen and bathroom to a closed door, presumably leading to Billie's home.

'I should knock first,' she said.

'Good idea,' Sam said.

'I hope she's OK.' The woman looked up at him, her eyes perturbed.

'Me too,' Sam said. 'Could I have your name, ma'am?'

'Why?' Suspicious again.

'You're being very helpful,' he said. 'Very kind.'

'Why wouldn't I be?' She shrugged. 'My name's Jolene Baker.' The door squeaked as she opened it and called: 'Miss Smith?'

The silence was absolute.

'Mind if I take a quick look around?' Sam asked.

'Help yourself, Detective,' she said.

Billie's home was depressing. One small room and a bathroom; no kitchen, just an old, dented microwave and a small refrigerator. Through the narrow window onto the backyard, Sam saw that a barbecue he'd seen out back looked well used. Billie's own exit door had a double lock.

A framed photograph stood on a low white plastic table beside the sofa that he presumed opened into a bed. The photo of both her parents, Sam supposed, because although he'd never met Jill Smith, Larry's long, narrow frame and cheery grin were still instantly recognizable.

That aside, there was no clutter, nothing to make it feel like anyone's *home*. It was just a meager living space, without warmth, certainly no sense of the person who lived here. A young, beautiful, talented woman.

Not Sam's business.

His business here this evening – and even that was questionable – was to make sure that Billie wasn't sick or hurt.

'Better look in the bathroom,' Jolene Baker said, suddenly nervous.

There was just a shower stall and basin, a small, square mirror and shelf, yet Billie had squeezed in more personal items here than elsewhere: cosmetics, perfumes, headache pills and, taped to the mirror, a small photograph of herself on stage somewhere, wearing a little red dress and very high-heeled shoes, singing into a microphone. More than opera to her then and, perhaps, a whole world that Sam hadn't heard her talk about, either to him or anyone else at S-BOP.

'That's a relief.' The landlady backed out into the living room.

Sam followed. 'Would you mind if I check out the closet?'

'I'm not sure Miss Smith would like it,' Jolene Baker said, 'but I guess, since you're a cop and her "friend".'

Sam didn't care for the emphasis, but he thanked her anyway, took a swift and unobtrusive look in the small wardrobe – enough to see that her clothes were there – and then one more scan around the room.

Focusing, he remembered that Billie usually carried a large shoulder bag of soft pink leather and a fuchsia-colored wrap. No sign of either here.

'You done?' the landlady asked, growing impatient.

'Guess I am,' Sam told her.

No sign either of the *Carmen* libretto, which would seem to point to Billie having taken it with her when she left, intending to go to the rehearsal.

Certainly no indications of trouble here. The place was not over-scrubbed, but clean. No crumbs on the kitchen worktop, nothing in the sink. Just something on the floor that looked like seeds or grains, maybe tobacco.

He stooped, looked more closely, picked them up between his fingers, and sniffed, but the only aroma in the room was of something spicy that might have been cooked some time back, the kind of smell that lingered.

'That isn't what you think. I don't let my tenants do drugs.'

'I'm sure you don't,' Sam said. 'I wasn't thinking that.'

The landlady took a step forward, peered at his hand. 'That might be the tea she drinks. Herb stuff. She offered me some, but I like real tea.'

'Me too,' he said.

The woman shrugged, growing impatient.

Time to leave.

He told Jolene Baker that he was grateful, and she said she'd like him to exit through Billie's own door so she could be sure he'd gone before she locked the communicating door again.

'No offense, Detective.'

'None taken,' he told her. 'You can't be too careful.'

It was not yet dark outside, but Sam took out his penlight and directed its beam over the path and around the backyard, not knowing what he was looking for, or why, for that matter.

There were some footprints on the grass that were not his: they were small, probably a woman's, maybe Billie's own or someone else's. And there were some little round indentations on the dusty pathway, a set of them, repeated at regular intervals.

Could have been made by the heel of a woman's shoe or the tip of an umbrella or cane or even the base of a parasol – though the marks were small for that – and chances were they didn't mean anything. And he would have to explain his intrusion to Billie when she showed up, and if she got mad about it, he'd apologize.

But still, right now, he took out his phone and used its camera to take a few close shots of those marks anyway.

Because you just never knew.

May 21

Last evening's family dinner had been uncharacteristically tense. Everyone on eggshells around Mildred; David irritating her by being overprotective; Claudia having a depressed day and Saul in pain, having strained his back shifting a just completed oak table.

'It's hard seeing Mildred scared,' Sam had said later. 'Even if we know this is a minor procedure.'

'Not to her,' Grace had said. 'Though on the subject of fretting, I think you should call Billie Smith's parents.'

'I guess I could track down Larry,' Sam said. 'If it were Cathy, we'd want to know if there was a problem.'

'Hopefully there is no problem,' Grace had said.

He'd called a number of Lawrence and plain L. Smiths in Jacksonville first thing Saturday, had gotten nowhere with most and left voicemail on several more, identifying himself and asking Larry to get in touch.

After which he'd taken Grace and Joshua shopping and for lunch at Heavy Burger in Aventura, before dropping them home and driving back again to the Delgado crime scene to meet Martinez. Saturday afternoon a better time than most for a repeat canvassing of a residential neighborhood – but three hours later, Bay Drive had still yielded nothing fresh.

No sightings of mystery redheads with bags or black SUVs. Not a single useful memory forming itself in the victim's neighbors' minds. And still no known friends of Beatriz's to talk to.

Nor had they yet heard about any of Felicia's pals clamoring for news of the sick, bereaved teenager, making Sam feel more wretched for her than ever.

Lousy, miserable existence even before her mom's death.

They adjourned to Danny's Bar for a couple of beers, and Sam tried Billie's number and got voicemail again, then called Linda Morrison, who'd heard nothing and was starting to get very edgy about the production.

'So what happens to the show if the lead goes AWOL?' Martinez asked.

'I'm still hoping she'll be back for Monday rehearsal,' Sam said. 'If not, I don't have a clue.'

'You don't have stand-ins?'

'One of the other women sang the role Thursday, but she's soprano.'

'And that's not good?'

'Carmen's a mezzo-soprano role,' Sam said, 'but it's occasionally sung by sopranos, so it's not an impossibility.'

Martinez yawned, opera not his thing, though he would drag himself to the theater when Sam was performing, because that was what good buddies did.

Sam took out his phone again, scrolled through his photos to his shots of the indentations on the footpath outside Billie's home.

'What do you think might have made these?'

Martinez shrugged. 'Could be anything.'

'Helpful,' Sam said.

Martinez looked more closely. 'A cane maybe, or a gardening tool.'

Sam nodded. 'I thought maybe a cane.'

'And?' Martinez drank some Bud. 'It isn't a crime scene, man. Your friend probably just took off for a few days and hasn't thought about anyone else.'

'If she wasn't playing an operatic lead, I might buy that.'

'Stage fright?' Martinez suggested.

'Possible,' Sam admitted.

'You said she wasn't confident when she came to your place to rehearse.' Martinez paused. 'You also thought she was coming on to you.' He grinned. 'Need to watch that imagination, man.'

Larry Smith called Sam just after eight.

They spent a few minutes playing catch-up, and then Sam got to the point.

'Billie can sometimes be a law unto herself, Sam.' Larry sounded more wry than worried. 'She's been known to go off for days without telling anyone, so I wouldn't be too concerned.'

'I know she's taking classes at Lincoln Park Music School,' Sam said, 'and I know she's been waitressing, but I don't know where. It might be good to know if she's shown up for work.'

'Last we heard, she was working in a bar near the school, though I don't know the name, and that's not because we haven't asked.' Larry paused. 'I do know that *Carmen* means a lot to Billy, though, which is why I'm not going to mention this to Jill, OK? You know how moms can freak out.'

'Maybe Jill might know something,' Sam said.

'I doubt it,' Larry said. 'Do me a favor, man, call me Monday evening, tell me Billie's come to rehearsal.'

'Hope I can,' Sam said. 'Meantime, is there anyone you could call?'

'Couple of her friends,' Larry Smith said. 'Though they're from way back, before Jill and I left Miami. Things changed between us and Billie around then, I'm sorry to say. She didn't want to move, told us we were selfish, but at least it meant she'd be free to do her own thing.'

'Which was what?' Sam asked.

'Aside from her singing, damned if either of us really knew,' Larry said. 'Which worried us then and still does, but you can't live their lives for them, can you?'

May 22

It was Sunday, but no one was in the mood for another family get-together.

Which meant that Grace, Sam and Joshua got to go to the beach.

Exactly what the three of them needed.

They strolled and paddled and built a sandcastle, and *this* was what it was all about, what they had been so afraid of losing last year, and as Sam jogged slowly down to the ocean beside his little son, he was counting his blessings big time.

'David called this morning,' Grace told him a little later. 'Mildred says she wouldn't mind if I came by sometime this week.'

'This is you, without me, I take it,' Sam said.

That being a rarity, given that Mildred had often chosen him to confide in.

'I think I understand why,' Grace said. 'Lord knows, Mildred has less vanity than most women, but I'd imagine she hates the idea of you, of all people, seeing her so vulnerable.'

'But it's not happening till Thursday, right?'

'No, but she has to have more tests on Wednesday.'

Sam let his mind wander back to the early days of his relationship with his father's wife, when she'd held court on her bench now and then to grant him an audience.

Back then, her eyes had always been sharp, clear and canny.

Memorable eyes, special lady.

'Daddy, are you crying?' Joshua asked.

Sam blinked and swallowed hard, smiled at his son.

'It's just the wind,' he told him.

He watched them.

Mostly, he watched her.

He had been waiting around for several hours, knowing his vigil might be pointless, since it was Sunday, so if the husband was off-duty today, they might just have stayed home all day or have driven off someplace he could not easily follow.

He was not, after all, some stalker.

He just wanted to see her again.

And then they'd come out of their pretty white house and it was obvious where they were headed, with their brightly patterned towels and the big bag that Detective Becket was carrying, a red-and-white rubber ball protruding over the top, while she held their little boy – sweet, coffee-colored kid – by the hand.

He'd held back a little longer, then followed.

Had waited till they were settled, and then scouted out his own place, a decent distance away, and he hoped he looked like just another guy on vacation, a baseball cap pulled down almost to his sunglasses-shielded eyes; and he'd bought a book a couple of days ago, *Good Neighbors*, though reading in English wasn't easy for him, but he figured it was good practice, and he didn't want her noticing a guy reading a French novel and then maybe taking a closer look . . .

Hell, she probably didn't remember him.

But he remembered her, would never, ever forget her.

Had photographs to help him.

Not that he needed photos.

She was etched forever on his memory.

And even as he watched now, he was humming again, could not help himself.

'Je prends les poses de Grace Kelly . . .'

May 23

Sometimes, late at night, instead of reading, he pored over his collections.

Two apothecary cabinets, two antique leather doctor's bags, a considerable collection of instruments, antique and contemporary, a microscope and a medical mannequin, formerly used in some school.

Everything catalogued and labeled.

His own small, private museum.

He used the modern instruments periodically for extra-curricular practice, in the knowledge that no physician or surgeon could ever work to improve their techniques too often or too thoroughly.

Tonight, once again, his concentration was focused on vision.

He had another small collection, kept in a special compartment of his refrigerator, of porcine eyes, on which he sometimes rehearsed procedures, placing an eye under the microscope, sometimes using a Styrofoam head and cup, constantly refining his techniques and dexterity.

No practical work tonight.

Tonight, he was just looking over some of his instruments: orb indentors, membrane picks, foreign body forceps, curved scissors, serrated forceps.

He looked, did not touch, but spoke their names out loud, recited each one's purpose, saw in his mind the procedures and operations for which they had been created.

Very few people, he knew, would comprehend the pleasure his collections gave him, were he to try to explain.

Not that it mattered.

Ordinary people's opinions had never mattered much to him.

His patients mattered, what he could do for them.

As he had sworn by Apollo and Asclepius and Hygieia and

Panacea in the Hippocratic Oath, which had numerous versions, though he favored the classic translation.

'*If I fulfill this oath and do not violate it, may it be granted to me to enjoy life and art, being honored with fame among all men for all time to come; if I transgress it and swear falsely, may the opposite of all this be my lot.*'

He would not transgress.

A doctor, first, last, always.

Grace was typing patient notes in her office just before noon on Monday, when Magda knocked and came in.

'Mr Delgado just called to ask if you would see Felicia.'

Grace sat back. 'Is she speaking?'

'I didn't question him,' Magda said. 'Are you willing?'

'I'll need to speak to him first,' Grace said. 'There are considerations.'

Magda handed her a blue Post-it note with a phone number. 'When you're ready.'

Grace thought for several moments, then made the call.

He picked up on the first ring, and she introduced herself.

'Before we go any further,' she said, 'there might be certain issues precluding my visiting your daughter at the Foster-Pérez Clinic. For one thing, I don't have practice privileges there.'

'I already assumed as much,' Delgado said. 'Which is part of the reason why Felicia is coming home tomorrow. I'm taking on a private nurse, and my housekeeper is fine with the arrangements.'

'And is her doctor in agreement?' Grace asked.

'Doctor Pérez will continue seeing her at my home.'

'That's good.' Grace paused. 'Three more things. You might want to take time to check out my credentials.'

'Already done, Doctor.'

She asked the most significant question: 'Has Felicia begun speaking?'

'Just a few words,' Delgado said, 'and nothing about her mother. But she has begun.'

'That's very good news.' Grace went on. 'There's one more major issue here, though it represents no conflict at all from my professional standpoint.'

'Your husband,' Delgado got there first. 'Detective Becket.'

'Quite,' Grace said.

'I'm sure you respect each other's confidentiality issues.'

'We do.'

'Then I have no problem,' Delgado said.

Sam took fifteen minutes out to drop by at Lincoln Park Music School to find out if Billie had been attending classes.

Except no one would tell him.

Which was, of course, as it should be.

If Billie's parents wanted to check on their daughter, they were going to have to contact the school directly.

Still no sign of her at evening rehearsal, nor had anyone heard from her.

Faced with major decisions to be made, Linda, by now intensely stressed, had turned to Sam to share the load, linking arms with him and moving away from the rest of the group toward a big old banyan tree.

'I really don't want to give it to Carla,' she said quietly. 'However fine she is, it's just not a soprano role.' She sighed, frustrated. 'Though it would obviously be a thousand times easier to find another Micaëla at this stage than another great Carmen.'

'Frankly' – Toni Petit came from behind, holding a cup – 'I'm more concerned about what might have happened to Billie.'

'We all are,' Sam said, and the delicate fragrance from Toni's drink reached his nose. 'What's that?'

'That's my chamomile tea, with honey and vanilla,' Linda said. 'Get you some, Sam?'

'Not right now, thanks.' He paused. 'Does Billie drink herb tea?'

'Not to my knowledge,' Linda said.

'It'd be healthy for her,' Toni said. 'Wherever she is.'

'I wouldn't worry too much about our Miss Smith.' Tyler Allen joined them. 'I have her down as a Grade-A mini-diva.'

The rest of the group were making their way over the lawn.

'You couldn't be more wrong,' Sam said to Allen.

'All this chopping and changing Carmens isn't exactly a picnic for me,' Jack Holden complained.

'You said you enjoyed my interpretation on Thursday,' Carla said.

'"Interpretation",' Tyler mocked. 'You were a good stand-in, darling.'

Sam shot him a look.

'You have a problem with me?' Tyler asked.

'Just with the barbed remarks,' Sam said.

'How about we get down to some work?' Linda took control.

'And anyone who's not needed first –' Toni raised her voice – 'I'd like to check measurements.'

Sam called Larry Smith from the Saab after rehearsal to tell him that the school needed to hear from him before releasing any information.

'I'll call first thing,' Larry said. 'But what if she hasn't been there? I mean, I guess she can't be called a missing person, not if she's probably just gone off someplace.'

'Any luck naming the bar where she works?'

'Nope,' Larry said.

'Maybe Jill knows,' Sam said.

'Jill's not feeling too great right now,' Larry said. 'Which is why I don't want to stress her. It's also why I can't just drop everything and come down to Miami – we don't even know that Billie's *in* Miami.'

Sam told his old school friend that he'd see what he could do.

Billie troubling him even more now.

May 24

On Tuesday morning, shown into Felicia Delgado's bedroom in her father's condo by the gentle-mannered nurse, Grace found the room cool and dimly lit, the drapes closed.

The teenager was sitting up in bed, her hands on the covers, her dark hair loose around her shoulders. The dark glasses she wore despite the semidarkness were as oversized as Sam had described.

'Hello, Felicia,' she said. 'I'm Grace Lucca. I'm a psychologist, and I'm here to help you, if you want me to.'

Felicia Delgado didn't respond, her expression impossible to read.

There was a chair against the wall over to Grace's right.

'Would you mind if I bring that chair a little closer, Felicia?'

She shrugged, and Grace picked up the chair and placed it about four feet from the bed, not wanting her to feel hemmed in.

She sat down. 'Do you understand why I'm here?'

'You're a shrink.' The teenager's voice was soft and a little husky. 'A shrink came to see me in the clinic, but I didn't feel like talking, so she went away again.'

No purpose in raising her brief appointment with Magda, Grace decided, especially given that it had taken place before her mother's death.

In another lifetime.

'Do you think you feel ready to talk to me now?' she asked.

'I'm not sure,' Felicia said.

'That's OK,' Grace said. 'We can just see how it goes.'

The only sound in the room now was the air conditioning's low hum.

Grace took a chance. 'I'm going to ask you to help me out with something, Felicia. But if you're not willing, that's OK, we'll manage.' She paused. 'I know you don't want to take off your lovely glasses—'

She saw the girl visibly flinch.

'—but because of them,' she went on, 'I can't tell how you're feeling.'

'I'm not taking them off.'

'I'm not asking you to,' Grace said. 'I know you have a problem with that.'

'I don't want to talk about it.' Felicia's voice rose a little.

'You don't have to. Not till you're ready.'

'I'll never be ready.'

'That's OK,' Grace said. 'I just want to explain that, from time to time, because so much of your face is hidden by your glasses, I might ask you questions about how you're feeling that seem dumb.'

'Oh,' Felicia said. 'OK.'

'Thank you,' Grace said. 'I only raised it because I'd like us to be honest with each other. So you know that I know about your problem.'

She allowed a decent pause.

'It's also pretty dark in here. Would you mind if I opened the drapes?'

Felicia didn't answer.

'I know I'd feel better,' Grace said. 'I often find first meetings quite hard, so it might help me if the room were a little brighter.'

'So open them,' the teenager said.

'Thank you.' Grace stood up, crossed over to the window, found a cord, opened the drapes and turned around.

This room had not, of course, been Felicia's home, but it was not an impersonal guest room, seemed like a place in which she might have spent time in the past. There were no posters, the only 'teen' thing a framed, signed photograph of three of the Harry Potter movie kids. A swift scan of the bookshelves revealed 'Extraordinary Hispanic Americans', a Bible and a Laura Ingalls Wilder novel, and Grace wondered if Felicia removed her dark glasses to read, if perhaps she waited until she knew no one would walk in on her, or if she locked doors.

Or maybe she never took them off at all in case she passed a mirror and caught sight of her own reflection.

'I'm sorry,' Felicia said. 'I know I'm not easy.'

'You have nothing to be sorry for,' Grace told her. 'You've been through an unimaginable ordeal, and you've suffered the worst kind of loss, and I wish I knew some easy way to help you quickly, but I don't. So I'm just going to see if maybe, over time, we can help each other find a way.'

Felicia Delgado's mouth lifted a little at the corners. Not exactly a smile, but something like it.

'What?' Grace asked gently.

'Nothing.'

'I thought perhaps I saw a trace of a smile.'

'And you could see that even with my glasses on,' Felicia said.

Being a smart mouth seemed to Grace a welcome sign of normality.

'Yes, I could,' she said. 'But why did you smile?'

'Because you talk like a real person,' Felicia said.

'I'm relieved to hear that,' Grace said.

There was a knock on the door, and Carlos Delgado looked in. 'How are we doing?'

Grace knew instantly and with regret that the brief connection was lost.

'I think we've been doing fine,' she said, staying focused on his daughter. 'Though I think you've probably had enough for one day, haven't you, Felicia?'

'I guess,' she said.

Grace stood up. 'Would you mind if I come back again soon?'

'If you want,' Felicia said.

'I'd like to,' Grace said. 'Very much.'

'Just so long as you don't think we're going to be friends,' Felicia said.

'Hey,' Carlos Delgado said. 'Don't be rude.'

'Your daughter's just saying what she feels,' Grace said. 'I want her to know she can be honest with me.'

'So how much did she say?' Delgado asked.

His living room was emphatically masculine, the flat-screen TV huge, the bar handsomely stocked, the furniture racing-green leather.

'We made a start,' Grace said.

'Did you ask about her mother?'

'No.'

'But if she was a witness . . .'

'We don't know that yet,' Grace said.

'If she's talking,' Delgado said, 'the police will want to question her.'

'They will,' Grace agreed. 'But I don't think she's ready to speak to them.'

'Will you tell your husband that?' Delgado asked.

'If Detective Becket asks for my professional opinion,' Grace said, 'that's what I'll tell him.'

Billie had not been to class for almost a week, Larry Smith reported to Sam that evening, and the school had no information to offer regarding any part-time work she might be doing.

'And so far, apparently,' Sam told Grace later, over bowls of vegetarian chili and couscous at their kitchen table, 'none of her fellow students seem to know anything.'

'You're really worried about her.'

'I'm concerned,' Sam said. 'But I guess it's her parents' decision as to if and when they regard her as actually missing.'

'I hope she's OK.' Grace paused. 'And it's all right, by the way, for you to ask me about Felicia Delgado.'

'I was waiting for you. Professional courtesy.'

'There's not much I can tell you, obviously,' she said. 'But you can ask.'

'Did she talk to you?'

'A little.' Grace paused. 'Is she ready to talk to you? Not quite yet, I'd say, but at least we made a start.'

'Meantime, every hour that passes . . .' Sam shook his head.

'Is wasted from the investigation standpoint,' Grace said. 'No help to you, though, if she shuts down again.' She paused. 'As it happens, we'd barely begun when her father came to check on her. I'll see her again as soon as possible.'

Sam put down his fork. 'Any chance he might have been deliberately cutting your time short?'

'He instigated my seeing her, didn't he?' Grace said.

'Point taken.' He thought for a moment. 'Where did you see her?'

'In her bedroom.'

'What was it like?'

'Comfortable. I thought she'd probably stayed over there in the past.'

Sam took another forkful of chili, then hesitated. 'Did you happen to notice if she had a Bible?'

'Why do you ask?'

'Did you notice?' he repeated quietly.

Grace supposed the question meant that Felicia had not yet been entirely eliminated as a suspect in her mother's death.

Just doing his job.

Didn't mean she had to like it.

'I did not,' she said, and knew that he sensed her lie.

His dark eyes on her were warm though, understanding.

That she liked.

May 25

At nine thirty-five on Wednesday morning, Magda answered a buzz from the office entry system.

'Is Doctor Lucca here?' a male voice, accented, asked.

'Do you have an appointment?' she asked.

'I'm afraid not,' he said. 'I'm here unexpectedly. We met recently in Zurich.'

'Your name?' Magda asked, just as Grace came into the entrance hall.

'Thomas Chauvin,' the voice on the speaker said.

'Good Lord,' Grace said.

* * *

The young Frenchman was apologetic for dropping by without notice.

'I'm in Miami for a month,' he told Grace and Magda, 'hoping to get material for a new project.'

'What's the project?' Magda asked.

'It's crime related,' Chauvin answered.

He offered nothing further, and neither woman pressed him.

'I'm staying in Surfside,' he said.

'In a hotel?' Grace asked.

'A vacation rental,' he said. 'A studio, one room and bath and a tiny kitchen.' He smiled. 'It's quite nice, and I have a car, so I can get around.'

'So you're all set,' Magda said brightly, and went to prepare for her ten o'clock patient.

'I'm afraid I don't have any time right now,' Grace told Chauvin.

She was finding it hard to conceal her irritation. She worked here on weekday mornings, while Joshua was at preschool. Now and then in the afternoons she saw patients at home, but mostly she liked to focus on her son and his needs. Had Chauvin given her notice, she would have done her best to fob him off, would certainly not have wanted him showing up at her place of work.

'I know I should have called ahead.' He looked repentant. 'But you're the only person I know in Miami, and all I could find was your business address.'

Better, perhaps, on reflection, than showing up at home.

'I'll do my best to schedule something, but this is a very busy time for me,' she said. 'I hope you'll understand.'

'Of course I do,' Chauvin said. 'I will take whatever crumbs you can offer.'

It was hard not to smile at such abject crawling.

He leapt on the touch of warmth. 'What I would dearly love is the chance to meet with your family and, most particularly, with your husband, so I could maybe ask him just a few questions to help with my research.'

That, at least, rang true. She said she'd do what she could, took the number of his prepaid local cell phone, and said she'd call when she'd had a chance to speak to Sam.

'But I can't promise anything,' she said.

'Even a cup of coffee would be wonderful,' Chauvin said.

* * *

'He's pretty cute,' Magda said, passing her in the hallway at eleven-fifteen.

'Don't even start,' Grace said.

'Very cute, if handsome young Frenchmen are your style.'

Grace ignored her and called Sam to put him in the picture.

'I told him we were both busy.'

'We have to invite him to dinner,' Sam said.

'We do?'

'Sure we do. You round up the family, fix up a time.'

'I don't think we should put your dad and Mildred through it,' Grace said, 'but I guess if the others don't mind . . .'

'They'll love meeting the guy who sent you flowers and then followed you all the way over the Atlantic.'

'Don't even joke,' Grace said.

'It's not my fault you're irresistible,' Sam said. 'Make it this evening, and Saul and I can rustle up a barbecue.'

'If I were you,' Martinez said to Sam, minutes later, 'I'd check him out.'

Sam grinned. 'What do you want me to do? Call Interpol?'

'If Grace were my wife, I think I might.'

'I think I'll just meet the poor guy first,' Sam said.

At eleven-thirty, Mildred and David arrived at the Adams Clinic on Indian Creek Drive for an appointment during which the curve of her cornea and the size and shape of her left eye could be measured again, after which there would be blood tests and a chance for her to ask any questions still on her mind.

If she was capable of speech, she thought.

She had rejected the suggestion she check in today and stay overnight ahead of the surgery, was determined to escape while she could.

'Very grand.' She looked up as they entered at the sign on the marble fascia of the building. 'I'd expect nothing less of the doctor.'

'You're still not overly fond, are you?' David said.

'It isn't his fault,' Mildred admitted.

For a while, her tension eased up a little. David had to go to the office to complete insurance paperwork, but everyone she encountered from the reception desk to the examination room was kind yet down-to-earth. Best of all, Dr Ethan Adams was not around, and instead there were two younger doctors, one a nice, modest man with curling fair hair called Dr Scott Merriam, the other with calm gray eyes, named Dr George Wiley.

'We've read Doctor Adams' notes,' Dr Merriam said, 'so we know you're a little nervous.'

'More than a little,' Mildred said.

'If we tell you there's no need to be,' Dr Wiley said, 'you probably won't believe us. Yet it is true.'

'Doctor Adams is the absolute best,' Dr Merriam said.

'If you've read my notes,' Mildred said, 'and if Doctor Adams has understood me at all, you'll know that it isn't belief in his skills that's my problem.'

'No,' Dr Wiley said. 'You're squeamish about eye exams.'

Mildred's mouth was dry, her insides tight as a drum.

'Which means you'd like us to stop talking and get the job done, so you can get out of here,' Dr Merriam said.

'Or better yet,' Mildred said, 'skip it altogether.'

'And get us fired,' Merriam said.

George Wiley's smile was gentle. 'You will be fine,' he said.

'Better than fine,' Scott Merriam confirmed.

Despite Grace having called him to arrange the barbecue, Chauvin came back twice more that morning, hoping she might have fifteen minutes to spare.

'I can give you ten,' she told him finally, at a quarter to one.

'Great,' Chauvin said, 'because I bought us lunch from a café in Bal Harbour.' He held up a bag. 'Some tuna salad and quiche – you choose – and crusty bread. OK with you? I brought enough for your colleague too.'

'She's with a patient,' Grace said. 'But thank you.'

They ate in Magda's kitchen, sitting on stools at her granite bar.

'Is it true,' Chauvin asked, 'that you used to see patients at your house?'

'I still do.' Grace paused. 'How would you know that?'

'I must have read it somewhere.' Chauvin saw her frown. 'Research is second nature for me, so I Google everyone I meet. It's become an addiction, I confess, but you can learn so much.'

He stopped, but Grace's hackles were already up, and most of the time she tried forgetting that her past was *out* there, and that people like this man, an aspiring photojournalist, were bound to be interested.

'Why are you really here, Monsieur Chauvin?' Her tone was sharper.

'I told you why.'

'Because if you've come here to pry into my private life or find some kind of story, then dinner and any further conversation are off the menu.'

'Not at all.' Chauvin looked distressed. 'The last thing I intended was to upset you. I swear I will never Google you again.'

Grace almost laughed. 'I guess I overreacted.'

'Not really, after what you've been through.' He shook his head. 'The worst kind of nightmare, and I've reminded you of it, but it was there for me to read, you know, and I wanted to be honest with you.'

Grace let the words hang for a moment.

'Let's just say I prefer not to talk about it,' she said.

'Understood,' Chauvin said.

'I hope so,' Grace said.

The evening slipped by pleasantly enough, with Sam, Claudia, Saul and Mel – and Joshua too for a while – all helping to make it relaxing for the visitor and for Grace. Only Cathy absent, delayed by an event at JWU, hoping to arrive in time to meet her mother's 'mystery Frenchman'.

Sam's barbecues were always easygoing, held out on their small deck, doors open to the kitchen and lanai, the calm waters beyond made occasionally choppy by boats whose skippers generally respected the laws and codes of the Atlantic Intracoastal Waterway that ran from Key West all the way to Norfolk, Virginia.

The conversation was easy too, Chauvin readily answering questions about his life and family at home in Strasbourg, though less forthcoming about his career to date.

'Not enough to tell yet,' he said.

'It takes time to build that kind of career,' Sam said.

'And luck, too, I guess,' Saul said.

'Which leads me to my very cheeky request.' Chauvin's blue eyes focused on Sam. 'Is there a chance that you might grant me a "tagalong" – I believe that's what you call it?'

'You want to ride in a patrol car,' Sam said.

'What I would really love, if it were possible,' Chauvin said, 'would be to ride with you and your partner.'

Sam regarded him for an instant, then nodded. 'I have no problem with that,' he said. 'I know journalists have to make use of anything that comes their way.'

'It's true, I guess,' Chauvin said, 'that we are all opportunists at heart.'

'Tomorrow morning,' Sam said. 'Though I'm going to call my partner, make sure we're not clashing on anything.'

'Thank you, Sam,' Chauvin said. 'I'll be forever in your debt.'

'I don't know how long we'll be able to give you,' Sam said. 'It's a busy time.'

'I can imagine,' Chauvin said, 'with this Black Hole killer.'

'You read about that,' Sam said.

'Thomas does a lot of reading,' Grace said.

Cathy arrived just before Chauvin left.

'*Dieu*,' he said when he saw her.

Grace glanced at him sharply.

'I'm sorry,' the Frenchman said. 'It was just the resemblance.'

Sam smiled. 'We know.'

'I hoped to be here earlier,' Cathy said, 'but things at college dragged on.'

'I gather you're going to be a great chef,' Chauvin said.

'I love to cook,' Cathy said, 'but so do a lot of people.'

'They're not all as beautiful as you,' he said.

'God.' Cathy laughed.

'If Cathy becomes a successful chef,' Mel said coolly, 'it'll be her talent and hard work that get her there.'

'Naturally.' Chauvin smiled at her. 'You're right to rebuke me.'

'Not that Cathy isn't gorgeous,' Mel allowed.

Chauvin held up his hands. 'I'm saying nothing more.'

'He seems a nice guy,' Saul said afterward.

'A little smooth and maybe naive,' Sam said, 'but I don't think there's any harm in him.'

'I hope not,' Grace said.

'He's clearly besotted by you, sis,' Claudia said.

'And not quite as young as you made out,' Sam said to Grace.

'I rather think it's you, the detective, he's after,' she said. 'Not me.'
'I thought he was cute,' Cathy said.
'He could get annoying in large doses,' Mel said.
'I'm concerned that he's here for a whole month,' Grace said.
'Don't be,' Sam told her. 'Al and I will help him out tomorrow, answer his questions, maybe suggest one more get-together just before he leaves, make it clear he'll have to fend for himself.'
'Isn't that a little rude?' Saul said.
'Grace saved his life,' Cathy said. 'She's allowed to be rude.'

May 26

The doctor was feeling tense tonight.
The way he often felt before important days.
All days were important to a doctor.
Every encounter vital to a patient.
He realized that. He *felt* their need.
He wasn't sure if they always comprehended his empathy.
Hard to tell when you were up on a pedestal.
The way all doctors deserved to be.
Some days were tougher than others. Long, arduous days when it was sometimes difficult to remember to rise above, to remind himself that he was entitled to his pride. When other people, often stupid people, got in the way of that.
His reading tonight was biblical, his need for inspiration; drawing it from The Acts, the story of Peter raising Aeneas from his sickbed through Christ.
On nights like this, he craved inspiration.

A missing person's report had come in early Thursday morning that had everyone in Violent Crimes on edge.
Marie Nieper, age thirty-four, divorced, living alone in a condo on Harding Avenue. Presently working on a home study course in interior design.
She had missed a lunch appointment with a girlfriend yesterday, and no one had heard from her or seen her since.
Bad vibes all around.

* * *

Thomas Chauvin arrived at the station at eleven-thirty.

Sam gave him a swift tour of the building, as promised, and then he and Martinez walked him along Washington Avenue to Markie's for a sandwich.

'Is this where all you guys hang out?' Chauvin asked.

'Not all,' Sam said. 'But Al and I like it.'

'Me too,' Chauvin said.

He ordered a club sandwich and Diet Coke, then asked if Sam minded him asking a couple of personal questions.

'Depends how personal,' Sam said. 'You can try.'

'I'm just interested to know how you and Grace met,' Chauvin said.

Sam glanced at Martinez, saw his partner's dark brows rise, then looked back at Chauvin. 'We met through work.'

'Great good fortune,' the other man said.

'Can't argue with that,' Sam said.

'Saul told me that you guys adopted Cathy,' Chauvin said.

'Yes, we did,' Sam said, wondering just when Saul might have told him that.

'Why don't you give us your research questions now?' Martinez said curtly.

'OK.' Thomas Chauvin opened his notepad. 'I have quite a few.'

'Great,' Martinez said.

'You did ask the guy,' Sam said.

The questions were straightforward, easy for them to answer.

Points of police procedure, mostly, relating to violent crime, nothing they felt it inappropriate to respond to.

They gave him thirty more minutes, then told him that if he wanted to do the tagalong, they needed to make a move.

'This is a great start to my trip,' Chauvin said.

'Glad to help,' Sam said easily. 'We'll drive around some—'

'And then you'll have plenty of time to take a long, slow look around by yourself,' Martinez said.

Mildred was scheduled to check in at the Adams Clinic at two.

However bad she'd been prior to and during her visits to Dr Sutter and Ethan Adams, David could not remember ever having seen her as jittery as she was today.

'What can I do?' he had asked her at ten.

'You could take me for a drive?' she'd said.

'You got it.'

She had wanted to go to South Beach.

They had parked the car and taken a stroll along the promenade, and then, seeing that her old bench was unoccupied, they'd sat down for a few minutes.

'Old friend,' she said, giving it a little pat.

David said nothing, giving her time.

'How about a walk on the beach?' Mildred said after a while.

They walked in silence, holding hands.

'Remembering Donny?' David asked at last, gently.

'Sure,' she said. 'But that's not why I wanted to come today. I've always wanted to do this here with you.'

'There'll be plenty more times we can do it, if you like,' he told her.

'Maybe.' Mildred smiled at him. 'Though I don't think I'll be needing to come here again, to this place. What you and I have is so much more.'

'What you had with Donny was the world to you,' David said. 'It's OK.'

'Back then, I guess it was,' she said. 'But I know different now.'

They walked back to the edge of the beach, shook the sand out of their shoes, and went back to the car.

The detectives were still in Martinez's Chevy, fielding Chauvin's questions when, almost over the Julia Tuttle Causeway, Sam answered a call from Joe Sheldon, who said that he and Cutter had just spotted a red-haired woman in overalls getting out of a black Suzuki SUV carrying two bags.

'Probably nothing,' Sheldon said, 'but she's knocking on someone's front door right now.'

'Address?' Sam said.

'Lenox Avenue, near 7th, east of Alton Road.'

'There in ten.' He twisted around in his seat. 'Gonna have to drop you off, Thomas.'

'Can't I come along?' Chauvin asked.

'Afraid not,' Sam told him.

'I promise to behave.'

'Where'd you leave your car?' Martinez asked.

'I came on the bus,' Chauvin said.

'Good.' Martinez waited until they were on Arthur Godfrey, and pulled over. 'Have a nice day.'

'Thanks, guys.' Chauvin opened the door. 'I hope I get to see you again.'

'I'm sure you will,' Sam said. 'Give me a call at the start of your last week and we'll fix something up.'

Chauvin got out and shut the door.

Martinez gunned the engine.

Just before two p.m., in the offices on Collins Avenue that Dr Bartolo Lopez shared with several other physicians, Mrs Angela Valdez – one of the part-time receptionists, just back after two weeks' vacation – was catching up on a few things with the doctor.

'A terrible thing happened,' Dr Lopez said. 'I'm not sure if you were still here or not.' He paused. 'The Delgado murder?'

Angela Valdez's eyes widened. 'Who got murdered?'

More than one Delgado on their books.

The doctor filled her in, and the receptionist's horror grew, recalling the last time she'd seen Beatriz Delgado, when she'd had an argument with her daughter in the waiting room.

'Just one day before I went to Portugal,' she said.

Lopez looked at his calendar. 'Your last day was the tenth, right?' He shook his head. 'If I'd known they'd been here, I would have told the police.'

'You think it could be important?'

'I think everything could be important when it comes to the last few days of a murder victim's life.'

Angela Valdez crossed herself. 'Should we call the police now, Doctor?' She glanced at the clock on the wall. 'Though your next patient's due.'

'It's waited this long,' Lopez said. 'I'll call them later.'

Mildred was all checked in.

Her room was comfortable, furnished in soft apricot tones, and if it had not been for the array of call buttons and sockets for emergency equipment on the wall behind the bed, she might almost have been in a hotel.

The last time they'd been in a hotel had been on their honeymoon.

Boston first, then New York City. David had encouraged her to see her elderly parents, from whom she'd been estranged for many years, but they'd seemed almost like strangers. Too much had happened to her over the years, the void between them too deep, but they'd all behaved well, and Mildred was glad she had seen them again.

After all, she could not be certain of seeing anyone clearly again . . .

Stop that, she told herself. Cataracts were nothing, her surgery a mere trifle to Ethan Adams.

Yet still, she'd been dealing with a brand-new sense of dread, unrelated, she felt, to her ridiculous squeamishness.

It had begun plaguing her about a week ago.

The dread that something might go wrong.

That something bad was going to happen.

'Dollar for your thoughts?' David's voice broke in.

She smiled at him. 'Not worth a penny.'

There was a knock, and Dr Merriam poked his head around the door. 'Welcome, Mrs Becket,' he said. 'It's good to see you again.'

'I tried heading for Mexico, but my husband stopped me,' Mildred said.

'I thought you said you were going to behave,' David said.

'Is there anything you need?' Scott Merriam said.

'Sedation,' Mildred said. 'The sooner the better.'

'Doctor Wiley and I are both on duty,' Merriam said, 'so if you need anything.'

'I'll ask, thank you.'

'Meantime, you just try and relax,' the doctor said.

'Huh,' Mildred said.

Sam and Martinez took over from Cutter and Sheldon on Lenox Avenue.

The SUV was parked right outside.

'No tinted windows,' Sam said.

'The Naples neighbor could have been wrong about that,' Martinez said.

The redhead answering the door was African-American and male by gender, a pin on his white overalls identifying him as 'Marilyn', with curves to match. He looked Sam over with approval, voiced no objection to admitting two Miami Beach detectives into the apartment.

'This isn't my home,' Marilyn said. 'My clients asked me to get the door.'

The 'clients', waiting in the living room, were both in their late sixties, wearing skimpy towels. Both partway through Brazilian waxes, according to Marilyn.

That thought alone enough to make the detectives' eyes water.

Dead end, and they both knew it.

They went through the motions, asked 'Marilyn' very politely for ID, and the redhead did not refuse, handed over a driver's license in the name of Dewayne Jones with a soft, resigned sigh.

'Nothing illegal happening here,' Dewayne/Marilyn said.

'Except maybe your entry,' the old guy said to the detectives, showing the first sign of resentment.

'We knocked,' Sam said.

'And this person let us in,' Martinez added, looking at Jones.

'Would it kill you to say "lady"?' Marilyn said.

'No, ma'am,' Martinez said.

'We're sorry to have disturbed you,' Sam said.

'Not at all,' the female client said. 'You're kind of hot, Detective.'

'Thank you, ma'am,' Sam said, then turned to Dewayne/Marilyn. 'I wonder if you could do me a big favor? It may sound kind of strange.'

Marilyn smiled. 'I think I can cope.'

'Would you mind if I sniffed the contents of all your products?'

Martinez groaned. 'This just gets better and better.'

'There's no dope here,' Marilyn told them.

'We're not looking for drugs,' Sam said. 'I'm just trying to track down a particular scent that beauticians sometimes use, but I've been unable to identify – you know how that kind of thing can bug you?'

Marilyn shrugged. 'Sniff away.'

'Pardon me for breathing,' the old guy said, looking down at his towel, 'but what happens when this stuff stays on too long?'

'Oh, my God,' Marilyn said.

'Jesus,' Martinez said.

* * *

'Not what you signed on for when you married me,' Mildred said to David.

It was just past three-thirty, and though her surgery was not scheduled until five, Dr Merriam had come by a while ago to give her something to settle her nerves.

'A dependent old woman,' she went on. 'If anything goes wrong, that is.'

'It won't,' David said. 'It really won't.'

'But if it did . . .'

'Then that would be exactly what we both signed on for,' David said. 'After all, who knows which part of *me* is going to crumble next?'

'It can't,' Mildred said. 'I might need you to guide me.'

'What I'll probably need is help stopping you running around too soon.'

'I'm not so sure.'

'What happened to positive thoughts?'

'I'm not sure of that either,' Mildred said.

David's cell phone vibrated in his pocket.

'Take it,' Mildred told him. 'It might be important.'

There was a knock, and Dr Wiley came in.

'I'll take this outside,' David said.

'Just wanting to know how're you doing, Mrs Becket?' Wiley asked.

'Not too badly,' she said. 'Thanks to the pill Doctor Merriam gave me.'

'That's good.' The doctor took her pulse, and she smiled, closed her eyes. 'Very good. You just relax.'

'Might as well.' Mildred opened her eyes. 'I've signed the consent forms.'

'No going back then.' Dr Wiley smiled. 'Any questions?'

She shook her head. 'I just want to get it over with now.'

'Waiting's always the tough part,' Wiley said, and patted her hand.

Mildred usually found hand-patting patronizing, but from this young man she didn't seem to mind too much. His hands were gentle and his eyes intelligent, and his exam careful as he listened to her heart and then felt her abdomen, though Mildred couldn't quite imagine why it needed to be so thorough when all they were going to do was . . .

She shuddered involuntarily, and Dr Wiley immediately removed his hands. 'Was that painful, Mrs Becket?'

'No,' she said. 'Just nerves. Please take no notice of me.'

'All done anyhow,' George Wiley said.

David came back into the room.

'Everything all right?' he asked Mildred.

'Everything's peachy,' she said.

'My cue to leave you both in peace,' Dr Wiley said.

'What time is the anesthesiologist coming to see my wife?' David asked.

'Soon, I imagine,' Dr Wiley said.

At three forty-five, Grace was home alone, Claudia having taken Joshua to her house after preschool, freeing Grace to visit Mildred.

'I doubt she'll want visitors,' Grace had said.

'Please don't spoil my nephew time,' Claudia said.

'I wouldn't deprive Joshua of his Aunty time,' Grace had said.

She'd just come back with Woody after a walk when the doorbell rang.

With the dog barking loudly, Grace took a look through the den window and saw Thomas Chauvin standing on the path, a bag over one shoulder, another bouquet of flowers in his right hand.

Already irritated, she told Woody to cut it out and opened the door. 'Thomas,' she said.

'I know I should have called first,' he said.

'Yes, you should,' Grace said. 'I'm afraid I'm in a hurry.'

'Always in a hurry, Grace.' He held out the flowers. 'For you and Sam, to thank you for your hospitality and to thank Sam and Detective Martinez for the tagalong, even though it was cut short.'

Grace took the bouquet, saw they were pink roses again.

'I hope you like roses,' Chauvin said. 'These are my favorites.'

'They're lovely, thank you,' she said. 'But completely unnecessary.'

'Absolutely necessary,' Chauvin said, then hesitated. 'I'm embarrassed to ask, but I wonder if you'd mind if I use your bathroom? I've been out a long time, and . . .'

'Of course.' Grace opened the door wider to let him in. 'Just there,' she said, pointing to the door near the staircase.

'A thousand thanks,' Chauvin said.

Grace shut the front door, looked at the bouquet, even more aggravated because now she had little choice but to offer him a cup of coffee. She went through to the kitchen, laid the roses on the worktop, then ran water into the coffee machine.

'You read my mind,' Chauvin said from the door.

'I take it that's a yes to coffee?'

'Always.' He stooped to pet Woody, who allowed his ears to be fondled, then trotted to his bed and lay down.

'Espresso or regular?'

'Espresso,' he said, 'definitely.'

'Pull up a chair,' Grace told him.

'*Merci*.' He rummaged in his bag and brought out a camera. 'I hope you don't mind. I meant to take some photos last night, but I forgot.'

It was a sharp-looking camera, Grace thought, larger than most of the neat little digital devices almost everyone used these days.

She brought over his small cup.

'OK with you?' Chauvin turned on the camera.

Grace wished she hadn't offered him coffee.

'Just a snap or two,' he said, 'for my collection.'

'Collection?' She went back to the counter, set up the machine for her own cappuccino.

'Travel memories, you know,' Chauvin said. 'I'm sure you and Sam take pictures when you go places.'

'Sure,' she said.

'Smile for me?'

Grace turned, smiled, and the camera whirred and flashed.

'Another please?'

She didn't turn around this time, but she heard the camera go again, ignored it, looked at her watch and shook her head.

'I'm sorry, Thomas, I can't even have a coffee with you. I really do need to get going.' She switched off the machine, turned around.

Chauvin took another photograph.

Grace blinked. 'No more, please.'

He said something softly in French.

'I didn't catch that,' she said.

'I was just thinking aloud,' Chauvin said, 'about your amazing resemblance to the late Princess of Monaco.'

Grace laughed.

'But it's true,' he said.

'I have blonde hair,' she said. 'That's about it.'

'No,' he said. 'You have the same wonderful bone structure, beautiful eyes.'

Grace felt a real flash of discomfort. 'I think it's time you were leaving.'

'Just a couple more photos, please.' He raised the camera again.

'No more photos.' She was firm.

'Are you going to confiscate my camera?' He grinned. 'You sound like a teacher, scolding me.'

'I have a lot to do,' Grace said.

'OK.' Chauvin leaned down, put the camera into his bag, picked it up and rose. 'You're right to be cross with me. This was an intrusion.'

'Not at all.' Grace went ahead of him into the hallway. 'But you really need to call first. Sam and I both have very hectic schedules.'

At the front door, Chauvin stopped. 'You know, back in Switzerland I thought that the resemblance between you and the other Grace was almost uncanny, but then, last night, when I met your daughter, that really took my breath away.'

'Really,' Grace said, and opened the door.

'You must have noticed it, surely?'

'Never,' Grace said.

'Now that would be fun, to photograph Cathy as Kelly – perhaps as she looked in *High Society*, or maybe *Dial M*—'

'I don't want you bothering my daughter, Mr Chauvin,' Grace cut in sharply.

'So hostile.' He looked disappointed. 'From Thomas to Mister.'

Grace moved away from the door, and Chauvin stepped over the threshold.

'Goodbye,' she said. 'Enjoy the rest of your stay.'

She closed the door.

Discomfort had turned to unease.

She went back into the kitchen, picked up the phone and keyed Cathy's speed-dial number.

'Leave a message and I'll call you right back,' her daughter's voice said.

'Cathy, I may be overreacting, but if Thomas Chauvin tries to contact you, please don't have anything more to do with him, and call Sam. I have reason to feel a little uncomfortable about him. Call me anyway, please, as soon as you get this.'

She ended the call, made another one, to Sam.

Voicemail too.

She left a message.

When Sam got back in the car, Martinez had just finished a call.

'Cutter says the Delgado doctor called. Doctor Bartolo Lopez. Says he only just found out that Beatriz and daughter visited his practice on the tenth. Cutter and Sheldon are going to talk to him.' Martinez paused. 'Your nose tell you anything in there?'

'Nothing,' Sam said. 'The stuff Marilyn says she uses for "chemical peels"' – he grimaced – 'was closest, but I'd be reaching.'

Martinez had found a couple of speeding tickets for Dewayne Jones, nothing more significant or sinister, and had returned his driver's license with thanks.

'The problem with remembered smells,' Sam said, 'is you're never sure they're accurate.'

'Even if you had nailed it in there,' Martinez said, 'how would that help us with about a thousand "technicians" in Florida using that stuff.'

'I know it,' Sam said, checking his phone, still wishing he had nailed it.

He'd love to nail *something* in this case.

He listened to Grace's message, returned her call.

'I'll pay Chauvin a visit on the way home,' he told her. 'If he comes back—'

'I won't be letting him in,' Grace reassured him. 'And I've left Cathy a message telling her to call you if she sees him.' She paused. 'I'm going to the clinic at around five, spend some time with your dad while Mildred has the procedure.'

'He'll appreciate that,' Sam said. 'You think Chauvin's more than just a nuisance?'

'No,' Grace said. 'But I think he may be obsessive, and Cathy does not need someone like that in her life, I'm sure you'll agree.'

'Did you get his address?'

'No, I'm sorry, but I didn't want to show that much interest. But he'd have to have given his address when he entered the country, wouldn't he?'

'First address of his stay,' Sam confirmed.

Didn't mean he had to have given the right one, though.

'Leave it with me,' he said.

Mildred's surgery had been delayed.

Dr Merriam had come to tell them that Dr Adams had been called to Miami General to carry out emergency eye surgery on an accident patient.

Scott Merriam was apologetic. 'I know how much you want to get this over and done with, Mrs Becket.'

'Can't be helped,' Mildred said.

She'd have liked to offer sympathy for the poor soul whose eyesight might be hanging in the balance, but the knowledge that she was going to have to go on waiting made it hard for her to speak.

'How long?' David asked.

He understood emergencies, but Mildred had disliked Adams from day one. There were other excellent ophthalmologists in Miami, and suddenly he found himself considering calling this off, taking her home.

'It's hard to say exactly, Doctor Becket,' Dr Merriam said. 'Hopefully not more than a couple of hours, but one can never tell with these things.'

David looked at his wife.

'No, David,' Mildred said, her voice returned.

He smiled.

'Am I missing something?' Dr Merriam asked.

'Just my wife reading my mind,' David said. 'I was contemplating asking her if she'd rather reschedule.'

'I couldn't bear it,' Mildred said flatly. 'So we'll just send our good wishes to Doctor Adams's much needier patient, and go on waiting.'

'You're very understanding.' Merriam looked at David. 'Is there anything we can get for you, sir, while you wait?' He cast another apologetic glance at Mildred. 'Nothing for you, I'm afraid, but if Doctor Becket would like some coffee, or—'

'Nothing for Doctor Becket either,' David said. 'I'll sit it out with my wife, and eat something when she's allowed too.'

'That's just silly,' Mildred said. 'If you're hungry.'

'I'm not,' David said.

'Me neither,' Mildred said.

All her energies concentrated on resisting the urge to burst into tears.

ICE – Immigrations and Customs Enforcement, the main investigative arm of Homeland Security – would provide the address Thomas Chauvin had given on entry to the US, but it would take time, and Grace's reaction to the Frenchman's unscheduled visit had made Sam uneasy.

Still, they were back at the office and there was work to be done.

Especially after the kind of downer that always hit when a potential break came to less than nothing.

His thoughts swung briefly to 'Marilyn' and her line of work, how well it suited her, probably infinitely more than anything an unfulfilled Dewayne Jones was likely to have done with his life.

And then his mind turned back again to Chauvin.

To the word Grace had used about him.

Obsessive.

Where their family and that kind of individual were concerned, he was not prepared to take chances. Christ knew they'd been through more than enough in the last several years.

He'd seen Chauvin's rental car last night, a white Ford Focus, but he hadn't seen the tag, had had no reason to look at it. And he'd tried Cathy twice since Grace's call, knew she was probably not home yet, knew that she sometimes turned her cell off, which was fine, though at moments like these . . .

He called Saul, but his brother's phone went to voicemail too.

He turned to Martinez. 'Remember what you said about Interpol?'

Martinez nodded. 'Maybe not such a crazy idea after all?'

Cathy often forgot to check her voicemail after lectures. Through so much of last year, when they'd been under threat, Sam had insisted they all call in regularly. These days, she sometimes frankly enjoyed the freedom of being out of touch for a while.

Hell, she was a grown woman, living with her uncle – even if they were more like brother and sister – and in daily contact with her parents. And however much she loved them all, she needed to build up her own life structure again if she ever wanted to have the independent existence she was striving toward, and she was doing OK at JWU, and if all went well, come next year, she had plans.

For this evening, though, with Saul and Mel going out, her only plan was for a cool shower and then . . .

She saw him.

Waiting outside the front door of their building.

She remembered the way he'd looked at her when they'd met last night at her parents' house.

Parking her Mazda, she checked her reflection in the rearview mirror.

As she turned off the engine, he was already walking toward her.

Cathy smiled.

Best-laid plans . . .

Cutter called Sam on his cell number.

'What do you have, Mary?' Sam put the phone on speaker, motioned to Martinez.

'Doctor Lopez says the reason he didn't know the Delgados had come to his office on the tenth was because they never actually made it in to see him. He says his list was full that afternoon, and the on-duty receptionist went on vacation next day, so only just mentioned it to him. It's a fairly hectic multiphysician practice – on Collins and seventy-fourth street – so Mike and I think that's credible.'

'Go on,' Sam said.

'Lopez hadn't seen Beatriz Delgado for five years, by the way,' Cutter said. 'And regarding her phobia, he says he once tried suggesting she got help, but she became very agitated, and he's never been approached for her records.'

All of which lent further credibility to Delgado's statements.

'He wouldn't breach confidentiality about Felicia,' Cutter said, 'though he did imply there was nothing to breach. And he said he'd never met Carlos.'

'Hey, Mary.' Martinez leaned toward the phone. 'We goin' somewhere with this or not?'

'The receptionist, Angela Valdez, wasn't there today,' Cutter went on. 'But she told the doc that on the tenth, Felicia refused to see him, and she and Beatriz argued about it. Felicia called her mom a hypocrite, said she was cruel to make her come, then stomped out. Beatriz apologized to Mrs Valdez and went after her.'

Sam considered the effects of that on other waiting patients.

'That must have attracted some attention,' he said.

'Mike and I raised that. Lopez says Valdez didn't mention anything about other patients, but he's left a message for her asking who else was there at the time, though there might be confidentiality issues there too.'

'The doc going to let you know?' Sam asked.

'Doctor Lopez and Mrs Valdez both have my cell number,' Cutter said.

At ten after six, Dr Merriam came in to Mildred's room.

'We have lift off,' he told her.

'I'd say "whoopee",' she said, 'but I guess you'd see through that.'

'I've brought goodies,' Dr Merriam said.

'Premed?' David looked at the small basin the doctor was carrying, at the small hypodermic within it. 'For such a short procedure?'

'Doctor Adams wants Mrs Becket to feel as relaxed as possible,' Merriam said.

Mildred extended both arms to him. 'The more the better.'

'My wife, the new junkie,' David said.

'Needs must,' she said.

'You don't mind needles?' Merriam asked.

'I don't especially love them,' Mildred said. 'How is that poor patient doing?'

'Better than he was,' Dr Merriam said. 'Doctor Adams is a great surgeon.'

David watched him swab his wife's arm and smoothly administer the injection.

'OK?' Scott Merriam asked her.

'Swell,' she told him.

'It can't be working already,' David said.

'Believe me,' Mildred said wryly, 'it isn't.'

He'd started creeping Cathy out a little less than five minutes after she'd invited him into the apartment.

Taking photographs.

She'd offered him a cup of coffee, but he'd asked for mineral water, and he'd taken out his camera, which she'd admired, and he'd focused the lens on her and started snapping away even while she was taking two small bottles of Zephyrhills out of the refrigerator.

'Hey,' she told him. 'Enough.'

'I can't help it,' Chauvin said. 'You're a great subject.'

'I didn't ask to be a subject,' Cathy said.

She remembered abruptly that Grace had seemed a little annoyed by him last night. Mel, who was usually a good judge, had seemed unimpressed, too, though Sam had just said he'd thought him 'smooth'.

Chauvin took another photograph.

'Come on,' Cathy said, and handed him his water.

'Where to?' he asked.

She smiled. 'I meant "come *on*", cut out the Annie Leibovitz routine.'

'Wow,' Chauvin said. 'If you're trying to flatter me, go right ahead.'

Not so much smooth as a dope, Cathy decided.

'Let's sit on the terrace,' she said.

'May I bring my camera?'

'If you can't bear to be parted from it.'

'Aspiring photojournalist, remember?'

'How could I forget?' Cathy said.

David had come down in the elevator and walked alongside Mildred and an orderly named Benjamin as far as the broad, code-secured doors that led to the OR area. He had held her cold hand and knew that, despite the light premed, she was still more anxious than he'd hoped.

'It'll soon be over,' he told her.

'I know.' Mildred's voice was quiet but steady.

'I'm proud of you,' he said softly.

She pulled a self-deprecating face, and he told her that he loved her, and she told him the same, and then he kissed her forehead, and Benjamin assured them both that he would look after her, and then they were through the door and gone from sight.

Suddenly, David felt intensely nervous.

Lying on the gurney in the room outside the OR, staring up at a clock on the wall telling her it was now six thirty-three, something remarkable happened to Mildred.

Benjamin was still hovering, and two nurses were busy with something over to her right, when Dr Ethan Adams appeared out of nowhere.

And something inside her changed.

She felt better. Safer. And it was not because that injection had suddenly taken effect.

It was because of *him.*

There he stood in his green scrubs, looking as clean and spruce as if his own nanny had just dispatched him, and he bent slightly from the waist and spoke to her.

'This is going to be much easier than you could possibly imagine, Mrs Becket,' he said. 'I know you've had general anesthesia before, so you already know you'll go off to sleep in no time, and when you wake, it will all be done, and I'll come and talk to you again.'

The words were no different than Mildred had expected, but the amazing thing was that she *believed* them. She believed *him*, because suddenly, for the first time since they'd first met, Ethan Adams's eyes were not just sharp and keen, but kind, too, even empathetic, and it occurred to Mildred that maybe this was where he felt at his most confident, became most able to communicate with his patients.

The anesthesiologist – a friendly woman with a gentle touch and reassuring smile – began to talk to her then, but Mildred found she was hardly listening.

It was OK, she thought, just before she began counting backward as instructed. It was going to be OK after all, and what a foolish old woman she'd been, worrying about . . .

She slept.

Cathy led the way out onto the terrace, sat down and unscrewed the top of her bottle. 'So you're serious about photojournalism,' she said.

'Very.' Chauvin sat to her left, set his camera down on the table.

'So long as you're not practicing the journalism part now,' she said.

'You looked very serious as you said that,' he said.

'I guess I am,' Cathy said.

'I can understand why,' Chauvin said.

'Meaning?'

'Meaning that I know a little of what you've been through.'

Cathy put down her bottle. 'Let's get this cleared away,' she said. 'I don't want to talk to a virtual stranger about old personal business.'

'I'm not exactly a stranger,' Chauvin said. 'I'm a friend of your mom's, and I spent time with your father this morning.'

'Only because he was too polite to refuse,' Cathy said.

'Ouch,' Chauvin said.

'I'm sorry,' Cathy said. 'That was rude.'

'But truthful.'

'Not really.' She felt guilty. 'Sam wouldn't have agreed to the tagalong if he hadn't wanted to. He wanted to be helpful.'

'And he was,' Chauvin said. 'And I met the rest of the family last night, but had too little time with you, and I'm only here to take a couple of snaps for my Florida album, and then I'll be out of your hair.'

'Oh,' she said. 'OK.'

'Which is gorgeous, by the way.'

'Oh, stop.' She just stopped herself reaching up to touch her hair, which had been cut very short, but was now a kind of midway shaggy bob.

'I like your style altogether,' Chauvin said.

He picked up the camera again.

'You've taken your snaps,' Cathy said. 'Please, no more.'

And Chauvin sighed.

Grace sat in a waiting room with David.

The place had every comfort, except, of course, the one that every waiting relative or close friend ever really wanted when they sat in a room like this. Namely good news about their loved one.

Not that Mildred was in any danger, but still, when David had called earlier sounding stressed about the delay, she'd promised that she would still come and keep him company when they did finally take Mildred to the OR.

Now, he looked wretched.

'It's seeing her so vulnerable,' he explained. 'I wish the shoe was on the other foot. She's always been so strong for me.'

'As you have for her – for all of us – when anything's wrong,' Grace said. 'No woman could ask for a more supportive husband. Besides which, Mildred's anxieties aside, we both know this is a straightforward and almost miraculously effective surgical procedure. And you don't have to worry about her fears, because she's sleeping.'

'Which is the reason I encouraged general anesthesia, but now . . .'

'Mildred's healthy,' Grace said. 'It's a short anesthetic.'

'I know,' David said. 'Still, things sometimes go wrong.'

'Very seldom.' She looked at the craggy face with its hawk nose, remembered other times when he'd had terrible reasons to be fearful, saw that he was afraid now. 'You really are nervous.'

'I am.' David looked puzzled. 'Mildred hasn't talked about it, but I've sensed that her fears have snowballed into something stronger these last few days. It's been almost as if she had some kind of warning intuition.'

'So now that she's happily asleep, you've taken on her irrational fear.' Grace reached for his hand, squeezed it gently. 'Over soon.'

'Taking pictures is just what I do,' Chauvin said to Cathy. 'It's become second nature, when I see something or someone special. I didn't mean to make you uncomfortable.'

'You did, a little,' she said. 'But it's OK.'

'Good.' He paused. 'Where is Saul, by the way? I was hoping to see him too. And Mel, of course.'

'He's on his way home,' Cathy said.

And then she flushed, because she was not a seasoned liar, and the small untruth made her more uncomfortable. She stood, picked up her water, walked back into the living room.

'Are you OK?' Chauvin asked from the terrace.

'Sure,' she said.

She remembered, then, that she hadn't turned on her phone since leaving JWU, so she retrieved it from her bag and did so now.

She watched Chauvin stand up, wander over to the edge of the terrace and gaze out over the Intracoastal, expected him to take some shots, especially as it was overcast, and Florida skies were often fascinating when spring storms threatened.

The jazz tone on her phone told her she had messages.

She listened to the first, which was from one of her college friends, asking if she wanted to run with her early next morning.

The next was from Grace.

Cathy listened.

'Cathy, I may be overreacting,' the voicemail began.

She went on listening.

Chauvin turned away from the Intracoastal, picked up his camera and stepped back inside.

He raised the Nikon again, focused on her, made some adjustments.

Then started shooting again, rapidly, one photo after another.

Cathy heard Grace's message to the end, kept hold of the phone.

'I thought I asked you not to take any more,' she said tightly.

'Just a couple more,' Chauvin said. 'Please.'

'No more,' Cathy said.

'Is something wrong?' he asked.

'Yes,' Cathy said. 'I'd like you to stop.'

He lowered the camera. 'Was that a message from your mom?'

'I can't see that's your business.'

'I'm sure it was,' Chauvin said. 'And I can imagine what she said, because I was taking photos of her, too, just a while ago, and she became a little testy about it. And then, when I remarked about your amazing resemblance to the other Grace in my life, and said how much fun it would be to photograph you as . . .'

'I think I'd like you to go now,' Cathy said.

'Have you guessed who that other Grace is, Cathy? Only you're very young, so you might not think of her right away, but as I told your mother, you look so much the way I imagine she might have looked as a young woman in this century.'

Cathy looked back at her phone, saw there was a second message.

'Would you consider posing for me,' Chauvin asked, 'as the princess?'

Realization struck Cathy. 'God,' she said. 'You're talking about Grace Kelly.'

'Of course I am.'

She laughed.

'That's just what your mother did,' Chauvin said.

'I'm not surprised,' Cathy said.

Her phone – her landline – rang.

'Excuse me,' she said, walked into the kitchen, picked up.

'Cathy, are you OK?' Sam's voice asked her.

She heard Chauvin's soft tread moving from the living room into the hall.

And then the sound of the front door, opening, then closing.

'Hold on,' she told Sam.

She walked into the hallway, checked the living room and the terrace, just in case he'd played a trick, was waiting for her.

'Cathy?' Sam said sharply.

'I'm OK,' she said.

She checked the rest of the apartment, grimly aware that a normal young woman, who'd led a less scarred life, would not be going to these absurd lengths . . .

No one there.

Chauvin had gone, without another word.

Cathy went back out into the small hallway, looked at the front door.

Locked it.

'Hi, Sam,' she said. 'If this is about Grace's weird Frenchman, he's been and gone, and I'm perfectly fine.'

'Are you sure?' Sam hesitated. 'He isn't still there?'

Cathy laughed. 'You're even more paranoid than I am.'

'Only your mother thinks he's got some obsession about—'

'Grace Kelly,' Cathy said. 'Tell me about it.'

Saul returned Sam's call, said that he'd been delivering a walnut cabinet when Sam had left his message, but that he and Mel were at the apartment now, and Cathy was fine.

'So you can stop stressing, bro,' Saul said.

Yet still, Sam left Martinez waiting at the office in case anything transpired from the Interpol inquiry, jumped in his car and drove north to Sunny Isles Beach, checked around their building, inside the garage and around the pool area, then got back in the car and drove up and down North Bay Road and around several blocks, looking for a white Ford Focus rental.

It was seven-thirty, and the light was starting to fade, but he was as satisfied as he could be that Chauvin was gone, and unless Martinez hit on something, there was certainly nothing official to be done about his visits to Grace or Cathy. They had both invited Chauvin in, and even if they had both asked him to stop photographing, taking too many snapshots of acquaintances might make him a bore and just possibly a weirdo, but did not constitute any crime or even misdemeanor that Sam could think of.

Still, Chauvin could whistle for any more help with his research if he asked.

And for now, Sam had more important things to dwell on.

The squad's continuing lack of progress in finding and stopping Black Hole.

Marie Nieper still on the missing list.

Felicia Delgado still not ready to talk.

Mildred's surgery was probably over by now, but David had Grace for company, so Sam wasn't needed at the Adams Clinic, though he would check with his father in a while before deciding whether or not to drop by the rehearsal.

They weren't running his scenes tonight, but he liked showing interest.

And Billie Smith was still on his mind.

A cup of coffee was what he suddenly felt he needed. The real thing, not decaf. Maybe even a shot of espresso, his very first since giving up, and maybe a little sharpening of his senses now might sweep away some of this useless negativity, help him pinpoint something they'd all missed so far.

Mildred was in recovery, and would soon be back up in her room.

Ethan Adams had come to find David.

'Everything went beautifully,' he assured him, smiling at Grace.

'Thank you, Doctor.' Relieved, David shook his hand. 'I'm very grateful to you, and Mildred will be too.'

'Just doing my job,' Adams said.

David introduced Grace to the doctor, and Adams made a courtly bow from the waist and told her it was a pleasure, then returned his attention to David.

'Your wife may have a few difficult days, simply because of her issues. The drops are a simple matter for most, but . . .' He gave a small shrug.

'I don't think she'll mind, now that it's done,' David said.

Adams smiled. 'Let's hope so.'

'And when she's ready, I expect we'll be back for the second round.'

'I'll be seeing her a couple of times before that,' Adams said, 'but in the meantime, if you'll excuse me . . .'

'Of course,' David said. 'Many thanks again.'

'My pleasure,' Ethan Adams said, and left the room quietly.

David sat down again, feeling a little shaky.

'Better now?' Grace asked him gently.

'I will be,' he said.

'You'll be perfect,' Grace said, 'just as soon as you see your wife.' She bent to pick up her bag. 'You should get straight to her room.'

'You don't have to leave,' David said.

She smiled. 'I think I do.'

Martinez called Sam just after eight.

'How's Mildred doing?'

'Good,' Sam said. 'I just talked to my dad.'

'More good news,' Martinez said. 'Marie Nieper showed up an hour ago, safe and well, got bawled out by her family, said she had no idea anyone was worried about her.'

No idea they'd feared she might be Black Hole's seventh victim.

'I got nothing yet on our creepy snapper, but I'm still on it.'

Sam thanked him, told him to go home, mentioned the espresso he'd just finished and his hopes for inspiration.

'Nothing,' he said.

'You give it a rest too,' Martinez said. 'You going to visit Mildred?'

'She's too tired,' Sam said, 'and my dad's OK, so I'm going to look in at rehearsal, just in case Billie's turned up too.'

'Here's hoping,' Martinez said.

'Not a word,' Linda told Sam, as soon as she saw him. 'I'm sorry to say I'm going to have to think about recasting.'

She looked tired, and the atmosphere in Tyler Allen's backyard felt strained all around.

'The kid's a diva, I told you,' Allen said.

'I'm just so worried about her,' Linda said.

'Without your lead,' Allen said, 'I'd save your worries for the production.'

'I'm female,' Linda said. 'I can worry about more than one thing at a time.'

Sam laughed.

'I'm glad you're here, Sam.' Toni Petit came up behind them, dressed in black T-shirt and jeans. 'I have your costume to fit.' She shook her head. 'I brought one of Billie's, too, but . . .'

'Not tonight, I'm afraid,' Sam said.

'Linda's getting really upset about it.' Toni led the way into the big converted garage, all the way to the back where she'd leaned a tall mirror against the wall.

'I don't blame her.' Sam spied his plastic wrapped matador outfit hanging on a rail. 'Let's hope Billie gets to wear her costumes.'

'Let's hope.'

Toni drew the wrapper up, unzipped some fasteners, then took it down off the rail in two parts, first the gilded jacket and then the narrow pants.

'It looks terrific,' Sam said.

'We'll see,' she said.

There was something not right about her this evening, Sam felt, as Toni got down on her kneeling pad and regarded the fit of Escamillo's pants. He'd often seen small vertical lines of concentration form between her eyebrows, but tonight they looked deeper and her mood seemed distracted.

'You OK?' he asked as she took two pins from the small black velvet cushion held by elastic on her left wrist.

'Mm-hm.' She stuck the pins between her lips.

'Only you don't seem your usual self.'

She took one pin out of her mouth, shrugged and bent to her work.

Toni Petit not the shrugging kind, as a rule, always precise and wholehearted about her work.

Aside from her work with the company, of course, Sam realized that he knew little about her – which was true of most of the S-BOP family. They were drawn together because of opera, worked hard as a group until after the crescendo of performances, then went their separate ways until the next time.

Toni made an irritated sound, shook her head, began unpinning a seam.

'I don't know how you have the patience,' Sam said.

'All part of the job.' She transferred two more pins to her lips.

'I'd be worried about swallowing one,' Sam said.

'Never done it yet,' she said.

'Don't know how you talk with pins in your mouth.'

She didn't answer, went on, her fingers deft.

He waited till her lips were safe. 'Do you still have family in Louisiana?'

'No.' She sat back on her heels and surveyed his legs. 'Turn to your right, please.'

He turned, and Toni shuffled on the pad to get in position.

'I don't even know if you have family down here,' he said.

She looked away from her work for a moment, up into his face.

Something in her eyes.

Abruptly she took two pins from his pants seam and stuck them back into the velvet cushion.

The way she did that, like small stabs, jarred him.

Definitely something up with her.

'How about we take a break?' he suggested. 'I could make us both a cup of Linda's chamomile tea.'

'I'd rather finish this.'

'Sure,' Sam said.

And then suddenly, it struck him that it wasn't just a bad mood he was sensing about Toni this evening.

Something about her was manifestly *wrong*.

The small hairs on the back of his neck stood up.

Because suddenly, Billie had sprung back into his thoughts.

Sam was prone to hunches and gut feelings, and he'd had a minor one last Friday just before visiting Billie's home, which had taken him no closer to helping him find their missing Carmen.

But just now, when Toni Petit had stabbed those pins into the cushion, Sam had inexplicably experienced another jolt.

A medium to strong one on the Becket scale. About a 6.00, he figured. Nowhere near powerful enough to shake up anyone but himself, but still a *hunch*.

The kind that had often led somewhere over the years.

He took a breath.

'Toni?' he said.

'Mm?'

She leaned forward again, slid both hands down the fabric on his left leg, then tugged it gently, not looking up at him.

'How well do you know Billie?' He kept his tone conversational.

'Not well,' she said. 'Like everyone here, it seems.'

'But you're not really like the others,' Sam said.

'Why not? Because I'm not a singer?'

'No,' Sam said. 'Because you care about other people's needs in the company. Not just their costumes. You notice when they're sick or down.'

'I try,' she said.

She leaned back, removed another pin from the cushion, then slid it into place in the hem of his pants, and the motion was smooth enough, yet he noticed a tiny tremor in her right hand.

His hunch edged up to a 7.00.

'That's why I just found myself wondering if Billie might have confided in you,' he said. 'I don't necessarily mean immediately before she went missing, but in the past, in general.'

Toni sank back on her heels again. 'It's no good,' she said, then stood up with a grunt of effort.

'Are you OK?' Sam asked again.

'No,' she said. 'I'm not. I have a headache.'

'Bad one?' He was sympathetic.

'Bad enough,' she said.

'Are we done?' Sam asked.

'We're done for tonight,' Toni said. 'You can take it off.'

He did so with care, passed the clothes to her, stepped back into his pants.

'The costume's really terrific,' he said. 'You're very talented, Toni.'

'I try,' she said again.

He looked into her face and thought he saw the pain she'd complained of – though to him, fleetingly, it looked more like despair than the physical kind.

Up to an 8.00 now.

'Toni,' he began.

'No,' she said. 'Please.'

And without another word, she turned, still holding the costume, and walked away from Sam, out of the garage and into the backyard.

Leaving him unaccountably chilled.

He waited three minutes before following.

The rehearsal had gotten under way again, Don José singing with Micaëla, and Holden's throat seemed better and Carla's voice was beautiful, and if her heart wasn't really in this role with her sights set on the lead, no one could have accused her of short-changing the company.

Toni was standing by the table, a water glass in her hand, had probably taken pain pills; and maybe that was all this was, after all, maybe he could downscale to less than a 2.00, more of a knee-jerk than even a micro-hunch.

'Hey.' He kept his voice low as he approached. 'I was wondering if I could maybe offer you a ride home.'

'Thank you,' she said, 'but I have my car.'

Her small smile was insincere, but that too was probably down to pain.

'Is it a migraine?' he asked, still quiet, mindful of the rehearsal.

Toni nodded. 'Excuse me.'

She moved away from the table and from Sam, bypassing the performers on Tyler Allen's lawn, heading toward the pathway that led to the front of the house and to the road.

Sam realized that she was leaving. Without a word to Linda or anyone else.

There might be a precedent – Sam had been away from S-BOP for a few years, after all – but though Toni's presence wasn't mandatory, he couldn't recall her ever leaving before a rehearsal was over.

And though Sam was still wholly unsure why, his hunch magnitude climbed right back up to a 7.00, and after waiting sixty seconds, he went after her.

The taillights of her small Honda were still visible as she made a turn out of Lime Court.

Sam got in the Saab, started the engine, and followed.

Grace was not feeling relaxed.

Joshua had asked Claudia if he might spend the night at her house, where Mike and Robbie, her sons, always enjoyed playing with him, and Grace hadn't wanted to spoil their pleasure.

Perhaps, she thought, it was her slight concern that Thomas Chauvin might decide to put in another appearance, and in that respect she was doubly glad she'd let Joshua stay over in Sunny Isles, away from any possible unpleasantness.

Felicia Delgado was on her mind, too, disappointment that her father had not yet called her again.

Nothing she could do about that now.

She went upstairs, ran water into the tub, lit an aromatherapy candle.

She was, she realized, missing Sam and Joshua, and felt somewhat ashamed of that, because her little boy was safe and happy at her sister's, and Claudia's husband was never coming back, while Sam would be home soon enough.

And so far, at least, there had been no sign of the Frenchman.

If he did show up again, she would simply not answer the door.

On the South Dixie Highway, heading north, Sam was trying to rationalize his reasons for tailing Toni Petit's car.

The woman had done nothing wrong, either at Allen's place or on the road; had exceeded the speed limit a few times, but minor infringements only, her driving in no way erratic.

Sam was almost certain that she had no idea that he was following.

Still had no solid idea as to *why* he was.

Only that sense of something 'wrong' about her, and because something indefinable was telling him that she might possibly know something about Billie's disappearance.

Something had caused that brief look of despair after he'd asked a couple of questions about Billie – though probably it had been unconnected to that, could just have been a stress response to a fast-building migraine.

But was it just a headache that had made her cut and run so swiftly after a few harmless questions?

Except Toni had not really 'cut and run', Sam continued the dialogue in his head. She had taken his costume – had not rewrapped it, which was unusual but hardly a crime – and had walked out of the garage into the backyard, where he thought she had taken pills, probably for pain, and then she had *walked*, not run, out to the road and gotten into her car.

And now she was driving just a little faster than she ought.

But who didn't?

Still, he guessed he'd call Martinez as the Honda continued north on I-95.

Force of habit for them both, even off duty, checking in at unexpected moments like these.

He called him on his cell.

'I'm still at the office,' Martinez said. 'I'm going to wait a while longer in case I get something on our pal.'

'Give it up,' Sam said. 'Chauvin's my creep, not yours.'

'And I thought we shared everything,' Martinez said.

'Matter of fact,' Sam said, 'I might ask you to run a twenty-four on a tag number.'

'Shoot.' Martinez took it down. 'What's up?'

'Ninety per cent probability, nothing at all, just one of my gut feelings.'

'About?'

'Woman from S-BOP, name of Toni Petit.'

'The dressmaker, right?' Martinez said.

Sam kept his eyes on the car still up ahead, keeping two vehicles between them. 'I thought you never listen when I talk about opera.'

'It's the singing I try not to listen to, man. I don't mind hearing about the people – except I thought it was the choreographer you had a bad feeling about.'

'I know, and I have no real foundation for this, but I'm just keeping you in the loop, like always. I'm on Ninety-five going north, tailing this woman's Honda Civic, and there's no need to run the tag yet or do anything, because I'm seventy per cent sure this really is nothing.'

'Moment ago, it was ninety per cent,' Martinez said. 'You want me to come and join you, man?'

'I don't think so,' Sam said. 'But I'll stay in touch.'

'You do that,' his partner said.

Martinez hung up, not entirely happy because like all the detectives, they never went on calls alone. Though this, of course, wasn't official, this was just Sam Becket going on what sounded like a wild goose chase.

Except that Sam had used the words 'gut feeling'.

Which made Martinez a little uncomfortable.

Toni Petit was still driving carefully and steadily.

Which spoke against migraine, Sam thought, because people who suffered those tended to drive either erratically or too slowly, and those who got aura with their headaches often pulled over because their vision was impaired.

This woman was driving normally.

Even less of a crime than taking too many photos of a person.

Sam's mind flicked back to Chauvin, who had, albeit briefly, spooked his daughter and angered his wife, and his own hands tightened on the wheel.

His eyes moved to the rearview mirror, then narrowed and focused ahead again, concentrating on maintaining the tail on the Honda.

He wondered if Toni was going home or someplace else.

Either way, he was staying with her.

Mildred had been sleeping.

Her left eye was covered with a plastic shield, and she had a cannula in a vein in her left arm attached to a drip feed, and she'd asked David why she needed that, and he'd assured her that it would only be there until she felt well enough to eat and drink normally.

'If I hadn't had anesthesia, I wouldn't need it,' she'd said, shaking her head. 'Such a wimp.'

'But a happy one, who didn't need to know anything about her surgery,' David said. 'Remember to keep your head still.'

'Yes, Doctor.' Mildred had smiled at him, and drifted off to sleep.

Awake again now.

'I don't know why you don't go home.'

'Because I want to be with you,' David said.

The room was dimly lit, and she didn't know how her operated eye was doing because it was covered, but her right eye was just as before, and anyway, even without looking at her husband, she knew that he was doing his 'sentinel' thing. Keeping watch on her lest she experience the slightest problem.

Her problems behind her now, thank the Lord, at least for a while.

The remnants of the anesthesia still working on her very nicely.

There would, of course, be tomorrow to contend with. Dr Adams coming to check on his handiwork, maybe one of the other younger doctors doing the same. And then there'd be follow-ups . . .

Stop that.

She reminded herself how Ethan Adams had made her feel just before the procedure; almost confident, so far as she could recall.

And she did feel fairly confident of his skill now, so, provided it had worked and her vision was as improved as everyone said it would be, she might even agree to having the right eye done in due course.

Not that she would be hurried into that.

And she didn't need to think about it now. Not with this pleasant, sleepy buzz still coursing through her.

'You should go home,' she told David. 'Or at least go get some dinner.'

Right on cue, David's stomach rumbled, and he laughed.
'Guess you might be right about that,' he said.

For a while now, Sam had felt pretty sure that he'd picked up a tail of his own.

It was always hard to be certain on a busy Interstate, but it seemed to him that the driver of the car in question had been working hard to keep close but not too close, ducking in and out.

An amateur, for sure.

White car. Hell of a popular color.

Sam ignored it, stayed focused on Toni's car.

Three vehicles now between the Saab and Honda, but he saw her right indicator start flashing.

Exit up ahead.

Maybe heading to Miami Beach.

More choices up soon.

Sam took the right turn-off, checked and saw that the white car was still with him, just one pickup truck between them.

Starting to tick him off . . .

Not going to Miami Beach, Toni turned right instead onto West Hallandale Beach Boulevard, then left onto NW 2nd Avenue, and Sam followed, his own suspect tail coming with them . . .

And then, finally, on Foster Avenue, in a quiet, dark piece of Hallandale that neither Sam nor any other cop would have especially chosen to visit on their own, the Honda finally came to a halt.

Sam, holding back by a few hundred yards, slowed to a crawl.

He watched Toni Petit get out of her car, lock up, then walk toward a beat-up looking little house set well back from the road, and go inside.

Letting herself in, so far as he could see.

Still edging forward, he looked in his rearview mirror.

'Goddamn it,' he said.

He slammed on his brakes, got out of the Saab, sprinted back toward the other car.

A white Ford Focus rental.

Anger filling him.

'Get the fuck out of the car,' he told the driver.

Thomas Chauvin opened the door slowly, warily, and got out.

The five inches height between them suddenly seemed a whole lot more.

'I know,' he said. 'And I'm sorry.'

'What the hell do you think you're doing?' Sam demanded.

'Being an asshole, I guess.' Chauvin was meek.

'You got that right,' Sam said. 'What are you, eight years old?'

'I got a little carried away,' the Frenchman said. 'I guess I was in the zone, you know?'

'No, I don't know,' Sam said. 'Nor do I know what you thought you were doing in my house and my daughter's apartment earlier today, and we'll be getting back to that some time real soon. But right this minute I just want you to get back in this car, turn your butt around and get the hell back to Surfside, or I will get your ass kicked right out of this country.'

'Am I allowed to ask what—?'

'No,' Sam said.

'Just get in the car, right?' Chauvin said.

'*Now*,' Sam said.

David had given in, and had gone to get some dinner.

Hungry now. Food suddenly a metaphor for the goodness of the life he looked forward to sharing with his wife. A woman tough enough to cope all by herself for years on the streets, yet too fragile, too human, to want to face up to something she'd felt 'squeamish' about.

An understated word for something that had, of course, been a fear of phobic proportions. And yet, with a little help and encouragement, she had faced that too.

Great lady.

So now he could eat. Now he was suddenly starving.

Chops came to mind. With mashed potatoes and, maybe, a glass of wine.

Mildred was OK.

That merited a celebration.

More of that when they got her home.

Mildred was sleeping.

Dreaming.

In her dream, she was sitting on the smooth sand at South Beach, all alone, watching two men walking slowly away from her. One quite old, one young, but both walking evenly, their pace matched. Donny, her late fiancé, and David.

They were leaving her, but she did not feel sad because she was too compelled by what was happening up in the sky to keep her eyes trained on the men.

The light was dying, the sun itself slowly disappearing.

No clouds anywhere, a perfectly clear sky, yet darkness was spreading.

'It's just an eclipse,' Mildred said to herself.

'Don't watch,' Edith Bleeker, her mother, told her, 'or you'll go blind.'

But Mildred knew there was nothing to fear, and anyway, her mother had told her not to marry Donny, and she had thought him long dead, but there he'd just been, walking on the beach with David, so if she wanted to watch the eclipse, she was going to do just that.

And oh, Lord, what a sight it was as totality began, and the corona she'd only ever read about, only ever seen on television, blazed into the blackness, and oh, my, it was the most beautiful thing she'd ever seen, and there was nothing at all to be afraid of, and she was just going to look and look until . . .

'Mrs Becket?'

The voice woke her.

The brightness of the light from the corridor outside her room made her right eye blink.

Dr Wiley was looking in on her. 'How's my favorite patient doing?' he asked.

Which irritated Mildred, because he had broken her wonderful dream, and because she was sure that she was no one's favorite patient.

'I was sleeping,' she said.

'That's good,' Dr Wiley said. 'How are you feeling?'

'I don't know,' Mildred said pointedly. 'I was asleep.'

'No nausea?'

'No.'

'What about the eye?'

The eye was exactly what she had just been enjoying *not* thinking about, though she guessed the dream about the eclipse and, in particular, her mother's warning, indicated that her fears were still alive, and if she had been allowed to continue dreaming, maybe the worst would have happened, maybe she would have been blinded, so Dr Wiley might have done her a favor, after all.

'It feels all right,' she answered him.

'No pain?'

'A little discomfort earlier. Not really pain, and it's fine now.'

The doctor closed the door quietly, came over to the bed and took her hand, startling her a little in the semidarkness, her eye shield limiting her vision.

'What are you doing?' she asked.

'Just taking your pulse,' George Wiley said.

'I think my pulse is perfectly fine.'

'Just routine,' the doctor told her.

Mildred sighed.

'I expect you'll be glad to get home again,' Wiley said.

'Oh, yes,' she said. 'Though right now, I'd settle for some more sleep.'

'I'm sorry,' Dr Wiley said. 'Almost done.'

In the dim light she saw him take something from a pocket of his white coat. 'What now?' she asked, a little tetchily.

'Nothing for you to worry about,' he said.

Now he was starting to sound almost like Ethan Adams at his most irritating.

He was holding an ophthalmoscope, bending forward.

'What are you doing?' Mildred asked, startled again.

'Just going to take a quick look at the other eye,' he said.

'Doctor Adams said I was here tonight so I could rest. He said he'd be here in the morning to look at my eye.'

'Please just be still, Mrs Becket,' Dr Wiley told her.

Mildred felt suddenly too nervous to do otherwise, and she was almost getting accustomed to having her eyes examined, but that didn't mean she liked it, and certainly not when it wasn't necessary.

The bright light moved away, and she blinked.

'And now, we'll just take a look at this,' Wiley said.

Maybe, Mildred thought, this was another dream, and if it was, she decided it was probably about time she woke up . . .

The doctor was putting both hands around the back of her head, and she realized that he was feeling for the elastic holding the eye shield.

'I don't think you should be doing that, Doctor.' Now she felt agitated. 'I was told not to touch that.'

'Who's the doctor here?' George Wiley said.

Not a dream, she knew that now, yet still there was a strangely unpleasant quality to what was happening.

'Please,' she said, 'put it back.'

'Don't be silly,' Wiley told her. 'This is for your own good.'

She did not like his tone at all, and *what* was for her own good? She wished that David would come back, wished she hadn't pushed him to go out for dinner.

The shield was off and her eye felt naked, vulnerable.

'Please, Doctor Wiley, put back the shield.'

'Now, now,' the doctor said.

He leaned in closer again, placed one finger of his left hand on her eyebrow and his thumb on her cheek, and began to pull open her eye.

'What are you *doing*?' Mildred asked, alarmed.

'I told you, don't be silly, Mrs Becket,' Wiley said.

And then, with her other, better eye, she saw that he had some kind of instrument in his right hand.

'Get that away from me!'

The doctor leaned in even closer, and suddenly Mildred knew she had to do something she'd never done before.

She screamed – and then she pushed him away, and as he stumbled, his left hand struck her operated eye and she cried out.

'You stupid woman,' Wiley snapped.

The door opened.

'What's going on?' David took in the scene, saw his wife cowering against the pillows, the young doctor standing over her. 'What the hell are you doing?'

Wiley stepped away from the bed, slid his right hand into his pocket. 'Your wife's a little upset.'

'He had something in his hand, David.' Mildred was breathless. 'Some kind of instrument. I could see he was going to poke it in my eye, so I screamed and pushed him away and his hand – his knuckles – hit me.'

'Nonsense.' Wiley smiled at David. 'Your wife was having a bad dream. I saw that she'd pulled the shield off her eye, and I was trying to make sure she hadn't hurt herself.'

'That's a lie,' Mildred protested. 'I was asleep until you woke me, and started taking my pulse and shining lights in my other eye.' She felt something trickle out of her operated eye, gasped, raised her hand . . .

'Don't touch it,' David told her. 'It looks OK, but best not to touch it.'

He was shaking with fury now, the only thing stopping him from punching Wiley the knowledge that getting himself arrested would not help Mildred.

'I'd like to see that instrument,' he said.

Wiley laughed. 'There was no instrument.'

David turned and pressed the red emergency button on the wall.

'That's entirely unnecessary,' Wiley told him.

All traces of humor gone, anger now in his gray eyes.

Something else there, too, David thought.

The young doctor looked *thwarted.*

David picked up the phone from Mildred's bedside table, pressed O and waited briefly. 'Operator, I need you to find Doctor Adams,' he said. 'And this is to inform you that I am about to phone the police to report an assault.'

White-faced, Dr George Wiley quickly left the room.

Sam kept his distance, using the small night vision monocular that Saul had given him last Christmas to take a closer look at the house Toni Petit had entered.

Single-storey, frame construction, shingle roof, the house decidedly shabby on the outside, with some empty land to the right and what looked like a couple of garages.

He moved a little closer.

There were lights on in the front of the house, darkness around the back.

He put away the monocular, took out his phone and called Martinez again, got voicemail, gave his location, told him he was going to talk to Toni Petit now.

'And by the by, our French pal likes playing cop,' he added. 'I caught him tailing me here, just about stopped myself kicking the little jerk's butt. He's gone now. I'll call later.'

He slipped the phone back in his pocket and then, on impulse, took it out again and keyed in Joe Duval's number.

More voicemail, and didn't anyone pick up anymore?

'Hey, Joe, it's Sam Becket, not really sure why I'm leaving this message. Just sharing a weird little hunch with you. No link at all with our case, but I'm out of jurisdiction, so I felt I should maybe tell you that I just tailed a woman named Toni Petit – that's Petit as in small – to Foster Avenue, Hallandale.'

He explained, quickly and quietly, about Billie Smith wanting to tell him 'something' on Thursday the nineteenth and having been missing since then, and about his sudden, probably irrational, suspicion of Toni, his sense that she might know something about the missing woman.

'Like I said, I'm almost sure this is nothing, but I'm here now.'

He logged the address, ended the call, looked back along the road, checking for Chauvin's white car or anyone else who might be watching, then returned his attention to the house.

He could not see or hear anything from out here. No TV or conversation or music, no windows open.

That *feeling* was still with him, a real buzz of something.

He couldn't officially call in a 'feeling', though, certainly not in Hallandale, and especially when it wasn't even related to a Miami Beach case.

Time to figure out what to tell Toni when he knocked on her front door.

If it even was her door.

For the second time, David hit the wrong speed-dial key on his phone.

'Damn thing.'

'Mind your blood pressure,' Mildred said from the bed, the eye shield having been carefully replaced by him. 'I'm fine.'

'And where the hell is Adams?'

'He's probably at home,' she said, 'or in some restaurant having a good dinner. I'm sure he'll come when he gets his messages.'

The door opened, and David swung around.

Neither Wiley nor Adams, but a young fair-haired nurse in a pale blue uniform asking if they needed anything.

'What we need,' David said, 'is Doctor Adams.'

'Doctor Adams is off duty,' she said, 'but we have two other on-call—'

'We need Ethan Adams here, stat, nurse.' David's tone was sharp.

'I've told the operator, and now I'm telling you to inform your boss that there has been an assault on my wife – his patient – by one of his doctors, and I'm calling the police.'

The nurse took another step into the room. 'Ma'am, are you hurt?'

'I don't think so,' Mildred told her. 'My husband's a doctor, so—'

'Will you please just do as I ask, nurse, and go find Doctor Adams,' David said.

'I'll do what I can, sir,' the nurse said.

'*Now*, please,' he thundered.

The young woman shot him a look of dislike, and departed.

'My,' Mildred said, 'I don't think I ever heard you really bellow before.'

David shook his head, returned his attention to his phone and, finally, keyed in Sam's speed-dial number.

Sam was three feet from the pathway to the Petit house when his cell phone vibrated in his pocket.

He answered, voice low. 'Dad? What's up?'

'Nothing bad, son, don't worry,' his father said swiftly. 'Mildred's all right. But we've had a problem here.'

'What kind of a problem?' Sam retreated a few steps. 'Dad, I'm in the middle of something. Can this wait?'

'I don't think so,' David said. 'One of the junior doctors here, a man named George Wiley, just assaulted Mildred.'

'He what?' Sam, horrified, moved farther into the darkness to the right of the house. 'Is she hurt?'

'Not really, and I'm hoping her eye's OK,' David said. 'But this guy scared her half to death.'

'Tell Samuel I'm fine, please,' Mildred's voice called.

'She says she's fine,' David said. 'Listen, son, I've told them to get Doctor Adams here and that I'm calling the police, but I wanted to run it by you first.'

'Sure.' Sam's mind raced. 'Dad, like I said, I'm in the middle of something, but since the clinic is in jurisdiction, I want you to call Beth Riley, or even the lieutenant. I'm not sure where Al is right now, but even if he was around, I'd rather not risk him losing his temper with this doctor.'

'How long will you be tied up?'

'Hard to say,' Sam said. 'Do you have those numbers, Dad?'

'Right here in my phone, just where you programmed them,' David said. 'I'll try Beth first. I don't feel right about bothering Mike Alvarez.'

'He won't mind,' Sam assured him. 'Neither of them will.'

'I'd still like it if you could come by when you're free, son.'

'Try keeping me away,' Sam said.

He turned his phone to silent.

Walked back toward the front door, and knocked.

Waited a moment, then knocked again.

He heard muffled sounds. Voices, he thought, then movement.

'Who is it?'

Toni's voice.

'Toni, it's Sam Becket.'

There was a brief silence.

'Sam, what are you doing here?' Her tone was unfriendly.

'Could you open the door, Toni?'

'Just a moment.'

A bolt slid and the door opened.

Toni still wore her black T-shirt and jeans, but her feet were bare, her toenails unpolished but neatly clipped.

'How did you know where I live?' she asked, then realized. 'Did you follow me, Sam?'

'I did,' Sam said.

Something passed across her eyes.

Fear, he thought, or maybe just anger.

'I was concerned about you,' he said.

'Do you always follow women you're concerned about?'

'You said you had a bad migraine, and I didn't like to think of you driving home alone.' He paused. 'Can I come in?'

'To be honest, Sam, it's getting late, and I think it's kind of creepy you following me like that.'

'It was an impulse,' he said. 'I'm sorry. I didn't mean to alarm you.'

'You have.'

She was not about to let him in, he realized.

'OK,' he said. 'I'll be honest too. I had a hunch, while we were talking, that something else, maybe something bad, was up with you, and I just wanted to ask if I could help you in any way.'

'Nothing's happened,' Toni said. 'I don't need any help, though I thank you for the impulse. It was kind.'

'How's the head?'

'Still aching,' she said tiredly.

Maybe that was all it was, after all, in which case he should leave her in peace, do what she wanted and go away.

People often said he could be like a dog with a big, juicy bone.

'I promise I won't stay long,' he said, 'but I'm very thirsty. Could you get me some water, or maybe we could have a cup of tea together?' He paused. 'Hey, come on, Toni. I'm not some stranger.'

She hesitated.

'Tell him to go away.'

Another voice. Female, too, but harsher, throatier, calling from somewhere inside the house.

'My sister,' Toni said. 'She isn't feeling too good.'

'I'm sorry to hear that,' Sam said.

Toni turned around, looking, he guessed, at her unwell sister.

Sam took the moment, and stepped past her.

Into the house.

Sam was not the only member of the family prone to intuition. Every once in a while, Grace developed an uneasy sense that something was not right.

At around nine-thirty, with no word from Sam – who'd told her he intended to do no more than drop by rehearsal – it occurred to her that something might have gone wrong with Mildred.

Unlikely, given that she'd been on her way back from recovery when Grace had left the clinic.

But still, Sam might have gone there . . .

She tried his cell phone first, got voicemail, left no message and called David.

'This is not a good moment,' he told her, tension clear in his voice.

'Has something happened? Is Mildred OK?'

'Yes.' He sounded preoccupied. 'I can't talk right now, Grace.'

'I'll let you go,' Grace said. 'Is Sam there?'

'No, he's tied up someplace,' David told her. 'Something going on.'

'With the case?'

'I guess.'

It was not like David to be short with her. Nor was it like Sam not to tell her if he was going to be late or out of touch.

On the other hand, she reminded herself, it had become *exactly* like her these days to start worrying at the smallest provocation.

She did so now.

'I won't stay long,' Sam said, just inside the front door. 'I only want to see if there's anything I can do to help.'

'I don't need help,' Toni said. 'As I told you.'

He cast around in his memory for any mention of a sister.

'If you and your sister are both sick,' he said, 'perhaps it's the same bug Carla and Jack had.'

'I thought you said you were thirsty,' the other voice said.

A woman came from the back of the house into the small hallway.

She wore black too, an ankle length linen shift, with small, neat silver sandals.

'I don't think we've been introduced,' she said.

'Sam Becket.' He held out his hand.

She didn't take it.

Sam couldn't tell if she was older or younger than Toni, partly because of the impenetrably dark glasses she was wearing.

Something clicked into place in his mind.

He'd learned a few tricks over the years when it came to moments of tension. To help calm down telltale physical reactions.

Useful in the kind of situation where you didn't want others observing you breathing too fast or breaking into a sweat.

He slowed his breathing, focused his thinking.

Looked at Toni.

'I would appreciate some water,' he said.

'Or tea, you said,' the other woman said.

There was a resemblance between them, Sam registered, but this woman was taller, less fine-boned, her dark hair long, tied back in a ponytail.

'Sam's the detective who sings with S-BOP,' Toni said. 'I've talked about him, remember?'

Warning her sister, Sam thought.

'How do you do?' the other woman said. 'I'm Kate Petit.'

* * *

'I wish you'd just sit down,' Mildred said. 'You're making me feel nervous all over again.'

'I'm sorry,' David said.

They were still waiting for the police and Adams, and he kept pacing the room, opening the door and peering up and down the corridor as if that would make them come faster.

If they didn't show up soon, he was going to get out there himself and find Dr George Wiley, make a goddamned citizen arrest if he had to, and he should have searched the man, found that instrument . . .

'Please,' Mildred said.

'OK,' he said.

'Not in the chair,' Mildred said. 'I need you closer, old man.'

David exhaled a breath of frustration, sat on the edge of the bed, took both her hands in his and gripped them tightly. 'It's just the thought of anyone hurting you.'

'I know,' she said. 'But I'm OK – at least, I hope my eye . . .'

David glanced back at the door. 'If I knew where the hell Adams was, I'd go get him myself.'

'He'll be here.' Mildred shook her head. 'It's so strange. When I met Doctor Wiley and the other young doctor . . .'

'Merriam,' David remembered.

'They were both so nice, both trying to make me feel better. But then, in the afternoon, when Doctor Wiley checked me over, I wasn't so sure about him.'

'You didn't say anything.'

'Because I'd already made such a production about Doctor Adams. I didn't want you thinking I was turning into some old fussbudget.' She held onto David's hand. 'You do know that his knocking against my eye only happened because I pushed him away, made him stumble? I'm not sure that really qualifies as assault.'

David's eyes narrowed behind his glasses. 'Remind yourself of why you pushed him away, Mildred.'

'Because I thought he was going to poke around in my eye with that . . .' She shuddered. 'Because he wouldn't stop when I asked him to – told him to. And he told me not to be *silly*.' Her expression hardened. 'He said that twice, and I did not like his tone.' She took a breath, steadied herself. 'And then he called me a stupid woman – though that was after I'd pushed him and . . .'

'It's OK,' David told her. 'I didn't mean to get you upset again, but just don't start acting like his defense attorney, saying you're not sure it was assault.'

'No,' Mildred said. 'You're quite right.'

They sat in silence for a moment.

'Do you think he was actually going to do something to my eye?' she asked. 'I mean, he was holding that instrument, and maybe it was nothing he was going to . . .' She broke off, abruptly nauseous.

'Hey.' David touched her cheek. 'Don't think about that.'

'No. Better not to.' Mildred paused. 'I did wonder if maybe some sixth sense had been warning me, but I know that's nonsense, because I've been squeamish for years.' She smiled. 'Doctor Wiley was just an added bonus.'

'The icing on the cake,' David said grimly.

Martinez had listened to Sam's message and called him back, but now Sam's phone was going to voicemail.

He considered for about five seconds, and called Grace at home.

'I'm glad you called, Al.' It was just after a quarter to ten, and she was in the den, sharing the couch with Woody. 'I was going to try you, but I figured you must be busy with Sam.'

'Not this minute,' Martinez said.

'Isn't he on the case?' Grace asked.

'Not as far as I know, though he did leave me a message about one of the opera women.'

'Billie Smith?'

'No, not her, though it might be connected.' Martinez paused. 'Grace, that isn't why I called. Sam asked me to check out the Frenchman.'

'You found something?' She grew tenser.

'Chauvin has a history. Not a criminal record as such,' he added quickly. 'But he's been accused of stalking a couple of times back in France.'

Grace's spine crawled, thinking of Cathy. 'Is he dangerous?'

'Doesn't seem that way,' Martinez said. 'But with Sam not home, I know he'd want me to tell you, so you don't let Chauvin in if he comes back.'

'Of course not,' Grace said. 'And I'll call Cathy right now, tell her the same, make sure Saul stays home with her.'

'And you make sure your alarm is set, Gracie,' Martinez told her.

They'd finally had a security system installed last year, but he knew they didn't always remember to set it.

'You really think that's necessary?' Grace asked.

Martinez decided there was no need for her to know that Chauvin had been tailing Sam.

'I'd be happier if you did,' he said. 'There's no reason to think Chauvin's going to come anywhere near you again, and I haven't seen anything that tells me he's dangerous, but the guy's definitely a creep.'

'I can't argue with that,' Grace said.

Martinez left Grace and tried Sam again.

Still going to voicemail.

He had also decided against mentioning Sam's *hunch* – he and Grace having both learned not to underrate those over time – or the fact that Sam had followed Toni Petit to Hallandale.

No sense in giving her more stress.

Sam had told Martinez not to run Petit's tag number yet, because it was probably 'nothing'.

But Martinez was going to run it anyway.

A sound pierced the silence of the house on Foster Avenue.

Like a moan.

'Who was that?' Sam asked, a chill tweaking his spine.

'I think it was an animal,' Toni said. 'Our dog, maybe, out back.'

Sam remembered the sound he'd heard in Tyler Allen's house, the choreographer's claim that it had been his Siamese cats, which might have been true.

This was very different.

'Didn't sound like a dog to me,' he said peaceably.

He turned to Kate Petit.

Who had gone.

The sound repeated, almost a wail.

Human suffering, Sam was almost certain.

He turned back to Toni.

'OK,' he said. 'What's going on here?'

'Nothing is going on, Sam.'

'I just want to help,' Sam said. 'I like to think we've all become a kind of family at S-BOP.'

Lame, he registered as he said it.

'I've told you,' Toni said tersely, 'I don't need any help.'

'My gut tells me you do.'

'Your gut is mistaken,' Toni said. 'I'd like you to leave, Sam. I didn't ask you to follow me.'

'I know. And I will leave, just as soon as I'm sure you really are OK.'

Toni shook her head, exasperated but giving in. 'You're right. Things aren't great.' Her voice was low, as if she didn't want her sister to hear. 'My life is not the easiest, if you really need to know.'

'I don't mean to invade your privacy,' Sam said.

Toni's smile was tired. 'Isn't that what cops do?'

'I'm not here as a cop, just a friend, and if you'd like to talk, I'm a decent listener.'

Another of those sounds pitched into the air.

Human fear, Sam was certain.

Coming from the back of the house.

Something very bad was happening here.

'Your dog again?' he said. 'Why not bring him inside?'

'Sam, listen to me.' Toni stepped close enough for him to smell her fragrance and feel the heat coming off her, and now he saw a plea in her black cherry eyes. 'You said it – we are a kind of family. Which is why I'm asking you, please, Sam, just let us be.'

'I will,' he said. 'Soon as—'

'My sister asked you to go.'

Sam turned.

Kate Petit stood there, hands behind her back, dark glasses still in place.

'I think you should listen to her,' she added.

His bad feeling intensified.

'I guess I will,' he said.

He started to turn around, toward the door.

'I guess I don't believe you,' Kate said, and brought her hands around from behind her back, linked them quickly back together.

Holding a gun.

Pointing it at Sam.

It looked like an old Colt semiautomatic pistol.

Maybe a Mk IV Series 80.

The kind used by Black Hole.

Sweet Jesus.

Sam had begun to think, from the dark glasses and from the way she angled her head when she spoke, that Kate Petit might be sight-impaired in her left eye.

She had some vision for sure, hard to say how much.

Hard to know just what she might be capable of.

'Hey,' he said to her now. 'Let's not get excited, Kate.'

'Who said I'm excited?' she said. 'And who said you could call me Kate?'

'I'm sorry,' Sam said. 'Ms Petit? Is that OK?

'Better,' she said. And then she added, to her sister: 'I told you we should have finished her.'

'Her?' Sam said, his stomach crawling.

'Her,' Kate repeated.

Billie.

Sam looked away from Kate Petit, away from the gun, at Toni.

'Why don't we all go sit down somewhere?' he said. 'Turn down the heat a notch or two, talk this through.'

'I'd like that,' Toni said.

'Would you really?' Kate asked her. 'Are you sure that's what you want, Toni?'

Toni nodded, and now her eyes seemed sad.

'I'm ready to talk, Kate. I need to.'

'I think it's a good idea,' Sam said.

'Did I ask you?' Kate said.

And raised the gun a little higher.

Lieutenant Alvarez arrived at the Adams Clinic with Sergeant Beth Riley just after ten.

Alvarez's presence a compliment to David and Mildred.

'You didn't need to come yourself,' David told him. 'Especially so late.'

'I can't remember a time when I was more embarrassed,' Mildred said.

She had started fretting about her appearance a few minutes earlier, had told David she wanted to get dressed, but David had been adamant she stay in bed until Ethan Adams had checked her over.

Word was he was en route.

'You mustn't even think that way,' Beth Riley told her now.

'Let's just say it's not the way I'd choose to entertain Samuel's senior colleagues.' Mildred tugged the covers a little higher.

'You entertained us rather well at your wedding, as I recall,' Alvarez said.

'But right now we need to verify a few things,' Riley said.

Getting down to business.

'I told you what happened,' David said.

'I know you did, Doctor Becket,' Riley said, 'and I know it's upsetting, but we do have to hear it from Mrs Becket.'

'Could we please at least stop being so formal?' Mildred asked.

Riley smiled. 'Sure we can, Mildred.'

Mildred took a breath. 'Not too much really did happen. Thanks to my husband coming back when he did.'

'Nothing at all would have happened if I hadn't left you alone.'

'You didn't leave me "alone",' Mildred said. 'You left me in a respectable clinic, with nurses and doctors you assumed I'd be safe with.'

Very calm now, she gave a precise account of what had happened.

'It doesn't sound like much now,' she said when she'd finished. 'Except for the end of it, for which I think I was a little to blame.' She glanced at David. 'My husband thinks I shouldn't be saying that because it was Doctor Wiley who scared me into pushing him away.'

'I agree with your husband,' Lieutenant Alvarez said.

'But for all I know, Doctor Adams might have authorized Doctor Wiley to do that,' Mildred said. 'To examine me.'

'To wake you, after nine, when you were meant to be resting?' David's anger resurged. 'After Doctor Adams had said that he was coming next morning to examine your eye? And then Wiley carried on after you asked him to stop, terrified you with some instrument he was holding.'

'Do you know what the instrument was?' Riley asked.

'I didn't see it,' David said. 'I wish I had.'

'I didn't get a good look at it,' Mildred said. 'He was so close to me, and it was quite dark in the room, but he never actually touched me with it.'

'But he as good as punched you in the eye.'

'That wasn't deliberate,' Mildred said.

'For the love of God,' David said, 'will you stop defending him?'

'I'm just trying to be fair,' she insisted. 'And I wish you would calm down.'

'He tried to make me believe you'd been dreaming,' he reminded her.

'Yes,' she agreed.

'You're sure . . .' Mike Alvarez looked uncomfortable. 'Mildred, forgive me for asking this, but you are quite sure that you didn't dream any of it?' He ignored David's furious expression. 'You said you were sleeping when he came in.'

'I was.' Mildred was composed. 'He woke me by asking how his "favorite patient" was doing, and then he took my pulse, and then –' She shook her head. 'I've already told you the rest, but no, I was definitely not dreaming.'

'Try not to shake your head like that,' David told her.

'I keep forgetting,' she said.

He smiled at her. 'I'm calmer now,' he said.

'Good.' Mildred looked at Alvarez and Riley. 'My main concern, now, I think, is that someone probably should deal with this man in case he really hurts someone else.'

'He hurt you,' Riley said. 'And he frightened you.'

'That he did,' Mildred agreed.

'I'd like to be there,' David said, 'when you make the arrest.'

'I don't recommend that,' Alvarez said.

'Will you be actually *arresting* him?' Mildred asked uncertainly.

'Let's just say we'll be talking to him,' Alvarez said. 'Initially.'

'And we'll need to speak to Doctor Adams,' Riley added.

'Where the hell is he, anyway?' David asked.

'Patience,' Mildred said.

Grace picked up the phone after one ring.

Not Sam.

Carlos Delgado calling.

'Doctor Lucca, I'm very sorry to call so late.'

It was ten-twenty.

'Has something happened?' Grace asked.

'It has,' Delgado said. 'Felicia just told me that she's ready to speak about her mother's death.'

'That's good news,' Grace said.

'But she says she won't talk to anyone but you. I said we'd have to wait till morning, but she became very upset. She says she has to tell you now, tonight, and if you don't come, I'm worried that she may get too worked up again.'

No option.

'Let me organize a few things,' Grace said, 'and I'll be on my way.'

'If it's what you both want,' Kate Petit said, 'by all means, let's talk.'

She turned to the right, led them into a living room.

Mushroom-colored walls, brown carpet, a single light fitting overhead. Little in the way of comfort and zero clutter; probably, Sam surmised, because of the woman's partial blindness, of which he was becoming increasingly certain. One worn-out couch, one armchair, a tapestry-covered footstool, a small round pine table with two cane-backed chairs and a low end table beside the couch.

The room was charmless and depressing, hard to connect with the chic woman who made beautiful clothes. Few books, no photographs, a small black hi-fi system on the floor in one corner, a stack of CDs beside it. No television. One painting, of a cornfield which might perhaps be a Louisiana scene, maybe a picture brought along to Florida.

On the wall opposite the painting, a closed door.

And, tilted in the corner to the right of the door, a black cane. Not a white folding cane that would have confirmed Kate's visual disability – but abruptly Sam recalled the indentations on the path and grass outside Billie's home.

The sound came again. More muffled than before, but just as chilling.

The sound of human fear.

Not coming from behind that closed door, he thought, but from farther back in the house.

'What would you like to know?' Kate Petit asked.

'Whatever you want to tell me,' Sam said.

She gestured with the pistol for him to sit in the armchair. Still the two-handed grip, though it seemed to Sam that her aim was a little off.

Not off enough for him to take a gamble.

Close enough to kill him.

Clearly, Kate Petit had enough sight for that.

Enough vision, therefore, hypothetically, to make her Black Hole.

Sam's chair sagged, felt lumpy, suggesting financial straits.

No financial gain anyone knew of from the killings.

Both women were still standing.

'Toni?' He looked up at her. 'You said you need to talk.'

Maker of theatrical costumes.

Sister, it now seemed possible, of a serial killer.

Of a monster.

Toni sat on the couch to Sam's right. She was pale, and if he'd thought she'd looked tired earlier, now he perceived the kind of weariness that ate right through to the bone.

Or maybe the soul.

She looked up at her sister. 'It's time, Kate,' she said. 'I want to tell him.'

Sam looked at Kate Petit, her eyes completely shielded by the glasses.

Dark glasses a recurring theme in the case, though not in all the killings.

Eye coverings of different kinds. Not covering *eyes* at all . . .

He suppressed a shudder.

'Your funeral,' Kate said to her sister.

She stooped to pick up a shabby, claret-colored cushion from the couch, then lowered herself onto the footstool, all the time keeping the handgun directed at Sam.

The cushion as a silencer perhaps, Sam registered.

Black Hole had used cushions for that purpose.

He looked at the muzzle of the weapon, and images of his loved ones passed swiftly through his mind, as they always had when he'd faced mortal danger.

One day his luck would run out.

Kate positioned the cushion on her thighs, rested her forearms on it.

Not just yet, Sam thought.

'May as well get comfy,' she said.

A little less harsh, perhaps; a note of something else, something almost seductive.

And deeply, intensely dangerous.

'What shall we talk about first, big sister?' Kate asked. 'How about life back in good ole Louisiana?'

Toni Petit seemed to sag a little, her narrow shoulders drooping.

And then she straightened, took a breath and began to talk.

The years dropping away.

On her way to Delgado's home, Grace had tried Sam again, and now, as she parked her car on Country Club Drive just before eleven o'clock, she called Martinez instead.

'Hey,' he said. 'What's up, Grace? You're mobile?'

Grace explained about Delgado's call, asked if Martinez had talked to Sam.

'No, but he left me a message. First chance, I'll tell him where you are.'

'And that Joshua's at Claudia's, so he doesn't need to worry about us.'

'You think this could be a breakthrough with the girl?' Martinez asked.

Grace knew he was talking about the case, not Felicia's health.

'Too soon to tell,' she said.

'And if it is, you won't be saying,' Martinez said. 'Just don't forget to tell us if you think she's ready to be interviewed, Gracie.'

'I won't forget.' She paused, her chest feeling tight. 'Al, is Sam OK?'

'He sounded fine. I'm on my way to meet him now. So you go do what you gotta do, Doc, and I'll go check on our guy.'

'Thanks, Al,' Grace said. 'And you both be careful, please.'

'Always,' Martinez said.

'And make sure he calls me when he can.'

'You got it,' he said.

Grace put the phone in her bag, took a moment.

Whatever he'd said, Martinez was troubled about something.

Didn't mean it had to be Sam.

But if Martinez was worried, then she was too.

She sighed, got out of the car, locked it.

Forced herself to direct her concentration on Felicia Delgado.

And whatever it was that she wanted to tell her.

'Will you be OK if I go get a little fresh air?' David asked Mildred.

Alvarez and Riley had departed just minutes before, on their way to find George Wiley.

'I wish you wouldn't,' Mildred said.

'I want to check on Adams, too,' David said. 'See what's holding him up.'

Mildred shook her head.

'Please try and keep your head still,' David reminded her. 'And rest a little.'

'I'll rest better if you stay with me.'

'I just need some air,' he persisted. 'A few minutes.'

'Please be careful,' she said.

'I know we have pollution,' David said lightly, 'but I don't think five minutes of Florida air's going to kill me.'

Mildred's uncovered eye looked at him hard.

'Please don't do anything foolish, old man,' she told him.

'I don't plan to,' he told her.

And was out the door in an instant.

'Oh, dear Lord,' Mildred said quietly.

They had lived on a farm in south Louisiana. A widowed father and his two daughters, soybean and corn their main crops, their lives comfortable and, to outsiders, contented and respectable.

Except that Jacques Grand – Jake to his friends, an attractive, hard-bodied, hard-working farmer – had been sexually abusing his older daughter, Antoinette, without compunction or constraint for years. Until one day in the fall of 1987 when she was ten, an hour after he had raped her once too often, Toni – as she was known – had summoned all her courage and had gone looking for him. Finding him in one of the barns, she told Jake that if he ever touched her again, she would tell her teachers exactly what he had been doing to her.

Toni had not seen Katherine, her eight-year-old sister, come into the barn behind her.

Had not realized that Kate had heard every word.

Kate, who adored their papa.

So that when Jake Grand had gone crazy, had called Toni a 'lying bitch whore' and thrown a pitchfork at her, Toni had ducked, and the big lethal tool had flown over her head and speared Kate's left eye.

In the local hospital, Jake said that Kate had tripped and fallen onto the pitchfork, and Toni, who had used up her resources of courage, did not contradict him because, after all, the pitchfork had been meant for *her*, and if she hadn't ducked, this terrible thing would not have happened to her little sister.

Kate had lost the sight in that eye. And because her right eye was already severely myopic, the child was now seriously sight impaired. Glasses were vital, but Kate had always disliked them. Now that she was virtually blind without them, she hated them more than ever, deliberately and repeatedly losing or breaking them. An optician suggested a contact lens, but Kate said it hurt her, wept when made to insert it, then took it out and stamped on it.

'I'm so sorry, baby, I'm so sorry,' Jake would tell her over and over, crucified with guilt because of what he'd done to her.

'It's OK, Papa,' Kate always told him. 'It was Toni's fault, not yours.'

For a while after that, Jake had left Toni alone, and so far as she knew, he never laid a finger on Kate. Yet her younger sister seemed sexually aware, and when the day came that Jake caught Kate masturbating, he yelled at her, said she was a whore, just like her sister.

The beatings started after that.

Always against Toni.

'Without you,' Jake lashed at her, 'your sister would have her sight! Without you, she would have remained *decent*.'

Kate knew all about it, saw Toni cowering, heard her cries of pain and fear, but since there was nothing she could do about it, and since she believed their father was right about it all being Toni's fault, she never protested, and anyway, Jake still did everything for her, was the perfect daddy.

And then one day in 1992, Toni couldn't take it anymore.

'It was during Andrew,' she said now, almost twenty years later.

It took Sam a second to realize that she was talking about Hurricane Andrew, which had hit Louisiana after it had smashed through Florida, and he was so sucked into Toni's tale that he might *almost* have forgotten the gun pointed at him.

1992. Toni would have been fifteen. Kate thirteen.

'Jake had two guns,' Toni said. 'An old Remington pump-action shotgun, and his Colt pistol.'

'This one,' Kate said.

It was the first time she'd spoken since Toni had begun, but there was excitement of a kind building in her now, Sam could almost feel it.

Whereas Toni, the storyteller, seemed calm.

In the eye of her own storm.

'Papa had beaten me that morning for no reason at all.' She shook her head, her dark eyes distant. 'The weather had made me feel strange – I'm often affected by storms, but not like that. It seemed to be feeding something inside me – strength, maybe.' She looked at Sam. 'I went looking for the Remington. I'd always admired it, and our father loved it. I'd held it a few times, trying to absorb its power, I guess, but it always scared me too.'

She stopped.

The room was silent. No more sounds except the low hum of cars and, now and then, farther away, sirens.

'That day, he'd used his belt and fists and he'd kicked me, too – and I was just so sick of it. And we'd all been hearing about the hurricane coming, and the wind was whipping up, and the storm was making me feel . . .' Toni tailed off, then blinked. 'So anyway, I found the shotgun, and picked it up and went looking for him. And found him.'

'Only I'd been following her again,' Kate said. 'I'd seen her take the gun.'

A slight tremor shook her hands, but she steadied herself, appeared very controlled, Sam thought, and the Colt that had once been their father's was still pointed at him, and he had to presume that her dark glasses were prescription, that the vision in her right eye was perfectly corrected . . .

'Kate saw me take aim,' Toni said, 'and she shouted out and ran at me, dragged the gun away from me. She was stronger than I'd realized, but still, if I'd fought her harder, I could have kept hold of it, but I remember being afraid that the gun might go off and shoot her, so I let her have it.'

Sam waited.

'And then a tree, a Bald Cypress – our very own Louisiana state tree – decided it couldn't take the wind one second longer, and it fell, and I could see that it was going to hit Kate, so I hauled her out the way, and the gun went off and hit our father right between his eyes.'

'It made a big, black hole,' Kate said, and shuddered.

A long shudder, seeming to pass all the way to her fingertips.

Yet still she held fast to the Colt.

'That was the moment when my mind came back,' Toni said. 'And when my little sister lost hers.'

Mildred's floor had been deserted except for a single nurse at the station near the elevators.

'I'm looking for Doctor Wiley,' David had told her casually.

'First-floor lounge.' She smiled. 'I just directed your friends.'

Friends and plain-clothes cops.

He'd debated. Four stories down. Old legs and heart. Had chosen the elevator.

He'd tried to sit it out with Mildred, just wait, like the retiree he was supposed to be, and let the cops do their job, and if anyone respected the police, it was surely David Becket, whose pride in his detective son frequently filled his soul to bursting point. And Mike Alvarez and Beth Riley were more likely than anyone, except perhaps Sam, to see to it that that man – that *doctor* – got his.

Yet he had not been able to sit it out. He wanted – needed – to see with his own eyes the moment when George Wiley was placed under arrest and removed from the Adams Clinic.

He needed to *know* that Mildred was safe from him.

On the first floor, he saw them. The lieutenant and the sergeant and *him.*

They were talking. Alvarez was just *talking* to the sonofabitch.

David strode toward them. 'Why haven't you cuffed him?'

'It's OK, Doctor Becket,' Alvarez told him, 'but I'd rather you stayed—'

'What's OK about it?' David erupted. 'This man needs restraining, he needs locking up.'

'We're dealing with it,' Riley told him quietly.

'Did you find the instrument,' David demanded, 'or did he get rid of it? Lord knows he had plenty of time.'

'I'm just giving these officers my side of the story,' George Wiley said. 'Two sides to every story, Doctor Becket, remember?'

'Don't you dare patronize me, you—'

'Hey,' Alvarez said gently. 'Let's take it easy here.'

'I was just telling the lieutenant about Mrs Becket's hysteria about her eyes,' Wiley said. 'The fact that her considerable overreaction to eye exams was well-documented even before she checked in here.'

'What the hell is going *on* here?' David turned on Alvarez. 'Why is this man being allowed to talk about my wife this way?'

'Diazepam before the simplest of eye tests,' Wiley went on. 'If Doctor Ethan Adams were not so understanding—'

'So help me,' David said to Alvarez, 'if you don't shut this man up, I will.'

'Hey,' Beth Riley said. 'Take it easy.'

She reached out to touch David's forearm, but he pulled away.

'I wouldn't have dreamed of mentioning such things,' Wiley went on, 'but medicine is my life, and I just can't allow a neurotic patient—'

'OK, that's enough.' Alvarez took a stand. 'George Wiley, I am arresting you on suspicion of simple battery.'

'*Simple*,' David said, still fit to explode.

'You won't make it stick,' Wiley told the lieutenant, then turned back to David. 'And you will regret it, Doctor Becket.'

In silence, Riley cuffed him.

'Anything you say,' Alvarez began.

'What a very nice scene,' a voice said from behind them.

Ethan Adams's eyes were angry.

'Thank God,' Wiley said.

'Shut up,' Adams said, and then, while Alvarez went on with the Miranda, he turned to David. 'I apologize most sincerely for the delay, Doctor Becket, but I suggest that our priority now is for me to see my patient.'

'Good,' David said.

'Doctor Adams,' George Wiley began.

And was silenced by one of the coldest, most damning stares that David Becket could remember seeing.

Adams nodded at Alvarez and Riley, then turned his back on Wiley.

'Shall we, Doctor Becket?' he said.

The stunned, lost expression on Wiley's face was satisfaction of a kind for David.

The rest, he guessed, could wait.

Her father and the nurse had been asked by Felicia to stay out of her room.

She would speak only to Dr Lucca.

Grace knocked quietly. 'Felicia, it's Grace Lucca.'

'OK,' Felicia's voice said.

Opening the door, it took a moment for Grace to locate her. The drapes were open, but her dimmed bedside lamp was the only real light in the room, and the teenager was sitting on the floor on the far side of the bed. She was tucked into the corner near the window, her body twisted so that she half faced the wall, her legs drawn up, arms wrapped around her knees. She was not wearing her big dark glasses, though they were close at hand on the bedside table.

She looked up at Grace. 'Can you close the door, please?'

Grace stepped back to do so, then stood still.

This had to be driven, at least initially, by Felicia. The glasses were off and her face was not concealed, yet her position and body language spoke of hiding, and Grace knew that if she pushed too hard, the girl might just shut down again.

'Where would you like me to sit?' she asked.

'I don't mind.'

The side of the bed might seem intrusive, Grace felt, the chair too formal and interview-like, but though choosing the floor would place them on the same level, it might also make Felicia feel trapped.

Grace decided on the bed, near the foot, giving the teen space.

'OK?' she said.

'Sure,' Felicia said.

'Your father called me,' Grace said.

'I asked him to.'

Felicia shifted a little, and with more light now illuminating her face, Grace saw that she had been crying. Her eyes were brown, and though the whites were pink from weeping, they appeared normal, healthy eyes.

'Don't read too much into it,' Felicia said. 'I often take off the glasses, usually when I'm alone.'

'It's nice to see your whole face,' Grace said.

'I don't know,' Felicia said. 'All that stuff, about my . . . You know.'

'Yes,' Grace said.

'It doesn't seem so important anymore.'

Grace waited.

Felicia licked her lips. 'Not when I think about my mom.'

She began to cry, very softly, and Grace wanted to get down and put an arm around her shoulders, but she stayed where she was, went on waiting for the fourteen-year-old to be ready.

And then, suddenly, she was.

'We had a fight,' Felicia said.

'We left that same day,' Toni said. 'While the chaos of the storm was still happening, everyone occupied. I wiped our prints off the Remington and put it in our father's hands, made it look as if he'd shot himself. And then I came back to the house and wrote a note for Mrs Larsson, my father's part-time housekeeper and, I figured, the next person who'd come by. I wrote that we'd found Jake's body, that he'd killed himself, told her where to find him, said that I couldn't take any more and that Kate and I were leaving.'

'I didn't want to leave,' Kate said. 'She made me.'

'Why did you leave?' Sam asked Toni. 'Your father's death wasn't Kate's fault. It was an accident.'

'I'd brought the shotgun, which made it my fault.'

'And she knew that if we stayed,' her sister said, 'I might have told them she was the one who'd shot him.'

'Is that why you ran?' Sam asked Toni.

'Partly,' she said. 'Mostly it was because I knew that even if they believed the truth, they'd have taken Kate into care, maybe locked me up, maybe not. Either way, I knew I was the only person who understood my sister's needs, so I couldn't let them split us up. I had to protect Kate.'

'What did you do next?' Sam asked.

'I took the Colt pistol and most of the cash in our father's safe – there was much more than I'd expected – a lot of cash, I mean a *lot* – I don't know where it came from. It was easy enough, because all I had to do was take his keys off him, then lock up the safe again and put the keys back on his belt, and I don't suppose anyone but Jake knew how much money he'd put away over the years, or where he got it from.'

She'd called that 'easy', Sam registered: returning twice to the horror of her father's body. Not many grown men, let alone fifteen-year-old daughters, would call that *easy*.

'And then we packed what we needed, got on the road, hitched a few rides and made our way to Florida.'

'Didn't anyone come after you?' Sam asked.

'I don't know, but they never found us. We changed our surname to Petit, and maybe they believed that Jake Grand had shot himself. It was crazy that night, trees falling, crops getting wiped out. One farmer less to make insurance claims, maybe. Two less kids to take care of, and no one to miss us. Mrs Larsson used to keep to herself, did her work and went home again, so I don't think she'd have cared.'

'She didn't like me,' Kate said.

Sam felt less intensity flowing from her now, wondered if she might tire any time soon.

'Did you make your name change official?' he asked.

'Of course not,' Toni said. 'I wouldn't have known how to take care of something like that without drawing attention. We had more than enough for our start, and I'd always been good at sewing, so I made a living from dressmaking. My customers pay me in cash or, sometimes, in the early years, I bartered for stuff we needed.'

'I don't work,' Kate said flatly. 'And I can't claim disability, because she made us run away.'

There was a moment's silence.

'Why did you take the Colt?' Sam asked. 'After what had happened?'

'Kate told me to take it,' Toni said. 'She was in a bad way. She said having the gun would make her feel safer. She said if we didn't take it, she wouldn't come with me. So I took it.'

'I'd been a bitch for two days,' Felicia said, 'because my mom had tried to make me go to the doctor because . . .'

Too hard to talk about her eyes, plainly.

'I know about that, Felicia,' Grace said gently, 'because your mother told Doctor Shrike what happened.'

'The other shrink,' Felicia said.

'Yes.'

'I was a bitch after that too.' She paused. 'I thought shrinks aren't supposed to say what a patient's told them.'

'That is mostly true,' Grace said. 'But Doctor Shrike wasn't repeating anything you said to her.'

'It doesn't matter anyway,' Felicia said, 'because what I'm going to tell you isn't secret. I just couldn't tell my father, and you . . .'

Grace said nothing.

Felicia took a breath, seemed about to speak, but more tears welled up.

'Don't worry,' Grace said. 'You cry if you need to.'

'But it's late.' Felicia looked at the clock on her bedside table, pulled two tissues from the Kleenex box beside it, blew her nose. 'It's almost midnight, and you've come here specially.'

'For you, yes,' Grace said.

'But it's so late,' Felicia said again.

'I have as much time as you need,' Grace said.

'You say you took the Colt so that Kate would feel safe,' Sam said. 'Who did she need to be kept safe from, with your father dead?'

'I'd never needed protection from my father,' Kate said. 'If you were paying attention, you'd know that, Detective.'

Sam had been in too many tight spots not to know how to try to navigate a conversation while under threat. But this situation was confusing as hell, because though he had thought something was *wrong* about Toni, he had not believed he was coming after her looking for a killer. And so far, these two women had only shared confessions about old crimes from which it might be possible for them to emerge free and clear, after so many years. Accidental death and theft. And though Sam found it perplexing that the Louisiana cops had not gone after the sisters back then, he had infinitely bigger things on his mind now.

Kate's use of those words 'big black hole', describing the wound in Jake Grand's forehead, had not been coincidental.

But the instant Sam asked these women about the Black Hole killings, the stakes in this room would rocket.

No way out for him that he could see.

And then Kate Petit took them there anyway, without being asked.

'He knows,' she said.

Toni Petit didn't speak.

She looked spent. Which was, Sam supposed, part of what he'd observed earlier at Tyler Allen's. Because this woman had to have been putting on a front for years, covering up for her sister who might, or might not, be insane.

Something had happened, something had *changed*, and maybe Toni had left that rehearsal tonight because she knew it was time for them to run again.

'You're the one who wanted to talk,' Kate Petit said now to her sister.

'You must have known we'd have to, finally,' Toni said.

'I always knew you'd betray me in the end,' Kate said.

Bitterness and a kind of satisfaction in the words.

'Oh, Kate.' Toni looked sad as an open grave.

Sam let the silence hover for another second.

And then he asked: 'Where is Billie Smith?'

May 27

Just past midnight, Martinez was outside on Foster Avenue.

Everything quiet.

Sam's Saab was parked a little way along from Toni Petit's house, and Martinez was engaging in a little silent debate with himself as to whether he should just wait out here, go knock on the lady's door or call the Hallandale PD.

Petit had no outstanding warrants.

Then again, so far as he'd been able to ascertain, there was no record of her existence, period.

He figured he'd take a look around.

His cell phone rang.

Mary Cutter telling him she'd had a call from Dr Lopez.

'The receptionist called him, said she'd been staying up late trying to remember who'd been there when Felicia Delgado got mad at Beatriz. And then it suddenly came back to her that two other people walked out right after them.'

'She just remembered this now?' Martinez said acidly.

'Go figure,' Cutter said.

Martinez kept his eyes on the house. 'So who were they?'

'One of them was a patient waiting to see a gynecologist; she thinks the other woman was just waiting with her. The patient's name was Toni Petit. That's Petit like in small, only no 'e' on the end.'

'Shit,' Martinez said. 'Would you believe I just ran her tag for Sam?'

'How come?' Cutter asked.

'Would you believe I'm sitting outside her house now?' Martinez paused. 'And Sam's inside.'

'Are we talking possible suspect here, Al?'

'I don't know what we're talking,' Martinez said.

And then he saw something.

Some*one.*

In the darkness at the side of the house.

There one minute, then gone.

'What the fuck?' Martinez said under his breath, cut the call, took his phone off the dash, turned off the ringer.

Very quietly, he opened his door and drew his Glock.

'Billie Smith is just fine,' Kate answered Sam's question.

'Where is she?' he asked again.

Uncertain whether he was notching down the tension in the woman holding the gun, or maybe lighting the fuse.

'Billie's all tucked up and comfy, waiting.'

The beautiful young woman with the stunning eyes and gorgeous voice, who had asked him for help and been turned away.

Making this Sam's fault.

No question.

At least Billie was alive, if that wail had come from her, and he had to believe that was true. And if they had her prisoner, then that alone explained the change in Toni. Because whether or not Kate Petit was the Black Hole killer, whatever had gone down with Billie Smith was too damned close to home, and Toni had to have known they were finished.

'OK.' Sam sounded reasonable. 'So the first thing we need to do right now is let her go.'

'Wrong,' Kate said.

Toni had stopped speaking. She seemed lost, Sam thought, elsewhere; and maybe she was back on their old Louisiana farmstead, or maybe she was with the victims.

Her sister's victims.

And then, everything turned upside down.

Kate stood up.

Unfolded from the footstool, with only a trace of unsteadiness.

She crossed the small room, keeping the gun trained on Sam, and sat down again, perching on one arm of the sofa.

'Hey,' she said, 'big sis.'

Toni Petit looked up at her.

'Here,' Kate said.

And, very carefully, keeping control of its aim, she placed the Colt into her sister's hands.

'Shoot him,' she said.

Sam saw shock in Toni's eyes.

'No,' she said.

Sam stopped breathing. If he was going to make a move, it had to be the instant this woman's grip wavered even a little, because Toni did not want this, so this had to be his best, perhaps his last chance.

Except the gun was still leveled at him, Toni's grip looking tighter and steadier than her sister's had. And Sam saw that the threat against him had just intensified, because suddenly Toni no longer looked *spent.*

Suddenly, she seemed replete with, fueled by, tension.

'You have to shoot him, Toni,' Kate said. 'You know it.'

'I don't know that at all,' Toni said, though her grip on the weapon spoke otherwise.

'No,' Sam said quietly. 'You don't, Toni. What you do have to do is show me where Billie is, and then you have to let her go. You have to do the right thing now, both of you, before it's too late.'

It was not enough, and he knew it.

Knew it was going to take more than that.

Like a SWAT team, maybe.

'Shoot him, Toni,' Kate Petit said again.

And Toni raised the gun.

'I've been so scared,' Felicia said to Grace.

Grace looked at the tear-stained face, at the dark, wounded eyes, always hidden away from the world because of a lifetime's fears of a different kind.

'Of course you have,' she said. 'How could you not be?'

'But what I've done is so bad.' Felicia reached up for her glasses, was about to put them on, then changed her mind, gripped them instead, took a deep breath. 'Not talking all this time, after what happened to my mom, and I knew I should tell, I *knew* it, but I just couldn't seem to do it.'

'And now?' Grace said, very gently. 'Do you think you can tell me?'

'I have to,' Felicia said. 'Except maybe it's too late already, and maybe they've already done it again to someone else.'

Grace heard the word, needed to be clear.

'They?' she asked, a chill running down her spine.

'I saw them,' Felicia said.

'Hey,' Martinez said.

Seeing the man now.

Seeing the window open at the back of the house.

The guy was climbing in, one leg already inside.

Thomas Chauvin.

Martinez trod silently up behind him, stuck the Glock right up against his back. 'What the fuck do you think you're doing, asshole?' he hissed in his ear. 'Get your butt out here right now.'

'I think Sam might be in trouble,' Chauvin whispered, still astride the ledge.

'You want to get out here,' Martinez said, 'and tell me why the fuck you think that.'

'I was watching when he went inside. Something didn't feel right to me.'

'I told you to get out here' – Martinez relocated the handgun to the other man's thigh – 'before I put a bullet through your leg.'

'I don't believe you,' Thomas Chauvin said.

And slid the other leg over.

Into the house.

'Sonofabitch,' Martinez said.

His cell phone vibrated.

'Shit,' he said, and slammed it into complete silence.

And then, swearing under his breath, he followed Chauvin over the window sill and into the house.

'Two women,' Felicia said.

The chill inside Grace turned to sickness.

Her conflict beginning, an almost painful tearing, because she was here as this child's psychologist, but Sam and all the other investigators were out there struggling to find this killer – and she had just learned more than any of them knew.

Nothing she could do about that now.

Not yet.

Just be here for this teenager, just listen.

'We had a fight,' Felicia said again, and stopped.

Not the prelude to another shutdown, Grace felt; rather that the girl was waiting for recrimination to rain down on her. Because she had fought with her mother on the last day of her life.

Felicia's eyes flicked to Grace's face, found no censure there, but could not hold her gaze.

Her hands played with the sunglasses. But she did not put them on.

'It was one of those dumb arguments,' she went on at last. 'And I was being a brat. Worse, I was being a bitch, and all it was about . . .'

Grace waited a few seconds.

'What was it about?' she asked, quietly. 'Can you tell me?'

'Maple syrup.' Tears welled up again, but she went on. 'Can you believe that? I wanted French toast with maple syrup, but there wasn't any, and Mama said why didn't I have cinnamon toast instead, but I said I wanted . . .'

She had to stop to weep again, and Grace passed her tissues and resisted her impulse to embrace and comfort, just laid a hand on her upper arm for a moment to connect, and Felicia did not shake her off, just cried for another moment, then blew her nose hard, angrily.

'I said I *had* to have French toast, and why couldn't she be like other, normal moms who made sure they had the things their kids liked? And Mama said she was sorry, and she would get some later, and I said that was going to be too damned late – only I didn't say "damned", did I? I said something much worse – to my *mother*, who was going to *die*, who was about to be . . .'

'It's OK,' Grace told her.

'It's *not* OK,' Felicia said. 'Oh, God, it's not OK, and it's never going to be.'

And the tears came again.

'What was that?'

Kate's head turned toward the hallway, her chin jutting as she listened intently.

Still sitting on the sofa's armrest, Toni on the seat beside her.

The Colt still leveled at Sam.

A figure appeared in the doorway.

Sometimes – the thought struck Sam in that microsecond – it really was hard to believe your eyes.

'Drop it,' Thomas Chauvin said.

And all hell broke loose.

Kate grabbed the gun from Toni.

Did it fast, in one smooth motion, so that it was still pointed at Sam, and there was nothing he could have safely done to disarm her.

'I knew you wouldn't do it,' she said. 'Call yourself a fucking sister.'

'Kate, don't,' Toni said.

She stood up, reached for the gun, but Kate stepped sideways, eluded her.

'I said *drop* it,' Chauvin said.

And hurled himself at Kate Petit.

Who pulled the trigger.

Joe Duval's black Dodge Magnum had just come to a halt about fifty yards along from Sam Becket's Saab when he heard it.

Unmistakable.

He grabbed his phone, punched in 911, identified himself and his location to the Broward Sheriff's dispatch for Hallandale PD and reported hearing a single gunshot.

'Officer inside,' he said. 'Request backup. One woman suspect believed to be inside, possibly more, and possibility of a female African-American hostage. Police officer also African-American, six-three, MBPD Detective Samuel Becket.'

Duval got out of the car, closed the door quietly, popped the trunk, pulled out his black bullet-proof vest and suddenly noted the Chevy Impala parked a little way along the road.

'Possible second MBPD inside, Detective Martinez, five-ten, Cuban-American. Note, both officers may be armed, so attending should ID themselves immediately. Request 10-40, no lights, no sirens. I'm Caucasian, five-ten, armed, wearing bullet-proof vest, and I'm going inside. 10-4.'

* * *

'No!' Toni screamed. 'Kate, *no*!'

'I'm OK.' Kate Petit scrambled to her feet, hands shaking but still gripping the pistol.

'Chauvin?' Sam addressed the man on the floor. 'You OK?'

'I'm shot.' Thomas Chauvin lay on the rug and groaned, clutched his bloodied left arm. 'She *shot* me.'

'Who the fuck is this joker?' Kate demanded.

'I don't know,' Toni said. 'Kate, I'm begging you—'

'Shut up, sis,' Kate said.

Sam stared at the gun, knew he was back in her sights, any chance of jumping her gone again, thanks to Chauvin.

He heard the soft creak of a floorboard *just* before a new voice rang out.

Oh, so familiar, and oh, so welcome.

'Like the man said, drop the fucking gun.'

Martinez stood in that doorway now, his Glock pointed center mass at Kate Petit.

Who turned her face briefly toward the newcomer, gave a strange, twisted smile. And then looked back at Sam.

Leveled the Colt.

With another scream, Toni Petit threw herself at her sister, wrenched the gun out of her hands and backed into a corner, weapon still aimed at Sam.

'That's good, sis,' Kate said, panting. 'That's more like it.'

'No.' Toni was parchment pale, bright tears in her eyes. 'Not this time, Kate. I can't let this go on anymore.' She took a breath, and a deep, gut-wrenching sob came with it. 'I'm so *sorry*.'

She moved.

Hardly more than a pivot.

Sam saw her trigger finger moving.

'Jesus, *no*!' he yelled and tackled her.

He felt the force of the gunshot, his ears deafened.

Kate Petit was beside him on the floor, blood pumping from her temple.

'I'm so sorry,' he heard Toni say again, very softly.

Sam stared up at her, saw the Colt turning, its black muzzle travelling swiftly up to her own forehead. He lifted off the floor, slammed into her, grabbed the gun, and Martinez pounced, pinioned her arms behind her.

'Jesus, man,' Martinez said, cuffing her.

A crash jolted the room, the front door being smashed open.

Special Agent Joe Duval entered, moving into the living room in tactical combat fighting stance, low, his personal use Glock 27 in both hands, as ready as he could be for whatever was waiting for him.

'Good to see you.' Sam's heart was pounding like a jackhammer.

Duval took in the scene, registered enough to straighten up. 'You guys OK?'

'We're good,' Martinez said.

'*Please.*' Toni Petit's voice was despairing, her eyes tormented, fixed on Sam. 'Please shoot me, Sam.'

Sam took a breath, his pulse calming. 'No can do,' he told her.

'Oh, God.' Toni's whole body was trembling. 'Oh, God, if you won't do it, please let me.' Still the appeal to him. 'I shot my sister. I just want to die.'

'Got a few questions to answer first,' Sam told her.

He knelt back down beside Kate, checked her pulse, shook his head, then carefully removed her dark glasses.

She had closed both her eyes while dying, but there was an old, ugly scar running from her left eyebrow down to just above her cheekbone.

The pitchfork's legacy, he supposed, as Toni began weeping.

'Backup on the way,' Duval said. 'Anyone care to fill me in?'

Still on the rug, just feet away from the dead woman, Thomas Chauvin groaned again. Sam moved over to him, crouched, took a look at his arm, his touch not especially gentle. 'You'll live, and you're damned lucky.'

'I saved your life,' the Frenchman said, hurt.

'What did you think you were doing?' Sam said. 'Playing some fucking fantasy game? You're a jerk, Chauvin.'

'You don't know the half of it,' Martinez said, and then, still holding on to Toni Petit, he started to call it in.

Sam straightened up, looked at Toni.

'Where's Billie?' he asked.

*   *   *

'So can you tell me what happened?' Grace asked.

Going as gently as she could.

'I stormed out of the house,' Felicia said. 'Said I was going out for breakfast before school, and my mom said she'd take me, but she wasn't dressed so I told her not to bother. I grabbed my bag and opened the front door, and she said I needed a ride, and I knew she was trying to be patient, I knew she didn't want to fight, but I didn't care, did I? I was too busy being a spoiled brat nightmare kid. So I left, and I slammed that door as hard as I could.'

Grace could almost hear its reverberation, could see the ravages of its repercussions in Felicia's face. A commonplace argument now forever elevated to something that had to feel like the worst sin she could have committed against her mother.

It had to be unbearable.

'She was right, of course,' Felicia went on. 'I did need a ride, because it was a long walk, but I was going to have my French toast if it killed me.'

She stopped short, that word hanging in the air.

'Go on,' Grace said, after a moment.

'I got my breakfast,' Felicia said, very softly, 'in a place on 71st, and I looked at it on my plate and knew I couldn't eat it, but I sat there anyway, feeling sorry for myself, the way I often do – and I know I do that, Doctor Lucca, same way I know how weird I am about my . . .'

Hands shaking, she finally put her sunglasses back on. Her mask back in place. Yet Grace was grateful to have been trusted this much by this poor, suffering child, and at least Felicia had not yet told her to leave.

Almost a minute passed in silence, and Grace sat calmly, waiting.

'Then I decided to go home,' Felicia said. 'I didn't feel like going to school. I was going to be late, anyway, and have to explain myself, and I hated the way I'd left things with my mom, didn't want to have to wait for hours till I could make it up with her.'

It occurred to Grace to ask Felicia how long she'd sat over that breakfast, because it was something Sam would want to know, but that kind of question might jar with Felicia, might turn her straight back into 'wife of cop'.

Here and now, she was Grace Lucca, here for Felicia.

'And if I'd gone straight back then, everything might still have been OK,' Felicia went on. 'But there was a phone store near the café, and I was sick of my cell phone, so I went in there and mooched around for a while until I knew I was really ready to go back.'

Grace waited again.

'I felt tired on the way,' Felicia said. 'Hot and sick, too, my stomach all tied up in knots because I was going to have to back down, and I always hated saying sorry to my mom.' Her mouth trembled. 'And now I'll never be able to say sorry to her again.'

She got up off the floor, her movements slow, weary.

Grace held her breath, afraid she was going to stop.

Almost as afraid that she would go on.

Felicia stepped sideways to the window.

The sunglasses had to make it hard to see much out there in the night, but Grace felt she was probably staring into space.

Back into the past.

To that morning.

When Sam opened the door to the room at the back of the house and saw Billie, despair almost poleaxed him.

Despair and rage.

He was too *late*.

Her eyes were covered.

Bandages this time.

Same stuff they'd tied her to the bed with.

No blood.

He registered that about a millisecond before she started screaming.

The sound reverberated in his ears, a hideous sound of sheerest terror from behind a sticking plaster gag, because Billie was *alive* and all she knew was that someone had come into the room and she thought she was about to *die*.

Wonderful sound, too, for Sam, because she was alive.

'Billie, it's Sam,' he told her, loud and clear. 'It's OK. You're safe.'

The screaming stopped and her body went rigid.

'It's only Sam, sweetheart, and I'm just going to touch your arm,' he said.

He laid his hand very gently on her right forearm, and she jolted, cried out.

'It's Sam, Billie. I just have to take a couple of photos, for evidence, and then I'm going to take the plaster off your mouth,' he told her. 'I'll try not to hurt you.'

He took three photographs quickly, then peeled the sticking plaster away very carefully.

Billie gulped in air and began to weep.

'You cry, Billie,' Sam told her. 'You just let it out.'

'I can't *see*.'

A new blast of terror shook him.

Flashes of Beatriz Delgado and Amelia Newton.

No blood, but . . .

His mouth was very dry.

'There's a bandage over your eyes, Billie.' He kept his voice steady. 'Did they do anything to them? To your eyes?'

'I don't think so.' It was a whisper, full of terror. 'I don't *think* so.'

'I'm going to take the bandage off now.'

Fear rose off her in waves and mingled with his own as he willed his hands not to shake and gently removed the blindfold, sending up a silent prayer. Her eyes looked fine externally, but they were squeezed shut, lashes quivering.

'Open your eyes for me, Billie,' Sam said.

They opened. The remains of panic still clouded them, but they were as beautiful as always. Their pupils were large, the whites reddened, but they were unharmed, and she was staring at him, and *alive.*

'Thank God,' he said. 'They're fine, and you're safe, and it's all over.'

He took out his pocket knife and began cutting her free, wondering if Kate or Toni had done this to her, or if it had been teamwork.

Billie's whole body shook with her weeping.

'I'm so sorry.' Sam began rubbing her freed hands and arms, felt how cold they were, knew they had to be numb. 'I'm just so sorry.'

'I tried to tell you.' Billie's voice was choked.

'I know you did.' He took a handkerchief from his pocket, carefully wiped her eyes. 'I know you did, and I'm sorrier than I can ever say.'

But even now, in the depths of his shame, his mind worked on.

Glad that of one thing, at least, there could be little doubt.
Black Hole was finished.

'I saw them when they were coming out of our driveway.'
Felicia still stared out into the night.
'They looked kind of familiar, but I didn't know why. Not then.' She paused. 'Not till *today*. A few hours ago.' She shook her head. 'I don't know why, but I suddenly remembered where I'd seen them before.'
Grace waited.
'They'd been in the waiting room the day my mom and I were at the doctor's. I only noticed them there because I thought one of them might be blind.'
More facts, Grace knew, that Sam desperately needed.
'But that morning, when I was coming back home and I saw them, I stood very still on the sidewalk and waited while they got in their car. It was a black SUV, and the woman I thought might be blind got in first, and the other one was getting in on the driver's side when . . .' Felicia's fists clenched by her sides. 'She saw me. She saw me looking at her. And I realized right away that she knew who I was.'
She turned around, faced Grace.
'She stared right at me for a moment, and then she put one finger up to her lips, like this.' She raised her right index finger, held it vertically against her own mouth. 'And then she moved the same finger up to her eyes, one at a time.' Felicia took a shaky breath. 'I didn't understand why, at the time. I didn't stop to think about it till later. After. All I wanted then was to go inside and fix things with my mom.'
She paused again, her mouth trembling.
'Do you mind if I sit next to you?' she asked Grace.
'Of course not.' Grace made space for her.
Felicia sat down slowly, removed her glasses, did not look at Grace.
'I let myself in.' Her voice was so soft, Grace had to strain to hear. 'Used my key. I went inside, into the hallway, closed the door behind me and called out.' She shivered. 'I called twice. "Mama. Mama". And then I had this feeling, this *awful* feeling.' Her voice was rising again. 'And then I went into her bedroom. I think I

knocked first.' She nodded. 'And then I opened the door.'

Grace was filled with horror and pity.

'I saw what they'd done to her. And I guess I knew, right away, that it had been them. But first, I went over to the bed, and I wasn't sure if she was dead or not, and she had these weird little white things on her face, over her . . .'

Grace remembered Sam telling her about the little lace doilies.

She started to feel sick.

'More than anything, I wanted her not to be dead, so I could tell her I was sorry, and that I loved her. But then I touched her.' She shook her head. 'There was so much blood.' She was whispering now. 'I'm not sure what happened next, except I think I tried to hold her, but then one of those *things* fell off from her—'

'It's OK,' Grace said.

'I think – I don't know – but I think maybe I put it back, because I couldn't . . . I don't *know*.'

'It's OK,' Grace said again.

Generally, when a patient halted at a crucial time, she let them pause, then encouraged them to continue, but suddenly she felt it might be better to slow this down for a while, because what Felicia had seen that morning in her mother's bedroom had been too much even for Sam, a seasoned homicide detective, and it was very late, the girl needed sleep, and there would be so much more for her to endure in time, not least her mother's funeral.

Intuition, rather than training, made her put an arm around Felicia.

'I think you need a break,' she said.

For a moment, Felicia leaned against her shoulder, but then she pulled abruptly away, all the terror visible now in her wide eyes.

'But that woman saw me looking at her,' she said. 'And then she warned me – her finger over her lips and then her *eyes* – she was telling me not to talk about *them*. And now I've told you, and I *shouldn't* have.'

The words vibrated, elongated by terror.

'It's all right,' Grace told her. 'You're safe.'

'How do you know?' Felicia said. 'I think I've been waiting all this time for her – for *them* – to find me. And now, if they find out that I've told you, then maybe they'll find a way to do that to me too.'

*   *   *

'What's the verdict?' Mildred asked.

Dr Adams's exam had been careful and gentle, but still, she wondered at her comparative calm. Partly fatigue, she supposed, dulling her senses, since it was almost one in the morning and she'd had anesthesia earlier in the day, not to mention the events of a few hours ago.

Mostly, though, she realized it was a case of relativity. Because after *that*, it was a relief to be in safe hands. Which was in itself a minor miracle; the acceptance that Ethan Adams's hands were safe.

The surgeon sat down, glanced at David, still standing tensely near the window. 'Why don't you sit too, Doctor Becket?'

David didn't move. 'Has he done any harm?'

'Remarkably little,' Ethan Adams said.

Mildred let out a shaky breath of relief.

'Go on, please,' David said.

'There is some inflammation,' Dr Adams went on, 'but I'm very happy to say that no real damage has been done. Though if it had been,' he added reassuringly, 'we could have fixed it.'

'So what now, Doctor?' Mildred asked.

'I'll be wanting to keep a careful watch on things because as you already know, in very rare cases, where the intraocular lens moves or doesn't function as it should, we might need to reposition or replace it.' He paused. 'I have to impress on you, Mrs Becket, how vital it is that you report any symptoms, and that you attend every checkup, because if there are problems, delay could lead to some visual loss. So long as you do keep showing up, however,' he added, 'that will not happen.'

David moved at last, pulled up the chair on the other side of the bed, sat down and took Mildred's hand. 'Good news,' he said.

'Oh, yes,' she said.

'Now then,' Adams said. 'I need to ask if you're willing to come to me for these checkups? Or might you be happier going elsewhere? I'd be very disappointed to lose you as a patient, but in the circumstances, I'd obviously understand.'

'I think we might consider going elsewhere,' David said.

'I can't imagine why you would think that,' Mildred said, 'so long as that man is nowhere to be seen.'

'That man will be going to jail,' David said, 'if I have anything to do with it.'

Adams nodded. 'I imagine you'll be consulting a lawyer about the incident.'

'I imagine so,' David said.

Mildred compressed her lips for a moment, then decided that was an argument that could wait.

'What I would like,' she said, 'is to go home.'

'Not now, obviously,' Dr Adams said.

She shook her head. 'I guess not. But in the morning?'

'We'll see,' Dr Adams said. 'I'd like you to keep as still as possible for several hours.'

'But you said there's no damage,' Mildred said.

'Just the inflammation,' the doctor reiterated. 'I'd like you to promise me to rest tonight, and I'll want to see you again tomorrow before discharging you. And when you do get home, try not to do too much bending or lifting heavy objects.'

'It seems to me,' Mildred said, 'that this is all my fault.'

'How on earth do you figure that?' David asked.

'If I'd had the procedure as a day patient under local anesthesia, I wouldn't have been lying here, waiting for Doctor Wiley to come in.'

'I cannot begin to express how sorry and appalled I am,' Dr Adams said.

'I'm sure,' David said wryly. 'But for the record, there is not one single aspect to this *crime* that was my wife's fault. May I presume we are in agreement on that score, Doctor?'

'You may most definitely presume that,' Ethan Adams said.

At two a.m., the body of Kate Petit still lay on the living room floor in the house on Foster Avenue, awaiting the arrival of the Broward County Medical Examiner, though two ambulances had already arrived and departed again, carrying Billie Smith and Thomas Chauvin to the ER at Hallandale General Hospital.

With officers from the Broward Sheriff's office having placed Toni Petit under arrest for the murder of her sister, the two Broward Homicide detectives now on the scene were in their rights to search the Petit property, though Joe Duval had cautioned Crime Scene and all investigators present to await warrants before conducting a thorough search.

A lot more at stake here, perhaps, he'd told them, than one

killing and one abduction. A whole lot more.

It was Sam who drew Duval outside while Broward secured the perimeter and made preliminary arrangements.

'We need to take a look in those, Joe,' he said, nodding at the two night-shrouded structures that looked like garages.

'They're on the property,' Duval said. 'So I'd say we can look.'

'Are we sure?' The last thing Sam wanted – last thing any of them needed – was to screw up any evidence that might turn their Black Hole suspicions into something more solid.

The lab would hopefully confirm that they had their 'smoking' Colt, and they had Toni dead to rights for the shooting of her sister and for the abduction of Billie Smith, but otherwise all they had was the late Kate Petit's bald statement, made only to Sam, describing the fatal gunshot wound between their father's eyes.

'It made a big, black hole.'

A statement deliberately made, for sure, a gauntlet thrown down.

Yet in legal terms, flimsy as hell.

Nothing.

'The neighbor on that side told one of the Broward officers that both sisters were always in and out of the garages,' Duval said. 'Toni Petit's under lawful arrest, so we're OK to look – but no entry and no collection.'

Martinez emerged from the house, holding a set of keys and a medium-size Maglite flashlight. 'You talkin' about those garages?'

'We sure are,' Duval said.

'Suspect just handed me her keys,' Martinez said. 'She said you'd be wanting to take a look in there, Sam, asked me to give them to you.'

Sam took the keys and handed them to Duval who, as FDLE, had jurisdiction here.

'Better safe,' he said.

The first of the small buildings was what it appeared. A garage.

Housing a black SUV. A 2003 black Ford Explorer with tinted windows.

Paid for, Sam was guessing, with some of Jake Grand's cash.

In the beam of the flashlight, it looked not recently cleaned.

Good news, perhaps.

They did not step inside the garage, the scene's potential too vital to risk contamination.

They moved on to the second structure.

Duval found the right key second time of trying.

He opened the door.

'Oh, Christ,' he said, his voice so low it sounded like a prayer.

'Holy fuck,' Martinez said.

Sam said nothing, just looked.

At first glance, it resembled a grotesque storeroom of a toy store.

Except that all the stuffed toys here had been made to look *dead*, even the ones appearing in photographs up on the whitewashed stone walls.

'We need to stay outside,' Duval said, loud and clear, finding his own small flashlight.

Sam took out his monocular for the second time that night.

No more *perhaps* about anything.

This was Black Hole's very own workshop.

Though not all of them *were* toys, he realized, zooming in on a deceased white rat nailed to a board, its little eyes hidden behind what looked like strips of black tape. And on another wall, an incredibly bizarre collection of butterflies, their eyes, too, concealed by tiny rounds of what looked, from a distance, like fabric.

Miniaturized versions of the little doilies that had covered what had been Beatriz Delgado's eyes.

'Man, this is way beyond sick.' Sam handed the monocular to Duval.

'Look over there,' Martinez said softly, standing on the balls of his feet to get a better view.

Sam, having the advantage of height, looked.

Saw a row of tiny coffins on a shelf.

Six of them.

One for every victim.

He thought about Toni Petit, small as her alias, presently handcuffed and being held in her own kitchen until a decision was reached as to how to proceed. And though it looked as if Kate Petit had been the real monster behind the killings, there was plainly no doubting now that Toni had, at the very least, been her accomplice, willing or otherwise.

It was hard to take in.

'We need to look in those coffins,' Martinez said.

'We need to wait for warrants,' Duval said implacably, but handed him the monocular while Sam took his partner's bigger Maglite and shone it around some more, coming to rest on a workbench by the opposite wall.

Rolls of tape and bandages on there, and a pot that held scissors and other implements that glittered under the flashlight's beam and might, Sam thought with a fresh chill, be surgical in type.

'Another coffin,' Duval said.

Martinez handed Sam back the monocular.

Sam located the coffin, small and white, lid open.

Could just see the doll inside. An African-American doll.

Which told him that if he had not blundered into the Petit sisters' private world tonight, Billie Smith would have gone the way of the other victims – though why hadn't that happened before? Why had they waited, and why in hell had they *taken* her?

'OK, that's enough.' Duval sounded hoarse. 'I'm calling the ASA.'

With no doubt left, but with everything still to prove, they needed the on-call Assistant State Attorney because there was strong evidence here in plain sight, and probably more in the house itself that could be linked to at least six homicides in five Florida counties; and Sam knew it was fortuitous that Duval was already here for the FDLE, but still, the construction of all the necessary warrants had to be as unimpeachable as possible, and the ASA was the person to ensure that.

Duval made the call.

Plenty more calls to follow, to the Office of Statewide Prosecutions and notifying investigators in Orlando, Jupiter and Naples. Fort Lauderdale already knew, were on their way; same deal for City of North Miami Beach, where Zoë Fox, the last victim, had lived and died.

'No one touches anything,' Duval said, 'until we get the warrants.'

No photographs to be taken, no evidence collection or preservation, not even sketches of the crime scene.

One of the Hallandale PD officers came out of the house.

'The suspect says she wants to talk to Detective Becket,' he told Duval.

'Don't you love it when they think they get to choose?' Martinez said sourly.

'I'm just passing on the message,' the officer said. 'She says she knows her rights, but she wants to waive them and talk to Sam Becket.'

'Getting to be a habit,' Duval said softly.

Sam knew what he meant. That request sounding too like what had happened last year, the interviews with psycho Cal the Hater coming back to him now like mental reflux.

No similarity here, he told himself. That monster had been playing a personal game. This woman, he hoped, wanted to unburden herself.

'I guess it might be the most productive way to begin,' he said. 'Tonight's craziness started with her telling her sister that she wanted to talk to me.' He paused. 'Though we're not the only ones who're going to want to interview Petit.'

'Can we take her to the Beach?' Martinez asked.

Duval considered, then nodded. 'Miami Beach is a close enough jurisdiction for us to kick things off there. The Delgado case is yours. So long as I'm there, too, I see no major problem.'

'Won't Broward want to process her first?' Sam asked.

Duval mulled another moment. 'I'm going to go speak to a few people, get everyone on board with this. You guys make sure no one even breathes near either of these buildings till I get back, OK?'

'You got it,' Sam said.

They watched him walk away, pass the officer at the front door, vanish back inside the house, and then Sam and Martinez stepped several feet apart, so they stood, one man blocking entrance to each structure.

Sentry duty for now.

Both Felicia and her father had given Grace permission to pass on the information about the two female suspects, but though she'd tried Sam twice, his phone was still going straight to voicemail and she didn't want to leave something of such importance in a message.

Back in her car, starting her weary way home, fear for her husband pushed its ugly way back into pole position and she pressed his speed-dial key again.

Third time a charm.

'How's Felicia doing?' Sam was keeping his voice low. 'Al gave me your message, but things have been a little wild here.'

'Felicia's doing better.' Grace prioritized, not wanting to waste his time. 'Did Al tell you what he found out about Chauvin?'

'He did, but the signal here's lousy, so I'll fill you in on the rest later.'

'I have news now,' she jumped in fast. 'If we get cut off, call me back.'

'Will do,' Sam said.

'Felicia did not witness her mother's killing at first hand,' Grace told him, 'but I'm fairly sure she could have seen her killers – that's killers, plural.'

'Go on. I'm hearing you.'

Grace heard his terseness, knew he had to be in the middle of something important; knew, too, that what she had to tell him might be his biggest break yet in the case.

'Two women,' she said.

'Two women,' Sam repeated. 'You're sure that's what she said?'

'You're not surprised,' Grace said.

'I wish I was,' he said. 'You'd better tell me what she said.'

'All of it?'

'Edited version, please,' Sam said. 'But everything you have about the women.'

The deal was that Duval and one of the Broward men would bring Toni Petit to Miami Beach as soon as things were organized, and Sam and Martinez would make their way back to the station in their own cars.

Which gave Sam enough time to make some phone calls while he detoured to Hallandale General to check on Billie and Chauvin.

His first call was to Larry Smith, to tell him that his daughter had been abducted but was safe and needed her parents to come down first thing – two people he owed a major apology for not having listened to their daughter in time to spare her this nightmare.

Then, late as it was, responding to an earlier message from his father, he tried David's cell phone, heard the number ringing and was about to cut off in case he woke him when his dad answered, his voice hushed.

'I had the phone on vibrate, son,' he said. 'I wanted to get out of the room so I didn't wake Mildred.'

He brought Sam quickly up to date.

'Alvarez came in person?' The only thing tonight that had made Sam smile.

'The lieutenant thinks a lot of you, son,' David said. 'You know that.'

'It's you and Mildred he thinks a lot of, Dad.' Sam paused. 'So she really is OK and resting?'

'Thank God,' David said. 'She was exhausted.'

'You must be, too,' Sam said. 'Couldn't you go home now?'

'I'm not leaving her,' David said. 'They've wheeled in a cot for me. You don't have to worry about us, though you might tell Grace I'm sorry for being abrupt with her when she called earlier.'

'She'll understand, Dad.'

Sam sent a kiss for Mildred, then hit the key for Grace's cell phone.

'I haven't been home long,' she told him.

He filled her in about the events of the night at the Adams Clinic.

'Dear God,' Grace said. 'Should I go over there?'

'Absolutely not,' Sam told her. 'They're fine now and resting.'

'And this man, this *doctor*' – she was incredulous – 'is in custody?'

'Alvarez arrested him,' Sam said. 'That's all I know for sure.'

'That's something,' she said. 'So now can you tell me what's been going on with you?'

He saw the hospital up ahead. 'Afraid not, Gracie, not now, but we have a prime suspect in the case to interview, and I'm seriously doubting that I'll be home any time tonight, so you get some sleep.' He paused, realizing what he still had not told her. 'And by the way, our French creep is in the hospital with a minor gunshot wound.'

'You shot him?' She sounded shocked.

'Not me. But he won't be going anyplace but home to France.'

'My God, Sam, are you and Al both safe?'

'As houses,' Sam said. 'A few dicey moments earlier, but all good now.'

'Did you say one suspect?' she asked, thinking about Felicia's sighting. 'Or is it two?'

'Two suspects: one in custody, one deceased.'

Grace was silent for a moment, and then she asked: 'Can I call Felicia's father? So he can tell her she doesn't have to be scared anymore?'

'Better hold off till daytime,' Sam said. 'I'd hope she's sleeping.'

'I'd hope, too,' Grace said.

Billie was sound asleep in her hospital room.

Doing remarkably well, a nurse had told Sam, given her ordeal.

As the sisters' only known surviving victim, Billie's testimony would be crucial. Broward would take her statement initially, and depending on how things moved forward, he and Martinez might participate in further interviews with her as the case against Toni Petit was built.

Not something he was looking forward to.

No more than he deserved.

'Sam,' she said, opening her eyes.

'Hey,' he said. 'I'm sorry. I didn't mean to wake you.'

'That's OK.' She started to sit up, looked woozy.

'Don't move,' Sam told her. 'You need to sleep.'

'I will.' She sat up anyway. 'I'm OK. I want to talk, need to tell you.'

'It can wait,' Sam said. 'You're safe here, Billie. You should sleep and we can talk all you like whenever you're ready.'

'I'm ready now,' she said.

Sam hesitated, then pulled up a chair and sat down near the bed. 'You were ready before all this happened,' he said. 'Only I wasn't listening.'

'No,' Billie said. 'You weren't.'

'I am now,' he said. 'But it's the middle of the night and you should be resting, and Broward officers are going to be taking your official statement tomorrow.'

'Can't you do that?'

'I'm out of jurisdiction.'

'And you should be home,' Billie said. 'But I still want to tell you what happened. I'm afraid that if I don't get it out, I might fall asleep and not remember it all tomorrow.'

No way that he was turning her down again.

He made notes and recorded her on his PDA as she began talking.

When Billie had called him on Thursday a week ago, it had been because she had wanted to talk to him about Toni. As she had at the end of the previous Monday's rehearsal, when Sam had driven away before she'd had a chance to say anything.

Toni had taken a call during that rehearsal which Billie had noticed she wasn't happy about, and when Toni had told her caller to wait while she found somewhere more private to talk, Billie had become curious – always a fault of hers, she confessed – and had followed her to the back of Tyler's garage.

'I heard Toni say that it was too late to start freaking out, that what was done was done. Sounded like Lady Macbeth,' Billie said. 'And then she said: "As far as I'm concerned, this was the very last time". It had to stop, she said. They had to get out.'

Kate on the phone, Sam figured, 'freaking out' after Zoë Fox.

And Toni had wanted out.

A couple of minutes later, Billie said now, she had asked Toni if she was OK, and Toni had given her a long, hard look, as if she knew Billie had been listening. And after that, Billie had felt that she kept on watching her, which had made her uneasy, which was why she had wanted to speak to Sam.

'Why did you wait till Thursday before you called me?' he asked now.

'Because I felt I'd done something to upset you that evening at your place. But then that thing with Toni kept on bugging me – she'd really sounded weird on the phone, and then the *way* she'd looked at me – and I just wanted to tell you about it before we all got together again at rehearsal.'

Only by then it had been too late.

Toni had shown up out of the blue at Billie's at around noon, bringing a plastic container of nutritious soup she said she'd made for the company because of the flu going around, and she'd been in the neighborhood and had figured she'd ask Billie to taste it in case it needed more spicing up before rehearsal.

'I was thrown, especially because I didn't think I'd told her where I lived, but I let her in,' Billie said. 'I didn't feel I had any choice, but then I told her that I wasn't hungry, couldn't face eating, that I'd try it later.'

Which was when everything had changed.

'Toni went to the door, and I thought she was leaving, that I'd offended her, but she let in another woman, wearing dark glasses, using a cane, carrying a bag, and Toni didn't introduce us, just said to the woman that I wasn't hungry – and then the woman came at me, barged me, knocked me off my feet, and I saw the cane swinging at me, at my head . . .'

She remembered nothing else until she'd woken up in the dark, tied down, and someone – she didn't think it was Toni, so it was probably the other woman – had fed her sandwiches a couple of times and juice, and Billie had known she had to eat something to survive, but she'd kept on getting sucked back down into this heavy kind of sleep, so she was sure they must have been drugging her.

'Who was the other woman?' she asked Sam now.

'Toni's sister,' he told her.

'They will go to jail, won't they?'

Which was when he realized how very little she still knew about why she had been abducted.

He told her no more than she needed to know. That Kate Petit, the woman with the cane, was dead. And that Toni was in custody and going nowhere for a very long time, probably forever.

'You weren't their only victim,' Sam said.

And then, seeing her start to tremble, he stood up. 'You have to rest.'

'You saved my life,' Billie said.

'You wouldn't have been there if it hadn't been for me,' Sam said.

In the ER, Sam established that Chauvin was still there, though the only medic Sam could find was too busy to give him more than a few seconds. He explained that Chauvin had witnessed a fatal shooting and that he needed to be sure they were keeping him overnight.

'The patient needs surgery, so I'd say he'll be here till noon or later.' The doctor paused. 'If he's awake, you can see him now.'

'Thanks, but no time,' Sam said. 'I'll be coming to take him home, but no need to mention to him that I was here.'

The doctor shrugged. 'I already forgot you were.'

Walking back out to his car, Sam had already decided how best to deal with Chauvin, to make sure he never came anywhere near his family again.

Then there was the scumbag who'd scared Mildred, and if his dad hadn't told him that Alvarez and Riley were on the case, he'd have had even bigger personal issues to fight right now.

But he and Martinez and Joe Duval – and whoever else was coming to join the party – had a suspect to interview.

Long session ahead.

He yawned.

Good job he'd gotten his coffee habit back.

Already hard to imagine a night into morning like this without caffeine.

* * *

The interview finally got under way at four a.m.

Toni Petit had been read her Miranda rights for a second time and, as previously, had waived them.

Duval checked with her one more time.

'Just so we're all clear, Ms Petit. You wish to waive your Miranda right to silence, and your right to have an attorney present while you speak to us?' He paused. '"Us" being myself – Special Agent Joseph Duval of the Florida Department of Law Enforcement; Miami Beach Police Department Detectives Samuel Becket and Alejandro Martinez; Detective Jerry O'Dea from Palm Beach and Detective Roberta Gutierrez from Fort Lauderdale.'

Five, the ASA had advised, was the maximum number for their side, tonight, if they wanted to avoid future challenges from whichever lawyer Toni Petit ultimately appointed.

'I'm clear on all that,' Toni Petit told him.

Sam was watching her closely.

A few hours ago, this woman had shot to death the sister she claimed to have spent almost two decades single-handedly protecting. It had happened in a moment of the highest drama and maximum stress, but Sam was as sure as he could be that she had known what she was doing.

Kate Petit had wanted him dead, but Toni had shot her dead instead, and then she had tried to turn the Colt on herself; had wanted, at that moment, to die.

Looking at her now, Sam felt that nothing had changed on that score.

She had nothing left to live for.

No reason, therefore – perhaps – to lie.

Her face was pale, her eyes dull, her expression remote, as if she had traveled a great distance, was not really here in this stark room with five officers of the law, all strangers.

Sam including himself in that, even if he had thought he'd known her for a number of years. There had been no friendship between them, no significant relationship, nothing to disqualify him from this interview.

He began by taking her back again – for the others present and for the record – to the multiple tragedies that had taken place in Louisiana, through to their escape to Florida and change of name.

Kate Petit's finger on the trigger of the Remington shotgun when it had gone off and killed Jake Grand, but Toni responsible for it, in her own heart and her sister's.

'I wanted to stop him,' Toni said.

'Because he'd been beating you for so long,' Sam said.

They had agreed in advance that this would be an interview rather than an interrogation; that they were, it seemed probable, dealing with an 'emotional offender', which meant that their technique would be friendly, even sympathetic, at least at the outset.

Emotional offenders were more likely to break.

This woman seemed already broken.

And ready to talk.

'Kate developed an obsession after we settled in Hallandale,' she told them. 'For a while, she started writing stories which all ended with some character being blinded, usually as a punishment. Eyes and blindness were always her theme.'

'Had she accepted by then that she had to wear her glasses?' Sam asked.

'When she chose to,' Toni said. 'When she didn't, she was almost blind.'

'Tell us about the Colt you stole from your father's safe,' Martinez said. 'The gun you shot your sister with tonight.'

'You want to know if it's the gun used in the Black Hole killings.' Toni paused. 'Kate liked that name.' She nodded. 'It was the gun used in all those killings, yes.'

And there it was already. Slam dunk.

They all looked at her hard, trying to penetrate the calm exterior.

Hoping for horror, Sam guessed, for shame.

For humanity.

Chauvin lay on his narrow bed in the ER bay, smiling.

Being shot had been a great shock to him initially, but he thought he might not have minded a slightly more serious wound if it had resulted in Sam Becket speaking to him a little more generously than he had.

'You're a jerk.'

That had hurt almost as much as the pain in his arm.

Yet still, Sam had come to check on him. Chauvin had heard his voice out there a while ago beyond the curtains, and though he hadn't been able to hear what was being said, it was enough, for now, to know that he had come.

He knew that Sam had been mad at him even before tonight, and he guessed he understood the big detective getting pissed at him for being there during those wild moments in that ugly little house – just remembering walking in on that, seeing the madwoman with her gun trained on Sam still made him shiver – but Sam would realize eventually that Thomas Chauvin really had saved his life.

And then they would be friends, and Grace and Cathy – or Catherine, as he had decided to call her – would love him for what he'd done.

His arm was starting to hurt a little again, but it scarcely troubled him because he had more important things to think about. Like what he would call Grace, in his mind, now that he had met Catherine – and pronounced the French way, it was a perfect name for her . . .

'Catherine,' he whispered.

His mind was fuzzy from medication, a pleasant kind of sensation.

He wondered when he would see her again, wondered if perhaps, after his surgery, Sam might invite him to come and stay with them while he recuperated, and then . . .

'*Grace-mère*' was what he would call Catherine's mother – almost like '*Belle-mère*', the French for mother-in-law . . .

'Catherine,' he murmured again, smiling.

And fell asleep.

Kate had never stopped complaining that glasses gave her agonizing headaches and contacts hurt her.

'I used to get mad at her,' Toni said, 'tell her she was choosing to be dependent on me, and sometimes she'd cry and rage, other times she'd be ice cold, but the bottom line was always that it was my fault, so "live with it".'

It was only, she went on, when Kate's urges struck, that her sister dramatically changed.

'Can you explain "urges"?' Sam asked.

'Sometimes, when we were out and Kate was wearing her glasses, she'd see a perfect stranger and become enraged. Sometimes, it was because she was very attractive or seemed very confident. Other times, it was because of the person's job. Kate hated opticians, anyway, but if she saw a woman selling mascara, she'd resent her too. Or she'd see a stranger just looking happy, *normal*, with her kids or partner. Or she'd decide someone was staring at her or talking about her.'

'And were they?' Joe Duval asked.

'I didn't think so.'

'Were they always women?' Sam asked.

'Usually.'

Kate complained almost daily about someone who'd infuriated her, either on TV or in a market or mall or on the street. Which was Toni's fault too, because if she hadn't made Kate wear her damned glasses, she wouldn't have seen them.

'Sometimes I actually hid her glasses for a while,' Toni said, 'but then she'd be so helpless, I couldn't bear it.'

Sam waited a moment.

'You referred to "urges",' he led her back again.

Toni nodded. 'Urges, rages, it's hard to describe what happened to her.'

'Try,' Jerry O'Dea said acidly.

Toni took a breath. 'Mostly, Kate kept herself under control. She would be seething, but keep it inside, building up until she could get home and explode in safety, without anyone noticing.'

'What happened when she "exploded"?' Sam asked.

'Sometimes she'd just cry and smash things,' Toni said. 'Other times, she'd go to the garage . . .' She looked at the investigators. 'You've seen Kate's "workroom" – that's what she called it.'

'We have seen it,' Detective Gutierrez said.

'Oh, yes,' Martinez said.

'Sometimes she'd go in there soon as we got home, and she'd take a toy or a doll – I bought them for her, because I figured it was a harmless enough outlet for her rage.' She paused. 'So anyway, Kate would take one and punish it.'

'How?' Sam asked quietly.

'She gouged out their eyes,' Toni said.

The silence in the room felt thick and ugly.

Sam broke the pause. 'I'd like to ask you about the other dolls in Kate's workroom.'

Toni didn't answer.

'Are you all right to go on?' Duval asked.

'You're talking about the special dolls. The ones that looked like the victims.'

'Yes,' Sam said. 'Did you buy those dolls too?'

'Yes.'

'When did you buy them?' Sam asked. 'At what stage?'

'I always had spare dolls,' Toni said. 'Different kinds. For when Kate got mad.' She paused. 'Not for when . . .'

Sam let that go.

'What about the clothes?' he asked. 'For the lookalikes, I mean.'

'Some I bought. Mostly I made them.'

'A little sewing sideline for you,' Martinez said.

'It was what Kate wanted,' Toni said.

'But it was what you liked doing,' O'Dea said.

'I *hated* doing it. But I still did it, same way I did everything she wanted.'

'Why?' Sam asked. 'If you hated it.'

'You know why,' she said. 'Because I owed her. Because if it hadn't been for me, her life would not have been ruined.'

Abruptly, she covered her face with her hands.

'Are you OK?' Sam asked.

'No.' Her hands dropped to her lap. 'I'm very tired. I'm sorry.'

'Would you like to take a break?' Duval asked.

'Yes, please.'

Sam wondered how she'd be after a rest break – which would be taken in this room, no other comfort offered unless she made demands; wondered if she'd go on talking then, or if she'd invoke her rights to silence and a lawyer.

It was a chance they had to take.

It was almost five in the morning.

One of the many terrible things about this endless night for Dr George Wiley was having nothing to read.

Graffiti didn't count, nor legal forms.

He had invoked his Miranda rights.

No *way* he was going to speak to those people like some common criminal.

He was a doctor, after all.

'I am a *doctor*.'

He had told them that over and over, but they just didn't seem to comprehend what that meant. And though Lieutenant Alvarez had treated him with a degree of respect, it had been apparent from the first that he and the red-haired sergeant already knew Dr Becket, and were, therefore, biased.

'I don't have an attorney,' he'd told them, because he'd never needed one, certainly not a *criminal* attorney, and they had told him that one could be appointed for him, that he would not necessarily need an attorney until his first court appearance, but that it was his decision.

He was going to get out. This night of abject humiliation would end, because he was going to 'bond out' – he had comprehended that much, that he would be bonding out on ROR – which stood for 'released on his recognizance' – and here was a whole new vocabulary which he refused to learn, he who had lived to learn.

They were talking about a charge of Simple Battery.

He had not *battered* the woman, had done nothing, deliberately, to hurt her, and if she had not reacted as she had, screaming and pushing him, he would never have stumbled and his hand would never have struck her eye. He would *never* have caused her intentional harm.

He was a doctor.

The instrument had been one of his own, a lid speculum, and opportunities to examine recently operated eyes were rare and valuable, helping him to perfect his skills, and he had believed that the Becket woman would still be sufficiently relaxed by medication to be compliant, so that he could gently examine her, so that in the future . . .

No future now.

They hadn't found the speculum on him because he'd disposed of it with hospital waste – and that irked him, the waste of a fine, expensive instrument, and maybe they would search for it, find it, but even if they never found it . . .

If he could only *read* now, to calm himself, feel more like himself, he might have been better equipped to control the fears.

As it was, reality was coming at him like a high-speed train.

Court was coming.

And with it, truth.

Because even though this would be the word of a documented hysteric against a doctor, George Wiley was no fool. Even if the case was dropped, those people would not let him forget what had happened – he'd seen that in Dr Becket's eyes. And he'd overheard something else tonight, that the retired doctor had a homicide detective for a son, which had to be bad news . . .

They would investigate him. Take him apart.

Destroy him.

All that time. All that learning.

All the *yearning*.

To be the best he could. The only thing he'd ever wanted to be.

A physician.

They were going to take it away from him.

He had seen that in Ethan Adams's eyes, too, in that cold, unforgiving stare.

Just before the great man had turned his back on him.

Already finished then, at the Adams Clinic.

And if they did begin to look more closely at him – which they would, he could see that as clearly as the ugly graffiti on the wall – then everything he had ever lived for would crumble away to nothing.

George Wiley shivered, closed his eyes and covered his face.

He could not bear it.

Could not bear what had been done to him.

Or what they would still do.

They would say that he had transgressed, that he had violated the Oath.

He could not bear that.

Would not.

While Toni Petit rested under guard at the station, Sam drove back to Hallandale General to check on Chauvin again and learned that the patient's surgery was scheduled for eight. Minor stuff, after which he should be ready for discharge by mid-afternoon latest.

Sam left the hospital and headed for home, feeling the need to touch base, to remind himself that his own world was clean and decent.

Not safe. He'd dropped that illusion a long time ago.

You just did your best, except, of course, that wasn't nearly good enough when it came to your own family.

He told his mind to shut the hell up, to allow himself to take a break, have a shower, see his wife without waking her.

She'd obviously done a great job, if Felicia Delgado had felt ready to describe those two women. Though Grace would see it as just one step toward her patient's long-term healing process.

He wondered, as he showered in their second bathroom so as not to wake Grace, if Felicia would ever feel strong enough to ID photographs, let alone testify against Toni Petit – though the way Petit's confession was flowing, they might not need to put the poor kid through any more.

He considered snatching an hour's sleep, decided it would only make him feel worse, went downstairs and made himself some toast and tea – plenty of lousy coffee to come later, back at the station.

He was glad in a way that Grace had not woken, because she'd have questions to ask, about Chauvin getting shot, about Beatriz Delgado's killing. And his answers, so far as he could give them, would lead to more questions, about Toni stopping Kate Petit from shooting him, then killing her own sister . . .

Only one of those questions he had an instant answer for.

Chauvin had implied to Martinez that he'd had some kind of intuition that he'd been in trouble, but the fact was the Frenchman had gotten himself shot because he was a moron. The rest was too damned complicated and grisly and, for the most part, unanswerable for now.

All down to what Toni Petit was going to tell them back at the station.

And how much of that would be the truth.

The Oath was everything to George Wiley.

Everything.

He'd been born Gregory Wendell, the only child of prosperous parents in Tampa, with whom he had never gotten along because neither John nor Frances Wendell had ever made any effort to understand him.

His life had *started* at age seven, after he'd broken an ankle and become mesmerized by the skills of the doctors who'd helped him heal and also to discover what he would do with his life.

He would become a doctor.

His industrialist father had other ideas. John Wendell loathed the medical profession, had blamed both his parents' deaths on doctors, whom he claimed were worse than murderers and far less honest. He ignored all advice given him by physicians and mocked his son when he disclosed his ambition – and if Frances ever disagreed, she didn't say so.

Nothing changed Gregory's mind. At school, he worked hardest on math, English and the sciences. In private time he read everything he could find about the aspirations and struggles of doctors, from Cronin to Erich Segal to the memoirs of the great physician, Thomas Starzl. When he wasn't reading, TV hospital shows sustained him; he'd been ten when *ER* and *Chicago Hope* had started, and soon Carter, Greene, Geiger and Shutt were his heroes alongside Pasteur, Fleming, Lister and Osler.

The afternoon Gregory told his father that he had been quietly concentrating on the subjects he was going to need for a medical career, so as to be sure of getting a head start, John Wendell suffered a stroke and died.

Frances blamed Gregory for her husband's death, and told her son that he could become an accountant or a janitor for all she cared, but that if he ever raised the subject of medicine again, she would disinherit him.

He chose accountancy, toed the line by day but used every cent that came his way to enable a secret education via books and, later, the Internet, setting complex passwords on his computer, encrypting texts, videos and lectures he downloaded for his *real* studies.

Three years into widowhood, Frances took a barbiturate overdose and tied a plastic bag around her neck, staging it so that her son would be the one to find her. Gregory buried her and the gruesome memory and set to celebrating – until he learned that her estate had firmly bolted the doors to medicine.

He could have waited till his twenty-fifth birthday, as stipulated, but that would have been too late because it took a decade just to get to the real starting gate, and though he'd heard tales of mature students battling through, Gregory knew that was not for him.

But he was no quitter.

If he'd had any real friends, they might have tried talking him out of his plans, but he'd never forged close bonds with anyone.

So, no living parents or other close family or friends.

No one to stop him.

* * *

Just after eight a.m., Toni Petit waived her rights again, and went on.

Every now and then, she said, one of Kate's urges would take her over so powerfully that she could not let it go.

'I tried turning it into a game,' Toni said, 'by making a plan.'

'What kind of plan?' Sam asked.

'A killing plan.' She looked at the others, then back at Sam. 'I won't pretend that I had no choice in any of this, because of course I did. I let my sister control me, manipulate me into doing what she wanted.'

'Your "killing" plan.' Sam drew her back on track.

'Kate loved that part. I'd come up with suggestions and she'd get excited, urge me on. It made her feel good.'

In the beginning, they talked about general factors like location. Kate suggested luring victims to cheap motels, the kind where they could pay cash for a room. She said they could wear disguises, then just walk out when it was over and leave 'them' to be found.

'Was this still a "game"?' O'Dea asked.

'I hoped so. It was all abstract, not real.'

'Locations,' Sam pressed.

'I told Kate that it could only work in the woman's own home.'

'Was "woman" abstract too?' Sam asked.

Toni didn't hesitate. 'The first was Arlene Silver. She lived in Fairview Shores, near Orlando.' She paused. 'Kate and I had gone up for a few days in January to look at houses – we sometimes fantasized about relocating, and I thought it would be a fun thing to do.'

They'd been in a drugstore when they'd heard a woman talking to a sales lady about a new brand of diet food. The woman said she was a serial dieter, said that she'd kill for the perfect figure, but she was an attractive woman with a good body, and Toni knew Kate was watching and listening, and getting mad.

'That was all it took. This perfectly nice woman called Arlene Silver – we heard her give her name to the saleswoman – and Kate perceived her as having everything, including beautiful, healthy eyes, but still wanting more.' She paused again. 'In Kate's mind, she needed punishing.'

They had followed her home and waited. When the man they assumed was her husband came home, Toni had thought that was an end to it, but Kate wouldn't let it go. They returned early next morning, the man left at seven and no one else emerged, and though Toni argued that didn't mean no one else was inside, Kate insisted they set to work on a *real* plan.

'I still believed it wouldn't come to anything. We were leaving in two days, and I was sure her rage would burn itself out, or maybe she'd just come home and take it out on a couple more toys.'

'Like that's real normal,' O'Dea said.

'Go on,' Duval said.

'We'd already decided about using drugs and minimizing any mess.' She paused. 'Neither of us were very good with blood.'

A swift, ironic nasal exhalation from Bobbi Gutierrez.

'I know it's hard to believe,' Toni said. 'But it's true.'

'You mentioned drugs,' Sam said.

'Diazepam,' Toni said. 'It had been prescribed in the past for Kate, for panic attacks, but she didn't much like taking medication. I kept a supply for when she needed it, bought the pills from a website. Occasionally, she asked for them. Other times, if she was getting really worked up, I put them in her food.'

'Did she know?' Sam asked.

'Not always,' Toni said.

They had discussed what they would need to bring along. The gun and ammunition. The drugs, sheeting, gauze.

'So you'd already decided on the gun?' Sam said.

'In a way.'

'What does that mean?' Gutierrez asked.

'Kate had always said that when we did it, it had to be like the dolls, only better.'

'What did she mean by "better", exactly?' Sam said.

'She wanted to shoot out their eyes,' Toni said.

Another brief, sickened silence filled the room.

'What did you say about that?' Sam asked.

'I still felt it was unreal,' she said. 'I was still sure it wouldn't happen. That either she'd burn herself out, or I'd find a way to stop her.'

'But neither of those things happened,' Sam said.

'No.'

'Why didn't you just put Diazepam in Kate's food?' Martinez asked.

'I thought about it,' Toni said.

'You had the drug with you in Orlando?' Sam asked.

She nodded. 'I always had some, in case.'

'But you didn't try giving some to Kate,' Sam said, 'to calm her down?'

'I might have, if we'd been home,' Toni said. 'But because we were still in Orlando, Kate would just have slept for a while. Then she'd have woken up and been mad at me, and still have wanted to do it.'

'Couldn't you have given her enough to knock her out and drive her back home?' O'Dea asked.

'She'd have been mad at me,' Toni said again.

'To clarify,' Sam said, 'you were in possession of the Diazepam.'

'It was in my purse.'

'Did Kate know you had it?' he asked.

'She knew I usually carried it.'

'You could have told her that you'd forgotten it,' Sam said.

'She'd have looked for it,' Toni said.

Sam moved on.

'Had you brought the gun along on your trip?'

'Yes. I never left it at home if we were both going away.'

'Did you ever go away without Kate?' Martinez asked.

'No,' Toni answered.

'But you did go out without her sometimes,' Sam said.

'You know I did.'

'On those occasions, did Kate stay home?'

'Yes.'

'And did you leave the gun with her then?' Sam asked.

'It was in a locked cupboard,' Toni answered. 'I kept the key with me.'

'You locked up the gun that you say you kept for Kate,' Sam said. 'But if she needed protection, she couldn't get to it.' He went straight on. 'To clarify again, on the Orlando trip, you, not Kate, were carrying the drugs and the gun?'

'I was,' she said.

Gregory Wendell had moved to Miami and gone through the motions of studying for his CPA exams, happily flunking them, excelling where it mattered, craving reading and learning the way some people needed junk food or drugs. His memory was superior, and he was a strict task master, creating his own exams, passing easily, setting the bar higher.

Wanting at least some of what was on offer to 'real' medical students, he began strolling into schools, learning their layout, finding out where security was lax, crashing lectures – and committing his first felony by obtaining a fake ID to grant him access where checks were in operation. He spent time at Miller and Dade Medical College, buying campus T-shirts, fitting in, listening but never voluntarily joining conversations, finding it easy to be the kind of guy nobody cared if they talked to or not.

He began collecting medical and surgical instruments at around that time, starting out with a stethoscope. He bought online and traveled to specialist sales, and if the estate trustees noticed what he was spending his money on, they never mentioned it.

What he still lacked was hands-on experience, but inspired by the Spielberg movie about impostor Frank Abagnale, he discovered how comparatively easy it could be to 'become' a doctor in a busy hospital. White coat, stethoscope, fake ID, pager, keeping moving, always watching, absorbing, copying minor procedures, escaping potentially dangerous encounters by saying he was needed elsewhere, equipped to name any department and even personnel.

He learned, too, when it was time to leave, period. If someone, say, had asked questions about him or looked at him curiously. Or, much worse, when he'd accidentally hurt a patient.

Not badly – he'd rather have died than cause serious harm – but no matter how often you practiced injections on an orange, you could still get it wrong with humans, whose pain thresholds and dispositions were so diverse.

He lost count of the number of unauthorized blood samples or swabs he'd taken. All he had to do was walk into a room and tell a patient what he'd come to do, and they let him. If a doctor came in and asked for a vein, they presented an arm. If he asked them to open their mouths or let him look in their ears, same deal. And sometimes, he just gave his time, listened to a patient, gave them comfort.

They thought he was a doctor, so they respected him.

It was a wonderful feeling.

His new identity as Dr George Wiley set him free.

Ready now, with enough knowledge and forged diplomas to get

a genuine position, sure that his work was excellent enough to earn him good enough references to climb to the next rung on the ladder.

It had worked out, because Florida was jammed with nursing homes and small clinics, most well run, personnel hired with care and scrutinized, but some run by the frazzled, idle or downright unscrupulous. In such places, patients were often grateful for extra care, which meant that Dr Wiley could give them the kind of thorough work-up they'd have been unlikely to receive otherwise. And if a senior, say, objected to something, it was easy to put it down to dementia or to note their tendency to be 'difficult' – and, thereafter, to avoid them.

He was good at his work, made no grievous errors, and his employers were always sorry to lose him when he left to take another step up.

And so, in time, he had worked his way to the Adams Clinic.

He'd found an extra benefit to working there, particularly with patients with bandaged eyes or who were enduring the uncomfortable positioning essential after certain procedures. A patient forced to lie face down after, say, the repair of a macular hole, was in no condition to argue, and the young doctor was careful not to cross the line, especially with the more well-informed individuals.

Dr George Wiley, gentle, approachable, obliging and on the up, thought he had pretty much mastered the art of judging who he could practice on and who it was advisable to leave alone.

Until the Becket woman had ruined everything.

'We had to work out the kind of person Arlene Silver would allow into her home. Best, we figured, for her to be expecting us.'

Everyone present was now way past tired, all listening intently to Toni Petit because this, to their knowledge, had been the first of the Black Hole killings, which made it the forerunner, in some ways perhaps the most crucial.

Sam's mind was swiftly running through legal ramifications of what she'd been telling them. Under Florida law, the Independent Act Doctrine applied when one co-felon who had previously participated in a common plan, did not participate in all the acts committed by a co-felon which fell outside the original collaboration.

No way now for Petit's lawyer-to-be to take that route.

They had created an invitation in a while-u-wait print shop telling

Mrs Silver that she was one of an exclusive selection of women in Orange County being invited to try a special treatment guaranteed to slim and tighten 'problem areas' after just one treatment or their money back.

Jerry O'Dea made a scoffing sound.

'I never thought she'd go for it,' Toni agreed.

The invitation stated that a unique combination of recently-discovered essential oils and a specialist massage technique was available in the area for one day only, after which the oils would not be available in the US for six months.

'We named it PN301, said it was its working name. PN as in *piel nueva*.'

'New skin,' Gutierrez said softly.

'We hand-delivered the invitation soon after the husband left next morning, and just after nine we knocked on her door.'

'And she fell for this?' Martinez was incredulous.

'She welcomed us, seemed so excited. I thought she might recognize us from the drugstore but we looked different – we'd bought wigs – I was a redhead and Kate was a blonde, and she wasn't carrying her cane.'

Partial affirmation of the Naples sighting, though it seemed improbable that anyone could have thought this slight, slim woman might be a man.

'She wanted to see the oils before we started, said she couldn't help feeling a little dubious, but then again, she'd try anything once.'

'You'd brought actual oils with you?' Sam asked.

'We'd bought some essential oils in tiny bottles from a natural health store and soaked off the labels. Kate let her sniff them while I told her about our special relaxing herb tea, asked if she'd like to try some.'

'And she'd try anything once,' O'Dea said.

'Did she?' Duval asked.

Toni nodded. 'If she hadn't . . .'

'Yes?' Sam said.

'I don't know,' Toni said. 'It didn't happen.'

'Did you bring any other treatments with you,' Sam asked, 'as part of your cover story? Anything containing acetone?'

She frowned. 'No.'

He logged that wrong turn down to experience.

Petit said that she'd made a cup of her 'special' tea with added Diazepam.

'What else was in the tea?' Sam asked.

'Ginger, bergamot, orange, honey.'

'How much Diazepam did you add?'

'I'd crushed several ten milligram tablets, more than enough to make her very sleepy, unless she was exceptionally resistant. We told her to keep stirring the honey that settled at the bottom of the cup.'

They'd sat down in Arlene Silver's living room, talking up the marvels of PN301, while the unsuspecting woman had stirred and drunk her tea, remarking on its sweetness and unusual flavor and talking about other treatments she'd tried.

'It surprised her when she started feeling drowsy. I told her that occasionally prescription medications interacted with the herbs in the tea, and she started to tell us about something she took, but by then she was too sleepy to talk.' Toni looked at Sam. 'She was never frightened.'

'Was that why you drugged her?' Still hoping for a trace of humanity.

'That, and the fact that Kate wanted to move her into her bedroom, which would be easier if she couldn't resist.'

Expediency then.

An almost gentle path up until the point of killing.

But not because of kindness.

Sam was becoming ever more certain that however often she said 'Kate wanted', Toni had virtually driven every stage, had been the sharp brain behind it.

Behind six horrific deaths.

'So then what?' Martinez asked.

'Kate made up the bed the way she wanted it. You've seen it.'

'Please describe it for the record,' Sam said.

She gave her account, the number of pillows, the sheeting.

And then she described the way they had helped the drugged woman to her bed, resting her head on the stack of pillows. There had been, Toni told them, a few flickers of surprise, perhaps because the bed felt different, but no fear.

And then she had been asleep.

* * *

Dr Adams had come in to see Mildred early that morning.

'You obviously don't need a lot of sleep,' she had remarked, impressed, and then she'd added: 'Are you sure you're sharp enough for this?'

'You're certainly sharp enough for us both,' he said.

David had noted what appeared now to be two-way respect. Which boded well, he hoped, for when it came time to attend to Mildred's second cataract.

The ophthalmic surgeon had seemed pleased.

'I'd say you're good to go, Mrs Becket.'

'Truly?' she said.

'Provided you're going to take care of yourself.'

'You don't need to worry, Doctor,' Mildred said quickly. 'I won't be doing anything to spoil your work.'

Just papers to be signed after that, and a wheelchair for Mildred, which she did not argue with; which caused David brief concern, being so out of character.

'You don't need to worry either,' she told him as Benjamin, the orderly who'd taken her to the OR yesterday, wheeled her from the elevator toward the world beyond. 'I'm just making sure I don't do anything to spoil our bid for freedom.'

David smiled. 'I guess, in the end, the surgery was the least of our troubles.'

They were almost through the sliding doors.

Mildred shook her head. 'Hard to know how a man like that gets to be a doctor at all.'

'Keep your head still, Mildred.'

'Yes, Doctor,' she said.

The morning air was very warm, but seemed delightfully fresh to her.

'Free at last,' Benjamin said.

Sam was finally ready to ask the question.

'Who pulled the trigger?'

'I did,' Toni said. 'Kate wanted to do it, but suddenly she changed her mind, said her aim might not be straight enough. She might screw up, and it might not be how she needed it to be. Perfect.'

'And you accepted that?' Sam asked.

'I told her no. I told her there was nothing to stop us leaving and going home. Arlene was sleeping. We could have taken our stuff – and her teacup – and we could have left, and all she'd have known was that she might have been doped. Nothing stolen but a teacup. No real harm done.'

'What did Kate say?' Sam asked.

'She got upset, said I didn't understand how much she *needed* this. And if I wouldn't do it for her, then she would fire the gun, but if she missed and it was hideous because she was almost *blind*, then she'd have nightmares for the rest of her life, and that would be down to me. The way all the bad things in her life always had been.'

'So you agreed,' Sam said.

'No, but I did it anyway,' she said. 'We'd taken a cushion from the couch to use as a silencer. I positioned the gun against it and aimed as accurately as I could. And I did it.'

'You shot Arlene Silver,' Sam said.

'Yes. Twice. One shot through each eye.' Her voice was soft. 'I remember worrying that the smoke detector might go off because the cushion was burning, but I threw it on the floor and stamped on it, and it was OK.' She paused. 'But then I had to look at her. At what I'd done.'

They were all silent.

'I'd never dreamed I could do anything like that. And then Kate said we had to go on, do more, make it look *right*.' She swallowed. 'We'd brought gauze with us, which I thought would be enough.'

'You had brought gauze for that purpose,' Sam said.

'Yes. But Kate started looking around the room and found something, said: "Hey, this is perfect." It was a sleep mask.'

The one that Arlene Silver had saved from a night flight.

'I put the gauze into the . . .' Toni's face was suddenly paler. 'I'm sorry, I can't, not about that. I mean, I did it, but I can't describe it.'

'Too hard, huh?' O'Dea said.

'That's OK,' Sam told her.

She nodded. 'And then Kate handed me the mask, and I put it on her.'

'You fastened it around her head?' Sam said.

'Yes,' she said.

'Were you wearing gloves?' he asked.

'Yes.'

'At what point had you put gloves on?'

'In the kitchen, when I'd made the tea.' Toni paused. 'And then I took them off until she got sleepy. And we were both very careful not to touch things.' She stopped again. 'I need to go to the bathroom.'

'We'll take a break soon,' Duval said.

'There isn't much more to say,' she said.

'You fastened the mask around her head and over her shot-out sockets.' Sam's voice was harder. 'What did you do then?'

'We cleaned up,' she said. 'We were both churned up, but I think we did a good job.'

'Not that good,' Duval said. 'You left prints.'

'Did we?' Toni said. 'Not so perfect, after all.'

Sam glanced at his watch, saw it was nearly ten, looked at the others, then at Joe Duval, who nodded.

Sam gave thanks.

'Interview suspended,' he said.

While Duval met with the ASA, Sam called Hallandale General and learned that Billie was well enough to be discharged and had already given a statement to Broward detectives. He also learned that owing to a backed up OR, Chauvin had only recently gone to theater, but that he would still probably be fit to leave that afternoon.

Sam asked the ER manager to tell Chauvin that he'd need his statement regarding last night's events, and to request that he sit tight, not leave the hospital until he returned.

'He won't be coming back to the ER, Detective,' the manager pointed out. 'Try the hospital operator later.'

He and Martinez went to Markie's for some breakfast, gave their order and sat in silence until the food came and they dived in.

'OK,' Martinez said after a while. 'I needed some energy so I can give you hell for walking into that *alone* last night, man.'

'I called you,' Sam said. 'Twice. And I called Duval.'

'You had a bad feeling, and you still went in alone. We don't do that.'

'I know,' Sam said. 'I'm sorry.'

They ate for a few more minutes.

'So what's your plan for the French dope?'

'Make sure Broward have seen him, then get him on a flight home.' Sam dipped bacon into yolk. 'Want to come along? Help make sure he gets the message?'

'Try stopping me,' Martinez said.

Toni had been given breakfast, which she had not touched.

Joe Duval kicked off with another Miranda, and she waived again.

The stories for the next three killings were horrifically similar. All three had begun one Saturday in February at a beauty therapies show in a downtown Miami hotel, where Toni had been earning some extra cash helping one of her dressmaking clients on her stand, and Kate had come too.

It was the day Kate had first seen Karen Weber, Lindy Braun and Amelia Newton and had become obsessed by them. All three had been given the PN301 sales pitch to suit their problems. All three had bought it.

The rest was history.

Sick, carefully planned, organized and ruthless.

Toni claimed that Kate had been unstoppable, that she had threatened her with what she had done to Arlene Silver, that it had not just been that threat which had made her comply, but the fear of what might become of Kate if she went to Death Row.

Abhorrence rippled through the room.

'I know I'm worse than she was,' she said. 'I do know that.'

No one disagreed.

Sam asked about the delay between Lindy Braun and Amelia Newton.

'Kate got sick after Naples, and I hoped it would be the last.'

'Sure you did,' O'Dea said.

'We told Amelia there'd been a delay with the product, but we didn't want to let her down,' Toni said. 'She was very grateful. They all were.'

The Delgado killing had come about differently.

With the argument between mother and daughter in the doctor's waiting room, overheard by the Petit sisters. Because listening to the hysteria over their eyes, Kate had become enraged, because they were so lucky, they *had* their eyes, but they did not deserve to see.

'She was worse than I'd ever known her,' Toni said. 'Wilder. She didn't want to wait, and though she despised them both, she knew the mother had to be the one responsible, the one to punish.'

They had followed them, kept watch into the next day, had seen Beatriz and Felicia go out that morning, the teen angry and upset again. And early the following day, they had seen Felicia storm out.

And had gone to the door.

Beatriz Delgado had answered.

Toni had apologized for the intrusion, explained that they had been in the doctor's office two days earlier, that it had been impossible not to overhear their argument, and that though they would understand if she didn't want to speak to two strangers, they really believed they might be able to help her.

'Even if she'd refused, Kate was so tightly wound, I thought she might force her way in. But it didn't come to that.'

Beatriz had invited them in, saying that she could not talk for long because she had an upset stomach. Toni had told her that by happy coincidence, she had an amazing herb tea in her purse that had recently settled her own stomach so well that she'd taken to carrying some, in case of need.

'Along with a Colt pistol,' Gutierrez said.

Beatriz had drunk the tea.

'And from there on, it was the same as with the others,' Toni said.

'And afterward, did you see Felicia Delgado outside?' Sam asked. 'And knowing that she was about to find her mother's mutilated body, did you raise your finger to your lips and then to your eyes as a threat?'

'I wanted to warn her,' Toni said. 'But I didn't tell Kate, because she'd already gotten in the SUV and hadn't noticed her. Because otherwise she might have wanted the daughter dead too, and I couldn't have done that.'

'You have some boundaries then, do you?' O'Dea said.

'I think it was a line I could not easily have crossed,' Toni said.

Zoë Fox had died because the sisters had been looking at new sunglasses at Shade City, and Ms Fox had told them that she remembered selling them a pair of ultra-large dark glasses earlier that month.

And if it had been in Miami Beach's jurisdiction, and if Sam had been one of those checking through the CCTV footage, he would have recognized Toni.

Still too late to have helped Zoë Fox.

'Kate felt she might be a danger to us,' Toni said. 'Because we'd used those sunglasses to cover Amelia Newton's eyes.'

'Kate felt that,' Sam said. 'Nothing to do with you.'

Her gaze was steady. 'I guess we both thought it.'

'So no uncontrollable *urge* about Zoë Fox,' Gutierrez said.

'I'd say we were both nervous of her.'

'Piece of work,' Martinez muttered, and received no warning glance from Duval, because if Petit stopped now and asked for a lawyer, they had enough to put her on Death Row five times over.

They'd had to use a different tactic with Zoë Fox, because she was young and beautiful. But she had a KISS tattoo on her shoulder, and Toni had asked if having the tattoo had hurt. Zoë had said she hated it now, wished she'd never had it done, and Kate said that oddly enough, that was Toni's specialty: tattoo removal with zero discomfort and no drugs.

'She said "Wow", and that she'd love to lose it. I said that it was clearly inappropriate to discuss it in her place of work, but if she wished, we could visit her at home.'

'And she agreed?' Sam said.

'She did,' Toni said.

Martinez and O'Dea shook their heads, everyone perturbed as hell by all the misplaced trust still out there.

The next day, Monday, May 16, had been Zoë Fox's day off.

By noon, she was already dead.

Toni said that Kate had wanted Billie Smith dead, but she had refused.

'But you had a doll resembling her all ready and waiting,' Sam said.

'Still,' Toni said, 'it felt different, because I knew her. And because I knew, right after I'd panicked and we'd taken her, that it was over. That if we didn't shoot Billie, it would be over because she would tell, and that if we did kill her, it would be just one wicked thing too many.'

She paused, seeming sunk deep in her thoughts.

And then she said: 'It felt to me, for a long time, as if we were both suffering from a terminal illness. At least Kate's out of it now.' She shrugged. 'Me too, I guess, one way or another.'

* * *

At two-fifteen, when Sam and Martinez – both functioning on caffeine and junk food – arrived at Hallandale General, they found Chauvin sitting dressed on his bed, arm bandaged and in a sling.

He looked sorry for himself, but glad to see Sam – even if he was traveling with his grouchy partner.

The gladness did not last long.

Broward had seen him, which was good news for Sam.

'I've taken care of your plane reservation,' he told Chauvin. 'I assumed you had a return ticket.'

'Where am I supposed to be returning to?' the Frenchman asked.

'Strasbourg is home, right?' Martinez said.

'Sure,' Chauvin said.

'Then that's where you're going.'

'But I'm not ready to leave yet.'

'I think you'll find that you are,' Sam said.

Chauvin's forehead creased, and he took off his glasses. 'I knew you were upset when I followed you last night, and then, even when the crazy woman was going to shoot you, and I—'

'We're wasting time,' Sam said. 'Your flight leaves Miami International at five-fifty, so we need to get you there for check-in.'

'That's not my flight.' Chauvin put his glasses back on.

'It is now,' Sam said. 'One-stop via Charles de Gaulle, Paris. We'll get you back to Surfside, and I'm even going to help you pack, and then Detective Martinez and I are going to take you to MIA.'

'Your very own chauffeurs,' Martinez said.

'That's all very kind,' Chauvin said. 'But what if I don't want to go yet?'

Sam looked at Martinez, nodded, and they sat down on either side of the Frenchman, closer than was comfortable for them, more so for him.

'Let's say we forget last night for now,' Sam said.

'Last night, when I saved your life,' Chauvin said.

'That's a moot point,' Martinez said.

'I'd rather backtrack,' Sam said, 'to when you were harassing my daughter.'

'Catherine,' Chauvin said, and smiled.

'Hey,' Martinez said. 'Don't be a smart ass.'

'What?' Chauvin said. 'Now I'm not allowed to smile?'

'And to two hours or so before that,' Sam went on, 'when you were doing much the same at my house, with my wife.'

'I brought her roses,' the Frenchman said. 'To thank her for dinner. And then I took a few pictures. Grace didn't mind.'

'Grace minded very much,' Sam said. 'But not nearly as much as I do.'

'About as much as the other blondes minded in France,' Martinez said.

Chauvin's cheeks grew red. 'I was innocent.'

'Sure you were,' Sam said.

'You were picked up in Monaco,' Martinez said. 'For loitering near the palace.'

'I was walking around, like any other tourist,' Chauvin said.

'Any other tourist obsessed with the late princess,' Sam said. 'They revoked your work permit, I believe.'

'I changed my mind about working there,' Chauvin said.

'Sure you did,' Martinez said.

'Makes your uninvited little photo shoots with my wife and daughter as unwilling subjects more than a little questionable, wouldn't you say?' Sam said.

'Not to me.'

'I'd call you a weirdo,' Martinez said, 'only that might be offensive.'

'I'd call you a stalker,' Sam said, 'following my wife in Switzerland and then all the way to Florida.'

'I don't see—'

'What I see,' Sam cut him off, 'is you going home today.'

'But the Broward detectives said I might have to come back as a witness in a trial,' Chauvin said.

'And if that happens,' Sam said, 'I'm sure you'll cooperate like the good solid citizen you are, but in the meantime, you're going home, today.'

'And that way,' Martinez said, 'you'll be real lucky and stick to standing in the witness box instead of sitting next to your defense attorney.'

'Accused of what?' Chauvin's cheeks were aflame.

'Section 784.048 on stalking.' Sam took a piece of paper from his inside pocket and read. '"Harass" means to engage in a course of conduct directed at a specific person that causes substantial emotional distress in such person and serves no legitimate purpose.'

He looked into the other man's eyes. 'Any person who willfully, maliciously, and repeatedly follows or harasses another person commits the offense of stalking, a misdemeanor of the first degree, punishable as provided in section 775.082 or . . . Do you want me to go on?'

'No,' Chauvin said.

'I have a little section I like a lot.' Martinez took out his own piece of paper. 'Any law enforcement officer may arrest, without a warrant, any person he or she has probable cause to believe has violated the provisions of this section.'

Chauvin shook his head. 'You're treating me like a criminal, deporting me.'

'If that's what you want to wait for,' Sam said.

Another headshake, followed by a defeated shrug, and Chauvin stood up, wincing. 'I need medication before I leave.'

'Already taken care of,' Sam said. 'Waiting for us at the pharmacy.'

'Don't I need a wheelchair?' Chauvin asked.

'Sure,' Sam said. 'Hospital rules.'

'We don't want to break those.' Martinez was up. 'I'll go get one.'

Chauvin looked at Sam, still sitting on the side of the bed. 'I have to say, I'm feeling very hurt and misunderstood.'

'Uh-huh,' Sam said.

Dr George Wiley had bonded out on ROR and was now shopping.

Never one of life's natural shoppers – most of his cherished books and instruments purchased in auction houses or by mail – he was surprised by the piquancy of this rather mundane expedition.

Though it was special.

Because it was the last time he would shop.

Buying things he'd need this coming evening and night. Not the kind of items that a doctor generally kept in supply.

Food and wine too.

For his Last Supper.

His perfect dinner. The kind of food he imagined a man like Ethan Adams had served to him at a nod of his silver head.

Calves liver with fresh sprigs of sage. Yukon Gold potatoes for mashing. Fresh asparagus. A fine half bottle of Pinot Noir.

* * *

He thought while he shopped and, finally, slowly, drove home, about his past.

About the small group of people who had pushed him to this final descent.

Who would, if he let them, take from him the only thing that had ever truly mattered to him.

Being the finest doctor he was capable of being. And he'd always known it would take time, but he had been getting there, would have succeeded but for *them*.

Lieutenant Alvarez and Sergeant Riley, who had handcuffed him.

Dr Ethan Adams, who he had so worshiped, and who had struck him down with a single look.

Mildred Becket.

And Dr David Becket. A man who'd already had a lifetime in pediatrics.

George Wiley would have been a better doctor than Becket, given time and an easier journey, decent parents, the education he had deserved, of which he'd been deprived.

He had counted up his crimes and their penalties, had done the math as well as possible. Practicing medicine without a license, forging diplomas, assaulting patients – since he supposed that an unlicensed doctor's examination probably qualified as some degree of assault, even if it had been done to *help* the patients.

Same as when he'd written prescriptions, given injections, pills.

Not forgetting the biggest crime, so far as the *law* was concerned.

Identity theft was a federal crime.

Up to fifteen years for that sin alone.

And if he survived it all, did his time, emerged alive, there would be nothing.

No more medicine.

No purpose left.

So he did not intend to wait.

Arriving at his Surfside rental apartment, Chauvin asked the detectives to stay in the car while he went inside to pack.

'We promised to help you.' Sam got out of the Saab.

'You're injured, after all.' Martinez opened the rear door.

They both felt the younger man's edginess noticeably heightening as they took the steps up to the second floor, keeping him between them as they moved toward his front door.

Chauvin fumbled with his keys.

'Allow me,' Sam said.

The narrow, white-painted entrance hallway was clear and clean.

The main studio room took Sam's breath away.

'Jesus,' Martinez said.

'Sonofabitch,' Sam said softly.

'They're just photographs,' Chauvin said.

True enough.

The walls were covered in them. Printed on matte paper.

Of Grace, mostly. And of Cathy.

Sam walked around the room, looking more closely. There could be no doubt for anyone that most of the shots of Grace in Switzerland had been taken without her knowledge. There were several of her on a conference hall podium, three of her with a man and a woman standing outside a restaurant – in one of which, Grace did appear to be looking right at the camera, though Sam was sure that Chauvin had simply timed his shot well.

The photos of Grace bothered him a great deal, but not quite as much as those of Cathy, knowing that she had asked him to stop and that he had not done so – not, at least, until he had happened to call.

Which was when Chauvin had left.

'What do you want to do?' Martinez asked Sam quietly.

'I want to take them down,' the Frenchman said. 'Since I have to leave.'

'I don't think so,' Sam said.

'You mean I can stay?'

Sam's mind worked swiftly through the facts. There was nothing overtly wrong with any of these pictures. Nothing in any way indecent. None of them appeared to have been manipulated or enhanced, which was not to say that Chauvin was not playing games of that kind on his computer.

He could keep the guy here, use these photographs as partial evidence of stalking, but he would achieve very little. An illegal search was pointless, and they had no probable cause to get a warrant. Which meant that the best way to draw a line under this chapter was still to get him out of the USA.

'Get packed,' Sam said.

'You sure, man?' Martinez asked, even lower.

Sam nodded, grim-faced. 'I want him gone.'

Chauvin nodded, reached up to remove one of the photographs of Cathy.

'Leave it.' Sam's voice was whip sharp.

'The prints are my property,' Chauvin said.

'Don't push your luck,' Martinez said.

'And while you're packing,' Sam said, 'I'd like to look at your camera.'

'No way am I giving you that.'

'I'm not going to keep it,' Sam said. 'I just want to admire it.'

'And to delete the originals,' Chauvin said.

'As if,' Sam said. 'But if you don't want to let me see it, I won't.' He shrugged. 'I'm guessing you've already copied them to your home computer, anyway.'

'Or sent them to some goddamned "*cloud*",' Martinez said.

Sam had taken out his iPhone and was taking his own snaps of the walls.

'Hey,' Chauvin said.

'You got a problem?' Sam tapped his wristwatch. 'Believe me, you will have if you miss your flight.'

'I don't believe you,' Chauvin said. 'If you were going to arrest me for something, you would have done it by now.'

'Believe this.' Sam went on taking photos. 'I want you out of my country more than I want your sorry ass in jail costing taxpayers' money, but if you waste much more time, that is what I can make happen.'

'Will you let me take these?' Chauvin nodded at the walls.

'Sure.' Sam shrugged. 'I have my own photographs now.'

'*Merde flics*,' Chauvin said, and began taking the pictures down, hampered by his injured left arm.

'What'd he say?' Martinez's dark eyes danced anger.

Sam grinned. 'Shit cops, I think.'

'Do I have to go on being polite?' Martinez asked.

'Just a while longer.'

Chauvin had all the prints and turned to the closet. 'I won't be long.'

'Don't forget your passport,' Sam said.

George Wiley had been home for a while.

A modest apartment of which he was fond, in which he had

felt safe as he'd read and studied and prepared for the next rung up.

Not to be.

Thanks to Mildred Becket.

He had cooked the potatoes and asparagus and flash-fried the calves liver, and had drunk the wine, and it had all tasted so wonderful that he had wept.

Because he knew it was his final meal.

He had cleaned up meticulously, as was his habit.

And then he'd sat down to read.

He couldn't settle, could find no perfect last reading, had strayed restlessly, browsing Sophocles, Shakespeare and Milton, moving finally to a thesaurus of quotations, searching themes that most closely fit his predicament and emotions.

Loss, grief and anger. And the need, if not precisely for revenge, then, at least, to have his loss *recognized.*

He found little that was apt. Except for a line from Izaak Walton's *The Compleat Angler*, which sailed so close to his personal truth that his throat closed with the pain of self-pity.

'No man can lose what he never had.'

He laid a bookmark on that page and moved on to his desire for an end, to reading of a more practical kind. Mostly to reaffirm the decision he had already reached.

He did not want a mundane death, nothing so vulgar as his mother's suicide. What George Wiley, MD wanted to achieve with his final act was something that would make him notable, if only by his dying.

He did not own a gun, did not want to cut himself and bleed messily to death; he lacked the courage to jump from a tall building or to commit seppuku – besides which, he had no sword, and a scalpel just wouldn't be right. Poison rendered people ugly, as did hanging.

Self-immolation appealed to him on several grounds. First, it was often regarded as a form of sacrifice, frequently of protest. He had read that some extreme Buddhists believed that it proved a disregard for the body in favor of wisdom – Wiley liked the dignity of that.

Finally, so long as he prepared carefully, it need not be the hideous torture suffered by poor souls burned at the stake in the past. Though it would be intensely painful at the outset, third-degree burns destroyed nerve endings, and suffocation and shock usually killed very rapidly.

He wanted it to have *grandeur*, but he also wanted it to be quick.

Death held no great fear for him, but he was as afraid as the next person of pain. He had seen good and bad deaths in hospitals, but most often it had seemed a release.

Whereas the prospect of shame in prison, of the deprivation of all he had striven for, was a thousand times worse.

He would never be considered a martyr, he accepted that, but he could at least anticipate that his final act might be of interest to psychologists and, specifically, students of suicide.

He might merit a mention in an essay or even a textbook.

More probably, his life and death would be reported in some local rag, maybe find its way onto the Internet, not even making Wikipedia.

Bitterness rose again in George Wiley MD, reminded him again how much those people had to answer for.

He looked at his watch.

Time to prepare.

It was dark again when Sam finally got home.

He and Martinez had seen Chauvin on his way back to Europe, after which they had dragged through paperwork back at the office, until his partner had pointed out that enough was enough and it was time to stop.

His son was asleep, and getting home too late for even a bedtime story had been happening too often lately . . .

'Let's take a break,' Sam said over dinner.

Eating with his wife, for once, and Grace had made *osso bucco* Milanese with risotto, and Sam was way past bone weary, and Grace had offered to bring him up a tray, but he'd wanted this more.

'Just a long weekend,' he said now. 'Maybe five days. I thought we could go up to New England, if you liked the idea.'

'What do you think?'

And after that they talked about whether they might go to Boston or maybe Vermont, about which would be most fun for Joshua, since what they both wanted was some family travel for the memory book.

After dinner, Sam took Woody out, and then they looked in on their sleeping boy, stroked his hair and kissed his soft cheek, and then the ten ton weight of his exhaustion overwhelmed Sam entirely and he crawled into bed ahead of Grace, vaguely aware of her telling him goodnight.

And then he was out.

* * *

May 28

George Wiley felt cold.

Not a physical chill. The night was warm and humid, and he was not running a fever, was not sick.

This was a chill of the soul, warmth already departing his body.

Even before . . .

He had arrived a while ago.

Had driven around the block twice – seen that the house was in darkness, that it was protected by an alarm, but that there were no police patrol cars in the vicinity – and then he had parked on the next side street.

It might have ended there, if someone had reported a suspicious guy heaving heavy-looking bags up toward Dr David Becket's house, then vanishing behind the white stone wall that all but hid the first floor of the house from Ocean Boulevard.

And if it had finished then, with another arrest, he guessed he'd have had to rethink, probably from inside prison . . .

That thought galvanized him.

He had not wanted to die. He *did* not want to die. He wanted to *live.*

But only as a doctor.

And that was finished now.

The books had been heavy, and the two gas cans, and his instruments. Everything else was pitifully light: framed diplomas, white coats, two fleece jackets for tinder, ten packs of wooden tongue depressors for kindling; his stethoscope, George Wiley's IDs, driver's license and Social Security card, two large boxes of matches and two safety lighters – he'd had to buy those, had never smoked in his life.

No one stopped him as he slipped around to the back of the house. No floodlights pinned him in their glare. The alarm stayed silent, would probably remain so, since he had no plans to break in.

He switched on his small penlight, looked around, saw all he needed.

Garden furniture made of wood.

Satisfied, he set to work.

He was not physically strong, but he had no reason to move the heaviest item, the table, from where it stood. He could have left the cushions and seatbacks in place, but that didn't mesh with what was in his head, so he removed them, tossed them silently onto the ground.

Table first.

Then stack the chairs.

Quietly, carefully.

He worked deftly, neatly, as swiftly as was safe and quiet, wanting no more time for thinking.

No turning back now.

It had not rained for several days, so the table and chairs were dry.

Almost ready now.

Then all he would need were his chosen spectators.

And flames.

And courage.

In this, at least, he hoped he might succeed.

Mildred thought, at first, that it was raining.

A storm, perhaps. Hailstones rapping on the window.

She had always liked thunderstorms, even during her years of living close to the beach. Sometimes they'd gotten a little scary, but it had been magnificent to watch the South Florida thunderheads sweeping along, to see the vast sheets of brilliance in those dark skies.

This was not hail.

She glanced across at David, saw, with her uncovered eye, that he was still sound asleep, then crept quietly out from under the sheet and over to the window.

And gave a soft gasp.

A man stood in their backyard on what looked, at first sight, like a sculpture, of which he was a part.

He was dressed in white, something hanging around his neck, and his right arm was lifting, swinging in an upward arc.

Throwing something.

She ducked, flinching, suddenly afraid.

The small stones struck the glass.

'David,' she said sharply.

He'd already woken. 'What's wrong?'

'There's a man in our backyard.' Her voice was a hiss in the semidarkness. 'Come look. Quickly. I don't know what he's doing.'

David was already beside her.

'What the—?'

She squinted with her one eye, saw that the thing around his neck was a stethoscope. 'It's him,' she said. 'It's Doctor Wiley.'

They both stared down at him, knew immediately that they were looking at a man gone mad.

And then they saw him bend, pick something up.

'Oh, dear God,' David said. 'It's gasoline.' He turned to get the phone. 'Come away from the window, Mildred.'

He had his spectators.

The gasoline was pungent in his nostrils and at the back of his throat, choking him, making him cough.

Almost there now.

He threw the first gas can away, picked up the second and poured, directing the fluid at the tinder and kindling and wooden furniture, and then he raised his right arm again, high above his head, and emptied the rest over himself.

He experienced a sudden burst of terror then, dropping the can, but still the *longing* was greater: for it to be done, finished. And yet, despite that yearning, he faltered just a little, had to remind himself . . .

Fifteen years in prison and nothing to emerge to.

Dr George Wiley gone forever, lost in ignominy.

This his only chance for a proud end.

He looked up at the window again as he picked up the first matchbox.

Another man might have thought of saying a prayer, but the only gods he'd ever set any store by were Apollo the Physician and the other god and goddesses who had witnessed his solemn oaths of Hippocrates.

Perhaps they were sealing his fate now, for his transgression.

He looked up at Mildred Becket, at her mouth open in horror, the eye shield in place, the other eye staring, and figured that the old man was probably calling Fire Rescue or maybe his cop son.

Now. It had to be done now, or they might come, try to stop him, and unless he was beyond help when they arrived, his end would be long and agonizing beyond comprehension.

He opened the box, and now his hand hardly shook.

He struck a match, dropped it, struck another, dipped that into the box, where it ignited the rest. That first tiny burn on his hand stung a little, and he winced, then laughed, looked down and saw that it was catching, and the explosion of heat was instantaneous, surpassing his imaginings, *beyond* heat, and the sounds, as the gasoline roared into flaming majesty, were terrifying and magnificent.

He took the second matchbox, dropped it onto the fire.

'I did try,' he said, looking up into the night, and then he hooked his arms around the tops of the chairs stacked on the table, so that when he passed out, he would not fall and risk being saved to linger on.

He felt it now, the devouring, all-consuming pain, and as he looked down, dazzled, to his feet, he saw them burning, flesh and bones melting, and his gut rebelled and his bladder screamed and he imagined that he heard the sizzle of his own urine spilling, and then he heard his own scream, which seemed to come from outside himself . . .

And then suddenly he saw that the fire was not being contained within his pyre.

It was travelling in fierce, spiking, flowing rivulets, toward the house.

'No!' he protested, though the word never formed, because his body was on fire now, and he was already dying, and maybe it was true that third-degree burns destroyed nerve endings, but oh, dear Apollo, the destruction was purest *agony*, and oh, Jesus, now his lungs were *broiling*, and his roasting flesh and bones and muscles and fat stank like the Devil's own barbecue, and he longed for death, but he was still living, *feeling* . . .

Able to see that gasoline had splashed onto the pathway, and tufts of dry weeds between stone slabs were feeding the hungry flames, and tongues of fire were lapping up the cushions that he had tossed aside, and an old swing seat with cushions and a fabric canopy stood close to the Beckets' French doors, and a sheet of blaze was reaching for the house itself.

'*No!*' his mind screamed, because now those old people inside might burn too, and he had not wanted *that* to happen, had not intended to endanger life, not even theirs. He had only wanted to alarm them, appall them, and he had sworn the Hippocratic Oath in three versions, had sworn it with utmost solemnity with only his books to witness it . . .

And his penultimate thought, as he burned on the funeral pyre of his own making, was that finally he *had* violated his oath, his covenant – even in that, he had failed.

And then, when he could no longer see, as his hair blazed, just before the coiled wonders of his brain began to melt, he realized that when Fire Rescue or whichever poor bastards came to collect and assemble and analyze his charred remains, they might already know that he was not truly Dr George Wiley.

That he had remained, from birth to death, an ambitious, pointless fool named Gregory Wendell, whose own parents had despised him, and who had been correct to do so.

They had come in time.

Fire Rescue in time to save the house, though the fire had blown out the French doors and taken out some soft furnishings and the old couch. The paramedics in time to check over the shocked elderly couple, who were physically unharmed, and who refused to consider hospitalization.

Sam in time to see the smoldering nightmare in their backyard, and to extricate his father and Mildred from the scene.

He brought them back to the island, where Grace was deeply disturbed by what she saw in their faces.

As good an imagination as she possessed, she knew she could never conjure up the sheer horror of what they had witnessed.

'How will they get past this?' she asked Sam, quietly.

'I have no idea,' he said. 'Though we know they're both very strong.'

'They'll need to be,' Grace said.

They spent the night in Cathy's old room, David insisting that Mildred rest, though he did not sleep at all, kept watch on her, dozing off periodically and waking with a start.

'I think we need to go back as soon as we can,' Mildred said suddenly, just after five a.m. 'If we wait too long, I think it might be worse.'

'Sam says we shouldn't think of going back until the repairs are finished.'

The smell of a house fire being a terrible thing even without . . .

David shuddered involuntarily.

'I keep seeing it,' Mildred said. 'Seeing him.'

'I know,' he said. 'Me too.'

'Was it because of us, do you suppose?' Her mouth trembled.

'It was not.' David was definite. 'Whatever was wrong in that man's mind was there long before I had him arrested – before he assaulted you, Mildred.'

'Poor soul,' she said. 'To be so tormented.'

'I know,' he said again.

'How will we ever forget it?' she asked him. 'I know it's selfish to even think about ourselves, but . . .'

'It isn't selfish,' David said. 'It's human. And I imagine time will ease it. As with most things.'

'You mean we'll try and bury it.'

'As deep as we can,' David said.

They were both silent for a little while.

'There is one small thing I am rather grateful for,' Mildred said.

'Mm?'

'My derrière will be very glad to be shot of that terrible old sofa.'

'You've always told me you thought it was comfy,' David said.

'Only compared to my old bench,' Mildred said.

June 1

The truth about Gregory Wendell, aka George Wiley, had begun to emerge quite swiftly after his suicide.

That he had never been a doctor.

That he had been a fraud, with no license to practice medicine, no genuine qualifications, guilty of several counts of identity theft.

A pitiful kind of a guy with grandiose ambitions, who had achieved for a time what ought to have been impossible, and who had, it appeared, believed that he was doing good, not harm.

Impossible, at this early stage, to know just how much harm he had done in his 'medical' career.

He had left behind in his apartment two apothecary cabinets, a microscope, a medical mannequin – formerly used for patient care training in a school – and a collection, in his refrigerator, of porcine eyes. He had also left a fascinating curriculum vitae, citing felonies and misdemeanors as credits and achievements, plus a bookmarked thesaurus of quotations and three handsomely printed versions of the Hippocratic Oath, naming Apollo as his witness.

And last, in the Google history on his PC: How to build a funeral pyre.

June 7

Thomas Chauvin was home alone in Strasbourg.

Alone, yet not alone.

Having his photographs to keep him warm.

Until recently, it had always been the other Grace who had filled his walls. Gorgeous big black and whites in every room, smaller, more intimate color shots in frames on side tables. Every book published about her on his shelves, along with all the available movies and TV shows she'd ever appeared in. Albums filled with clippings, all with pictures.

None of them *his* photographs.

All that had changed now.

He had started work on his shots of Catherine, had downloaded all the old news stories about her personal tragedy and later dramas, was anticipating more from his cuttings agency, had great plans for utilizing some of his own shots of her, and with Adobe's help and his own talent and flair . . .

One of his early efforts already filled the wall opposite his bed.

An inspiration that had gone off like a flashgun in his mind in her apartment.

Rear Window reborn. Little black dress with sheer shoulders. Triple strand of pearls. Not the Kelly look of shock, but certainly of consternation, almost of anger, taken in Catherine's living room while she had been listening to her voicemail, and she'd been a little mad at him because she'd asked him to stop . . .

So sexy.

He lay back on his bed now, and looked at it.

At her.

Mica's voice singing from speakers threaded through his apartment.

'*Je prends les poses de Grace Kelly . . .*'

Life was good.

Full of promise.
Would, one day, be even better.
Chauvin was sure of that.

June 10

Sam had known, right away, after he received the request, that he would go.

Martinez was against it, and just the thought of spending time, however short, with Toni Petit, gave Sam chills. But the killer had been hospitalized with severe stomach pains, was undergoing tests, and had put in a request for a visit from Sam.

Not as a detective, but as a man whose trust she had abused.

She wanted to apologize.

He was going, he thought, for himself. Because though he had never really believed in 'closure', it still troubled the hell out of him – as a man, not just as a detective – that he had spent snatches of time with this monster over several years, and had never suspected that anything was wrong with her.

'It isn't me you need to apologize to.'

The first thing he said when he went, on the second Friday in June.

She was in a locked ward, one of her ankles shackled to the bed.

She looked sick.

She wanted to write letters, she told him, to the families of the victims.

'Your lawyer tell you to do this?' Sam asked. 'To show remorse?'

'I don't know,' she said. 'I don't really listen to him, but no, this isn't about sentencing, Sam. It's something I feel I need to do.'

'So do it,' Sam said.

'But what if my letters open up their wounds?'

'You think those wounds are even halfway *closed*?' It was a relief to let out a little anger. 'You think getting a letter from you is going to make any of those poor people feel *better*?'

'Of course not,' she said. 'I just want to try to express . . .' She shook her head. 'There's no word that describes it. Remorse. Regret.' She struck herself on the chest with her right hand. 'Mea culpa.'

'Are you Catholic?'

'I have no faith,' she said. 'So no acts of contrition for me, and certainly no hope of forgiveness. Death Row and the fire is where I'm going and what I deserve.'

'So what do you want from me, Toni?'

He had used her first name unintentionally, was angry with himself for it, his thoughts with the victims and Felicia Delgado and Billie.

He wanted to leave.

'I've written a first letter,' she said. 'To Arlene Silver's family. I'd be very grateful if you would look it over, and then I could sign it and ask to have it mailed.'

'You should probably ask your lawyer to do that,' Sam said.

'I trust you more than any lawyer, Sam,' Toni said.

He noticed the sheet of paper to her left.

'Please.' She picked it up, held it out to him.

'I'm not reading it,' Sam said. 'You wrote it, you sign it, get it mailed, or throw it in the trash. It's all the same to me.'

He began to rise.

'*Please*, Sam.' Petit's voice rose in a plea. 'At least give me your pen so I can sign it – at least that'll be a start.'

He responded out of impatience, his desire to be done with her.

He took out a pen. Just an ordinary Bic ballpoint.

He handed it to her.

'Thank you,' she said, taking it.

And then she turned it around and stabbed the point hard into her left eye.

'Jesus!' Sam yelled as blood and vitreous gel splattered and she screamed.

He made a grab for the pen, but Petit hung onto it, and her fingers were *strong*, and two guards were running toward them, but Sam knew she was going to do it again, and no *way* was he letting her do that.

'*No!*' she screamed, twisted her arm, and dug the pen into the side of his neck.

'What the *hell*?!' he yelled and leapt back.

The guards were on her, restraining her, and Sam yanked out the pen – knew as he did it that it was the wrong thing to do – but though blood was flowing, it was not arterial, and he wasn't sure if he was madder at her or with himself for coming here, for being fool enough to give her the goddamned pen.

'My eye for her eye,' Petit cried out. 'Why did you have to *stop* me?'

'Jesus,' Sam said again, as a nurse began to steer him away to safety.

Even now, it was still about Kate, *her* lost eye.

Not really about the victims at all.

Not about penitence.

Black Hole still not finished.

Not until they lethally injected her, or she found a way to terminate herself or some other inmate did it for her.

July 11

The decision had been made to postpone the S-BOP production of *Carmen* until the next gap in their theater's schedule. There was no way, Linda had insisted, that Billie would be deprived of the lead after all she'd been through.

Cast and crew standing by.

Except, of course, for one.

Petit's costumes had been the only bone of contention.

'Waste not, want not,' La Morrison had said at a meeting in her condo.

A pragmatic, thrifty woman.

'I won't put anything that maniac touched next to my skin,' Carla had said.

Not the only one to feel that way.

'Too much time and money spent.' Linda had been adamant. 'And Toni's costumes are too beautiful to throw away.'

Sam fingered the new scar on his neck, understanding both viewpoints, personally just glad to know that they were all alive and well and would sing again.

Billie most of all.

They were rehearsing for the first time since the night that had culminated in Toni's arrest and Billie's rescue.

In Tyler Allen's backyard, as in the past, pitchers of water stood on the long table, the fragrance from the flower beds sweetening the night air.

Almost as if none of the ugliness had ever happened.

Billie's voice seemed to Sam lovelier than ever. Her defiance close to the end of the final act filled with fire. Carmen would never give in, she declared. She was born, and would die, free.

Sam let his thoughts wander for just another moment to the woman who had been part of this production; who had, perhaps, in her saner, more decent moments, regarded this company as a refuge, but who would now, almost certainly, spend her own final days on Death Row.

And then he left all thoughts of Toni Petit behind.

And gave himself back up to the music.

CPSIA information can be obtained at www.ICGtesting.com
Printed in the USA
BVOW03*0039060813

327720BV00002B/6/P